The Production Manager's Toolkit

"Our theater world is so much better with this book in it, and even better with Cary and Jay at the helm."

—David Stewart, Director of Production for the Guthrie Theater

The Production Manager's Toolkit is a comprehensive introduction to a career in theatrical and special event production for new and aspiring professionals, given by expert voices in the field. The book discusses management techniques, communication skills and relationship-building tactics to create effective and successful production managers. With a focus on management theory, advice from top production managers provides insights into budgeting, scheduling, meetings, hiring, maintaining safety and more. Through interviews and case studies, the techniques of production management are explored throughout a variety of entertainment venues: theatre, dance, opera and special events. The book includes references, tools, templates and checklists, and a companion website contains downloadable paperwork and links to other useful resources such as unions, venues and vendors.

Cary Gillett has worked as a production manager and stage manager in the Washington DC area for almost two decades. She teaches production management and stage management at the University of Maryland, College Park, and serves as the Production Manager for UMD's School of Theatre, Dance and Performance Studies. In addition, she has worked as a Production Manager for the Round House Theatre, the Potomac Theatre Project and the Helen Hayes Awards, celebrating theatre in the Washington DC area. She is married to director and educator Bill Gillett, and together they manage their biggest production, *Mary Louise*.

Jay Sheehan oversees the production management and stage management areas for the School of Theatre, Television and Film at San Diego State University. Jay created and leads the Certificate in Entertainment Management Program for the school. As the faculty Production Manager, Jay oversees all aspects of production for the eight-show main stage and student production season. When he isn't teaching, Jay also serves as the Logistics Coordinator for the president's campus-wide Arts Alive SDSU initiative, promoting the visual and performing arts on campus. Jay is also an Equity stage manager, and spent his early career at the Old Globe Theatre. Jay's other jaunts around San Diego have found him as the Director of Production and Operations for the San Diego Symphony and Director of Operations for House of Blues, overseeing the 20,000 seat Coors Amphitheatre in Chula Vista. Jay is also owner of Cue One Productions and is a freelance special event manager who produces nonprofit charity and concert events in and around the United States.

The Production Manager's Toolkit

Successful Production Management in Theatre and Performing Arts

Cary Gillett
Jay Sheehan

Routledge
Taylor & Francis Group

NEW YORK AND LONDON

First published 2017
by Routledge
711 Third Avenue, New York, NY 10017

and by Routledge
2 Park Square, Milton Park, Abingdon, Oxon OX14 4RN

Routledge is an imprint of the Taylor & Francis Group, an informa business

Cover image and interior part opener images by Hesh One

Library of Congress Cataloging-in-Publication Data
Names: Gillet, Cary. | Sheehan, Jay.
Title: The production manager's toolkit : successful production management in theatre and the performing arts / Cary Gillet, Jay Sheehan.
Description: New York ; London : Routledge, 2016. | Includes bibliographical references and index.
Identifiers: LCCN 2016002021 (print) | LCCN 2016004227 (ebook) | ISBN 9781138838840 (pbk. : alk. paper) | ISBN 9781315733777 (ebook)
Subjects: LCSH: Theater—Production and direction—Handbooks, manuals, etc. | Performing arts—Production and direction—Handbooks, manuals, etc.
Classification: LCC PN2053 .G53 2016 (print) | LCC PN2053 (ebook) | DDC 792.02/32—dc23
LC record available at http://lccn.loc.gov/2016002021

ISBN: 978-1-138-83884-0 (pbk)
ISBN: 978-1-315-73377-7 (ebk)

Typeset in Times New Roman
by Apex CoVantage, LLC

Printed and bound in the United States of America by Sheridan

Contents

Acknowledgements

UNITED STATES INSTITUTE OF THEATRE TECHNOLOGY (USITT)

We would not know each other, let alone have written this book, if it was not for the USITT annual conference. We owe a debt of gratitude to our amazing network, made possible by USITT. If production management is your chosen path, you must go to this conference! The possible growth and networking is endless! Specific thanks to David Grindle, Jack Feivou, Tayneshia Jefferson, Michael Mehler, Cameron Jackson, Rick Cunningham, Deb Acquavella and Tina Shackleford, among many others.

INTERVIEWS

This book would not have been possible without the wisdom and experiences from those we interviewed. The process of interviewing for this book was the most enjoyable part—talking for hours with fellow production managers about what we do and why we do it. It was inspiring, to say the least, and we are better production managers and people due to these conversations.

Jesse Aasheim
Kasey Allee-Foreman
Tom Bollard
Jamila Cobham
Linda Cooper
Rosie Cruz
Robert Drake
Vinnie Feraudo
Kim Fisk
Eric Fliss
Roberta Fliss
William Foster
Ken Freeman
Harris Goldman
David Grindle
Ben Heller
David Holcombe

Paul Horpedahl

Yvonne Kimmons

Joel Krause

Neil Kutner

Liza Luxenberg

Ouida Maedel

Naomi Major

Nancy Mallette

Anne E. McMills

Lee Milliken

Christy Ney

Rick Noble

Glenn Plott

Scott Price

Karen Quisenberry

William Reynolds

Michael Richter

Jennifer Ringle

Abby Rodd

Bronislaw Samler

John Sanders

Carolyn Satter

Paige Satter

Jenn Schwartz

Perry Silvey

Richard Stephens

David Stewart

Doug Taylor

Dixie Uffleman

Tracy Utzmyers

Jill Valentine

Deb Vandergrift

Mike Wade

Drew Wending

Jamie Whitehill

Rebecca Wolf

PHOTOS AND IMAGES

We offer gratitude to those who provided images, templates and photos for the book:

Stan Barouh

Kevin Berne

Brianne Bland

Tom Bollard

Michal Daniel

Jeanne DeLeifde

Kyle Flubacker

Neal Golden

Phil Groshong

Phil Hamer

Zachary Z. Handler

Ryan Knapp

Paul Kolnik

Neil Kutner

Bill Mohn

Chris Oosterlink

Karen Quisenberry

Jay Sheehan

Perry Silvey

David Stewart

Jenn Stewart

Ruth Anne Watkins

Rebecca Wolf

Jay Yamada

Adam Zeek

A special thanks to Hesh One for the outstanding cover and the interior graphics. Your work is inspiring. Thank you for sharing it with us.

OUR EDITORS

The support, inspiration, guidance and mentorship provided by our amazing technical editors is astounding. A special thanks from the bottom of our hearts to Carolyn Satter and David Stewart. And to our Routledge editors—Stacey Walker, Meagan White and Meredith Darnell—thanks for the guidance and encouragement. We're glad we stumbled into your booth at USITT!

SPECIAL THANKS FROM CARY GILLETT

Thanks to those who trusted I could be a production manager and hired me to do so—Cheryl Faraone, Danisha Crosby, Daniel MacLean Wagner and Linda Levy. Thanks also to all the horrible production managers I have worked with and for (who shall remain nameless). You have taught me what NOT to do.

To my current and former students—you inspire me every day to be a better production manager and teacher. Thank you to Scott Kincaid and Dwight Townsend-Gray for forcing me to start teaching production management and to Michelle Heller and Tarythe Albrecht for providing feedback and support throughout the book-writing process.

A personal thanks to my husband, Bill—you are my love, my friend and my editor. You put it all into perspective. And to my daughter, Mary Louise—thanks for your patience while "Mommy worked on her book." I hope you read this someday and are proud of me as I am of you every day.

SPECIAL THANKS FROM JAY SHEEHAN

In addition to those listed, heartfelt gratitude goes out to the following:

- In memoriam, to my first mentor, Douglas Pagliotti and the Old Globe Theatre for believing in a young stage manager enough to give me my Equity card.
- All of my students at San Diego State University, both past and present, who affect me daily and make me a better teacher, production manager and friend.
- San Diego State University School Directors, D.J. Hopkins, Randy Reinholz and Nick Reid, for believing in USITT and supporting my goals as a mentor.
- The theatre faculty and staff at San Diego State University, School of Theatre, Television and Film, who have given me daily opportunities to be a better production manager.
- Carolyn Satter, who taught me about relationships, lifelong friendships and where to park trucks.
- Paige Satter for her constant wisdom and guidance, especially during the writing of this book.
- Dan O'Rourke for his guidance and determination in helping me strive for more.
- My amazingly patient family, especially Kathleen Sheehan, whose editing skills I am so grateful for.
- And lastly, with special gratitude to Mark Sheehan, my guide, my light, my everything. I could not have done this without you.

Foreword

Networking. Communication. Compassion. Risk taking. I learned many of these skills from my parents as they molded me to be a good person, but I also learned a good deal from great friends such as Cary and Jay, the authors of this book. I am a huge fan of both of them and the institute that brought us together, the United States Institute for Theater Technology (USITT). USITT is indeed my second family; they are my friends who push me to continually learn, to be better and to believe in myself. The genesis of this book began out of that family.

I earned my BFA in stage management from Webster University. During a meeting with the incomparable Peter Sargent, Dean of Fine Arts, I asked him, "Where do you see me fifteen to twenty years from now?" He replied, "You will become a production manager." What? Who? What's that? Production management always seemed to be an accidental career for many. Skills honed by many hours in dark theaters, deep conversations with creative types. Disagreements over what we perceived as being "the right way" of doing something. And then, BOOM, someone anointed you as the Person in Charge. So, now I'm in charge; now what? Does this new role come with a "how-to" video? Osmosis? A book? Surely, there is a book. Wait, you must be kidding me. There are no books? Stage management? Technical direction? Done. Directing? Done times a thousand. How to manage a production from the 100,000 foot level? Sorry, there isn't a book on this subject . . . yet . . .

As an educator for fifteen years, I worked to train young managers how to become future leaders. Leadership and management are things that are vital to the health and progress of our industry, but those skills are so rarely taught beyond the primary concepts of stage management. When teaching the future production managers, where is it we educators go? Where do emerging production managers turn? How do we find a basic understanding of how to create dynamic teams and deal with difficult conversations? Ask any production manager what they think the best course of training is and you will get varied answers, but the truth of the matter is that there aren't any foundational resources to begin with. We, as leaders and managers, need to learn how to adapt not only to the changing landscape of theatre but to management and leadership as a whole. With new trends in leading diverse teams and how to create more equitable and inclusive workplaces, resources such as this book become even more critical in our continued quest for education and knowledge.

Our theater world is so much better with this book in it, and even better with Cary and Jay at the helm.

Read this book. Consume it. And now that you know better, do better.

David 'Dstew' Stewart
Director of Production for the Guthrie Theater

Introduction

WHAT IS PRODUCTION MANAGEMENT?

Production management is viewed by many different people as many different things. Simply put, it is the ability to manage a production—from beginning to end. But it's not just the physical production—it's the people, the resources, the facility, the money, the calendar, the temperaments, the list could go on. It is the ability to make sure the project happens on time, on budget, safely and with everyone still speaking to each other at the end. Production managers take their skills of organization, communication and strategic planning to provide structure for an idea and make it come to fruition. It may not seem to many as a creative position, but it is truly an art.

So why is it important to learn about production management? The truth is, very few of us who find ourselves in this job now started out wanting to do this. Many production managers come to this job via stage management or technical direction, and there are even a few who were designers or actors. We are doing a disservice to the production managers of tomorrow if we are not imparting our wisdom to them. Even if they might not know that they are destined to take over our shoes, they should be prepared nonetheless. All those in the production emphasis of study (though some could equally argue that performers, directors and designers would benefit too) should be required to learn about production management and, ideally, from those who have walked the walk.

HOW THIS BOOK CAME ABOUT

We met in 2013 at the United States Institute of Theatre Technology (USITT) annual conference. As this conference does for many, it connected the two of us based on common interests and areas of focus. We realized that we had similar jobs at similar institutions and that we both had recently started teaching production management. We swapped syllabi, discussed teaching techniques and then asked the age-old question: "What book do you use?"

Then in 2014, we met again at USITT, and the conversation about books quickly commenced again. We must have been pretty vocal about our unhappiness with the texts we were using because one colleague told us to stop complaining and write the book ourselves. Naturally we laughed—we're not writers! But it got us thinking. A group of us attended a session together later that day, and we sat right next to each other taking copious notes on the session (or at least that's what we thought the other was doing). In actuality, we were both composing the table of contents for this book. When we made that realization, we knew our decision was made. We struck while the iron was hot and walked down onto the expo floor to a publisher's booth and said: "We have this idea for a book." And the rest is history.

WHY WE WROTE THIS BOOK

The purpose of this book is to provide a tool to those teaching and studying production management as well as provide those new to the field with resources and ideas. Part one of the book focuses on not only the hows of the job (budgets, schedules, meetings) but the whys, too (to make artists' and clients' dreams come true). By providing techniques of management, communication skills and tips on building relationships, the entire scope of the job is represented. Part two looks at how to connect the hard and soft skills to the work itself, providing a well-rounded view of production management in America by looking at all of the various disciplines in which a production manager works.

Throughout this book, you will meet production managers from all walks of life and aspects of the performing arts. We knew the only way to write this book was to connect to the amazing network of production managers in this country. One thing we hope you will walk away from this book realizing is the power of a strong network and all it can aid you with. Each production manager quoted here has a unique perspective to share and a few great stories along the way too. We hope you enjoy their stories, and ours, as we take this journey together.

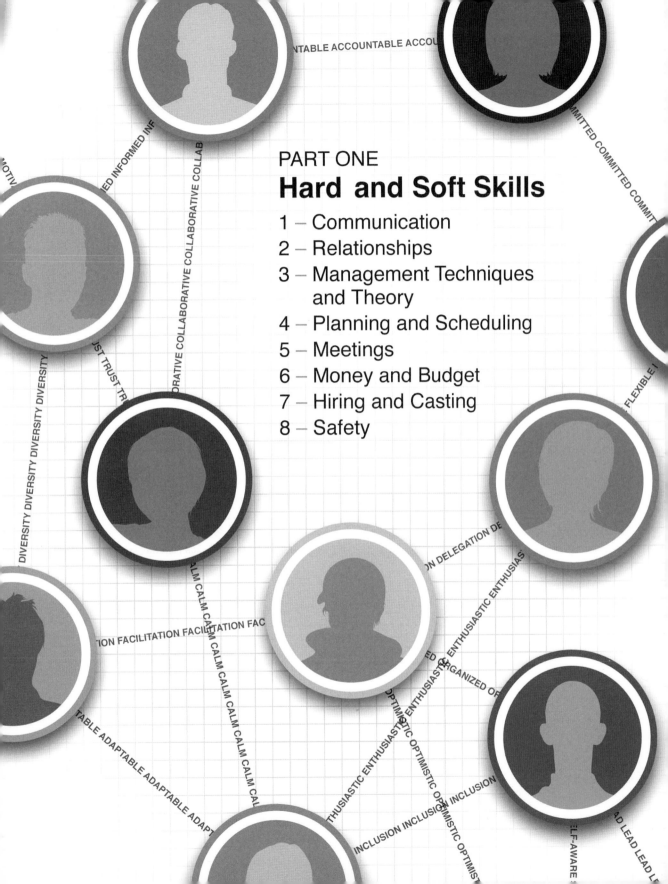

PART ONE
Hard and Soft Skills

Communication

Good communication skills are a necessity for any production manager. Day in and day out, we are communicating with all sorts of people and using every possible channel. This chapter provides techniques for communicating face-to-face, by phone and in writing. It will also explore the important role of non-verbal communication. Last, this chapter will discuss three very important points that production managers deal with all the time—saying yes, saying no and how to manage a difficult conversation.

In her book, *The Stage Manager's Toolkit*, Laurie Kincman offers three words as "key elements of successful communication"—*tactful, timely* and *specific*.

- To be *tactful* is to pay attention to what you are saying and doing and how it affects other people. Try not to upset or offend those you are communicating with.

- Communication is most effective when it is *timely*. If someone poses a question to you, get back to them as quickly as possible, or you risk sending a message that the communication with them is not important.

- Be *specific:* choose your words carefully so as not to confuse or complicate the situation.

"[These words] demonstrate respect for both the production and the personnel, and will enable [you] to facilitate creativity and collaboration in a highly successful manner," Kincman advises.[1]

To compliment these elements we, the authors of *The Production Manager's Toolkit*, offer up three more communication words—*genuine, respect* and *empathy*.

- To be *genuine* is to be honest, to yourself and to others. Many people can tell if someone is not genuine, and this can lead to distrust.

- *Respect* is reciprocal. If you respect the other person and what they are saying or asking, they will respect you in return.

- *Empathy* speaks to every person's need to be understood. Take a *moment* to put yourself in someone's shoes to truly understand what they feel and what they are experiencing. It will enable you to connect with them and their situation in a meaningful way.

"Be impeccable with your word." In his book, *The Four Agreements*, author Miguel Ángel Ruiz encourages us to make our word our vow.[2] Only speak the truth, and if you speak, know that you have made a promise to make it true. Next time you are speaking with someone, keep this in mind and pay attention to what you are saying and promising. Going back on your word, no matter how miniscule, could have a dramatic effect on the relationship you are building.

FACE-TO-FACE COMMUNICATION

In a world of increasing electronic communication, study after study has proved that the most productive and successful system of communication is face-to-face. Having the ability to give and receive full focus and attention is the best way to demonstrate that you are interested and engaged in the subject and in the person. The three major benefits of face-to-face communication are nonverbal communication, immediate feedback and paravocalics (the changes in tone we give our voices to make ourselves understood). Here are a few pointers for good face-to-face communication:

- Eye contact: Look into the other person's eyes when you speak to them. By engaging in this way, you connect deeply to the person speaking and are able to create a connection vital for good understanding.

- Listen, don't just hear: This can be a difficult skill to understand and master. To hear someone is to recognize the words they are saying. To truly listen is to understand what drives their need to speak, what concepts are being conveyed and the emotional content of these messages.

- Smile: Dale Carnegie, in his book *How to Win Friends and Influence People*, states that "actions speak louder than words, and a smile says, 'I like you. You make me happy. I am glad to see you.'"[3] People want to be liked, and a smile is an easy way to show this.

- Take your time: Just because the person is standing right in front of you does not mean you need to give an immediate response. It's perfectly acceptable to delay the response: "Thank you for bringing that to my attention. I need to look into that more and get back to you." Then make sure that you do. Remember what *The Four Agreements* teaches us— your word is your vow.

COMMUNICATIONS BY PHONE

Life is complicated and people are busy, so you can't always meet face-to-face. Communication by phone is a second-best option—you maintain the personal connection, but you are unable to connect with them visually. With no eye contact, you will need to find another way to let your partner know you are engaged. A good technique is to repeat back to them part of what they are saying or paraphrasing what you are hearing so they know you are listening. Listening is still vital here, and so is smiling. You can hear in someone's voice when they are smiling and attentive.

WRITTEN COMMUNICATION

When we talk of written communication, unless in unusual circumstances, we usually mean email. Email has changed the way we communicate, and in many ways NOT for the better. The three major benefits of face-to-face communication (nonverbal communication, immediate feedback and paravocalics) are removed in written communication. Communicating via email is not only impersonal but also less effective, as you remove all context of what you are feeling when you write it. Email is an inaccurate conveyor of tone. Email communications are best for distributing information or to follow up on a conversation that you had face-to-face: "Thanks so much for chatting with me today. Here is a list of the tasks we came up with."

Written communication requires a serious amount of scrutiny on the part of the writer. Once something has been sent, it is out of your control, so take time to choose your words and organize your thoughts. Because we remove the personal connection, it is also necessary to write in a formalized letter style so that our tone is not misunderstood. Unless you are intimately familiar with the person you are communicating with, you should format the email like a letter, with a salutation or greeting, subject or body of the letter, a closing (i.e. sincerely) and your name.

> **TIP**—Format an email response in exactly the way the person sending you the original email has done. If they have included all the structural elements of a letter, then you should do so too. If they become slightly less formal and remove the greeting or the closing, then it's generally okay for you to do the same.

In a world of ever-changing technology and social networking, our challenges with written communication increase. If email is challenging, texting is worse and instant messenger worse than that. It's important to create expectations for how you will communicate with people and how you expect them to communicate back. Choosing email over a social networking site as the main form of communication is usually the best choice. That's not to say that social networking is bad, but it can blur the line between personal and professional communication, which can be dangerous. It is also important to set expectations for communication tools like text messaging. Who is allowed to send you a text message and under what circumstances? Who do you choose to text, why and when? Not everyone uses the same technology and tools. There are people working in this profession who reject text messages and social media. Learn who you are working with, and tailor your communication plans to their needs and yours.

BODY LANGUAGE OR NON-VERBAL COMMUNICATION

Albert Mehrabian, a researcher in the field of body language, claims that the impact of a person's message is 7% the words they say, 38% how they use their voice when they say it (paravocalics) and 55% what their body says while they talk.[4] Body language is a fascinating and quite daunting field of study. To fully understand the minutia of how humans communicate non-verbally would take many academic degrees and years of study and observation. However, there is quite a bit you can pick up on if you know where to look and pay attention. Performing artists are quite gifted at reading body language. It makes sense, as many of them make a living using their bodies to make art, so they are often both self-aware and observant of others. Have you ever noticed how hard it is to lie to an actor? Not that you should make a habit of that, of course. They can read your body language and judge if you are telling the truth or not!

> **TIP**—A great way to study body language is to watch people. In a meeting where you are merely a participant or observer, pay attention to the people actively participating. Are their gestures matching what they say? Does one

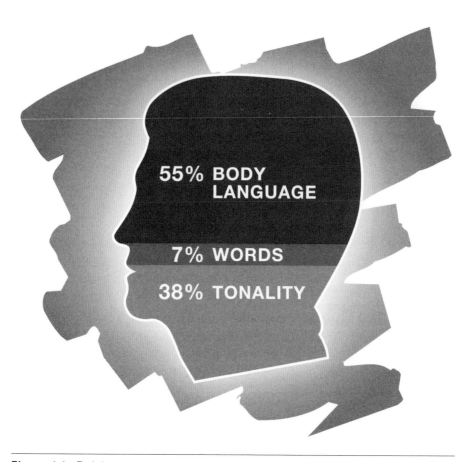

Figure 1.1 Body language percentages

Credit: Image by Hesh One

person say they are open to new ideas while tightly crossing their arms across their chest? Does someone agree with another while not making eye contact? What else can you observe?

We should not only be paying attention to people's body language but also their face. The face gives so much away without us even realizing it. Psychologist Paul Ekman has spent his career studying and mapping out facial expressions. He concludes that there are seven emotions with universal signals that cross race, culture and language—anger, fear, sadness, disgust, contempt, surprise and happiness. In his book *Unmasking the Face*, he speaks of "micro-expressions," or expressions linked to our emotions that we have no control over: "You feel fear, the expression begins to appear on your face, you sense from your facial muscles that you are beginning to look afraid, and you de-intensify the expression, neutralize it, mask it. For a fraction of a second the fear expression will have been there."[5] By learning to read another person's face, you can truly get a glimpse of what they are thinking.

You must also realize that YOU communicate with your body and face so it's important to take the time to observe your own actions. What is your resting face (your face when you aren't making a face)? Does it look angry or bored? That might give someone the wrong impression. You might need to actively keep a pleasant or engaged look on your face while you are talking with someone. What do you do with your arms while you speak? Are they held tight to your chest or stretched out with fingers crossed behind your head? Whether you realize it or not, you are sending a message. Be conscious of what that message is.

Our body language demonstrates how we feel, but it can also make us feel. "This is because gesture and emotions are directly linked to each other," experts say.[6] Studies have shown that if a person sits with legs crossed and hunched over (low status position) before an interview, they will feel less good about the outcome than if they stood up, with hands on hips and head held high (high status position). Sociologist Amy Cuddy speaks on this topic in her TED (Technology, Entertainment and Design conference) talk in October 2012. If you assume these powerful positions, you can in fact trick yourself into believing that you have that power. She identifies this not merely as "fake it until you make it," but rather "fake it until you *become* it."[7]

Another fascinating concept to consider is proxemics, or the study of people's relationship to the space around them. Anthropologist Edward T. Hall divided this study into two concepts—personal space and territory.[8] Personal space is the area around the body that shifts as we do. Each of us has a different expectation of how large that space should be, who can enter it and when. Personal space can be cultural: There are national or ethnic differences and differences between men and women and children and adults, as well as between people in different parts of the country. Territory is the larger space we inhabit such as a room, office, building, etc., and can be considered public, where we have no control over what exists inside of it, or private, where we have all of the control. To understand another's relationship to

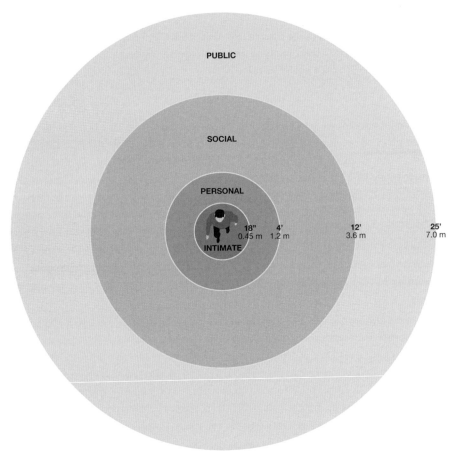

Figure 1.2

Credit: Image by Hesh One

personal space and territory can allow for either a positive or negative interaction based on how you choose to exist physically in relation to them.

Say for example you enter a rehearsal room to speak with a director. The rehearsal is still in progress, so you enter the space, cross behind the director, stand off to the side far back from them and wait until the break has been called. The rehearsal room is the director's territory,

Figure 1.3   The College-Conservatory of Music at the University of Cincinnati
Credit: Photo by Adam Zeek, www.zeekcreative.com

and until the break is called, their personal space should not be affected by others not directly involved in the rehearsal. What if you took a different approach? This time you enter the space, walk between the director and the performers and stand two feet from the director until they choose to acknowledge you. Which option sets up a successful conversation to come?

HOW TO SAY YES!

Saying yes seems like such an easy concept, but to a production manager, it can be quite a challenge at times. Artists have lots of ideas, many of them going beyond budget allotments and sometimes defying physics. Our job as production managers is to make our artists' dreams fly, not to shoot them down. Production manager Neil Kutner rightfully states that "one 'no' can negate twenty 'yesses.'"[9] By saying no, you can kill the professional relationship, and even worse, you can create a situation where the next time that artist has an idea, they'll do it without including you. So how do you take those ideas and make them a reality? Learn to say YES!

- Resist the temptation to immediately refuse an idea. Even if you know the idea is impossible, give it time. "No" is the easy way out but not always the smartest.
- Understand the why behind the idea. Engage the artist on a creative level, and allow them to explain the concept to you. Most artists are passionate about their ideas and want to talk about them. By allowing them that opportunity, you are cultivating the relationship.

Make sure you truly understand what they need. It's possible that a solution will arise that easily meets the needs.

- Challenge the obstacles in the way. Are there other people denying the artist's idea? Talk with these entities and understand the concerns. Often a "no" is merely a way to avoid dealing with a scary or unknown situation.

- Get the facts. (What are the laws of physics at play here?) Take this opportunity to learn something you did not know. Even if an immediate benefit is unclear, you never know when this information might be useful on a future project.

- Line up the right partners to get the job done. Maybe the request goes beyond the skill level of your team and specialists need to be engaged. Good production managers know their own limitations and ignorance, and they will find the right personnel to support the project.

- Try it. Who knows, it might be the most brilliant idea ever imagined . . . or it might not. Often, you will not know until you try. We learn more from our failures than we do from our successes.

> "Don't be afraid to fail . . . remember that good judgment is the product of experience and experience is the product of failure."
>
> - Tom Bollard, Production Manager / Technical Director for
> Meeting Services Inc.

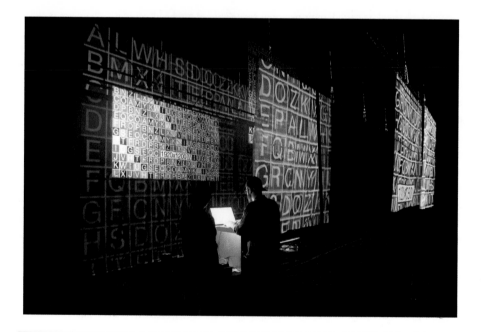

Figure 1.4 If you are not sure you can achieve something—do a test!
Credit: Photo by Ryan Knapp

HOW TO SAY NO

Sometimes it is necessary to say "no." Let's explore the best way to do this, save relationships and keep conversations going. In his book *The Power of a Positive No*, William Ury offers up a description of a "Positive No" as a *"YES! No. Yes?"* The first *YES!* protects your interests; it is the positive reason behind the no. The *No* asserts your power in the situation. The final *Yes?* keeps the door open for future possibilities and therefore saves the relationship.[10]

Here's an example of this technique in action: You get offered a job by a reputable company that you have been hoping to work with, but you are already engaged on another project, and you do not wish to burn a bridge by disappointing the company you are already working for. Your "Positive No" could sound something like this: "Thank you so much for the offer to work with your company. Unfortunately, I am busy with another job at the moment and would not be able to devote the time and effort that your project is due. I hope you will keep me in mind for future opportunities. It would be my pleasure to work with you soon." The *"YES!"* (or the positive reason behind the *No*) supports your best interests while supporting their project. The *"Yes?"* (or the relationship saver) is the connection to future work with that company.

Here is another example: A director requests four new costumes one week before tech. Due to the nature of the costumes, they would have to be completely built, which there is neither time nor money to accomplish. This "Positive No" could be along these lines: "As much as we would like to accomplish your request, we are not in a position to ask our staff to go into overtime to build these costumes, nor can we increase the materials budget to allow for the necessary items. However, we do have a substantial costume stock with many clothes from the same period. Would you like me to set up a time for you and the costume designer to look through them?" Here the *"YES!"* supports your staff as well as your bottom line and the *"Yes?"* allows for a viable option that in the end might prove better than the original request.

The most important key to successful communication is to keep the conversation going. If you immediately end a conversation or crush someone's ideas, you make future collaboration very difficult. Keep the conversation going. It's like you are all on the same train together headed toward the opening of a great artistic endeavor; don't hit the emergency break if you can avoid it! Remember: "one 'no' can negate twenty 'yesses.'"

Figure 1.5

Credit: Photo by David "Dstew" Stewart

DIFFICULT CONVERSATIONS

From time to time, we are required to cope with difficult or challenging conversations, either because of the subject matter or the person with whom you are communicating. In an artistic world, this will often be compounded by emotion and feelings of "high stakes." Let's face it; in the performing arts, the stakes always feel high. So what is the best way to approach these difficult conversations? Here are some pointers.

- Create a shared pool of meaning. Author Kerry Patterson advises: "When two or more of us enter *crucial* conversations, by definition we don't share the same pool. Our opinions differ. I believe one thing; you believe another. I have one history; you another. People who are skilled at dialogue do their best to make it safe for everyone to add their meaning to the *shared* pool—even ideas that at first glance appear controversial, wrong, or at odds with their own beliefs. Now, obviously, they don't agree with every idea; they simply do their best to ensure that all ideas find their way into the open."[11]

- Keep your emotions out of the way. This is easier said than done but is vital for good communicators. If you have done a good job with your communication, rarely is anyone attacking you personally. They are frustrated about a situation or a piece of news that you had the unfortunate luck to deliver. If someone yells, tell yourself they are yelling at you, not because of you.

- Allow the other person to express themselves or even vent. Sometimes people just want to be heard, and once they are, they are much easier to reason with.

- Don't feel you have to match their energy. If someone is yelling at you, resist yelling back. Try the opposite, and speak quietly or even whisper. Often, this will make the person realize that they are behaving inappropriately.

- Know your triggers. We all have certain things that spark our anger and trigger a fight-or-flight reaction. When you are aware of your instinctual reactions, you can succeed in resisting these urges. SCARF is a tool created by neuroscientists to assess how people respond to social threats and rewards. It stands for *S*tatus, *C*ertainty, *A*utonomy, *R*elatedness, *F*airness, which are the five domains of human interaction represented in the study.[12]

- Stand your ground. Don't let the heightened emotional situation lessen your scruples. If you believe firmly in something, make that clear. However, keep your emotions in check.

- Give it time. Perhaps a solution does not need to be found immediately. Allowing time or breathing room lets both parties contemplate all sides of the issue and perhaps return to the conversation later with a different perspective. If, however, a resolution is needed right away and time apart is not an option, make the best choice you can. Use your common sense to suggest a compromise.

To emphasize, the most important thing you can do is keep communicating. Keep connections and relationships with people thriving. In the moment, it might be hard to recognize the benefit of continual communication, but your patience will be rewarded. Those of us who work

Figure 1.6

Credit: Photo courtesy of the Guthrie Theatre

in the artistic community make up a very small percentage of the population. Chances are you will work with the same people again and again. Make sure that your communications are clear and positive not only for the happiness of your collaborators but also for your own happiness.

NOTES

1 Kincman, Laurie. *The Stage Manager's Toolkit: Templates and Communication Techniques to Guide Your Theatre Production from First Meeting to Final Performance.* Burlington, MA: Focal Press, 2013.

2 Ruiz, Miguel. *The Four Agreements: A Practical Guide to Personal Freedom.* San Rafael, CA: Amber-Allen Publishers, 1997.

3 Carnegie, Dale. *How to Win Friends and Influence People.* New York: Simon and Schuster, 1981.

4 Pease, Allan, and Barbara Pease. *The Definitive Book of Body Language.* Bantam Hardcover ed. New York: Bantam Books, 2006.

5 Ekman, Paul, and Wallace V. Friesen. *Unmasking the Face; a Guide to Recognizing Emotions from Facial Clues.* Englewood Cliffs, NJ: Prentice-Hall, 1975.

6 Pease, Allan, and Barbara Pease. *The Definitive Book of Body Language.* Bantam Hardcover ed. New York: Bantam Books, 2006.

7 Cuddy, Amy. "Your Body Language Shapes Who You Are." *TED Talk*, June 2012. https://www.ted.com/talks/amy_cuddy_your_body_language_shapes_who_you_are?language=en

8 Hall, Edward T. *The Hidden Dimension*. Garden City, NY: Anchor Books, 1990.

9 All quotations from experts in the theatre industry are from personal interviews conducted by the authors.

10 Ury, William. *The Power of a Positive No: How to Say No and Still Get to Yes*. New York: Bantam Books, 2007.

11 Patterson, Kerry. *Crucial Conversations: Tools for Talking When Stakes Are High*. New York: McGraw-Hill, 2002.

12 NeuroLeadership Group. http://neuroleadership.co.in/scarfsolutions/

Relationships

> "Relationships are created and maintained with mutual respect and open channels of communication."
>
> - Jesse Aasheim, Production Manager at Round House Theatre

A production manager cannot be successful working as an island. In order for the production manager to be effective in their position, it is important to have allies and good relationships with everyone. You wouldn't be able to get your work accomplished effectively and efficiently without having these relationships firmly planted in your toolbox. It is well known that stress levels are reduced when one has strong relationships. This is not only true for everyday life, but this is also true for the production manager, as it is in your best interest to keep stress levels in the workplace to a minimum in order to get the creative work done on time and on budget. As a production manager, you can act as a positive role model, especially in times of high stress. If you can remain calm in a stressful work environment, it will be much easier for your creative team and production staff to stay calm. That is the ultimate goal for the successful production manager, as having a calm staff can help lead to more meaningful relationships. A successful, "stress-free" relationship also leads to a better, more creative work environment for everyone involved. Let's face it, it is easier and more fun to get goals accomplished with less stress and with people who get along well together!

The collaborative team in the performing arts is a talented mix of individuals coming together for a common goal—to create a successful show or event. The production manager's team in all of the performing arts is fairly consistent. Scenic designers, lighting designers and audio designers are just part of the creative team involved with getting the show together. Stage managers, technical directors, shop staff and tech crew as well as general management and accountants are also vital members of the team. In the area of costume design and wardrobe, there are drapers, stitchers, dyers, make-up and hair staff that all contribute to this area. As they say, "it takes a village," and nowhere is that more evident than a busy theatre.

Figure 2.1

Credit: Image ©iStock

For those who work in a presenting theatre or produce special events (see chapters 14 and 17), the village is made up of the client that rents your building, your labor force of stage-hands, vendors and front of house staff such as ticketing and house management. All of these relationships matter, so take the time to create and maintain these essential connections. It will pay off for you in the long run.

So . . . now that you have been told to create and maintain relationships . . . how do you do that?

Answering this question is not always easy. Relationships take time and care to create and nurture. You can't just expect to sit down with every type of personality and passion level and get immediate results. Trust must be established, and trust takes believing in your team. There is no one way to create and maintain relationships. You will use various techniques and tools from your toolkit and this textbook in order to achieve positive results with relationships and relationship building. The important thing to remember is that every relationship at any given moment or situation can and will be different. Much like a chameleon that must change colors at a moment's notice in order to survive, so must the production manager be able to change tone of voice, body language and message delivery to the various team members on the project.

Creating and maintaining relationships takes hard work and a willingness to work on these relationships on a daily basis. We, and several other production managers from around the United States, have consistent opinions and messaging on how we create and maintain these very important relationships in order to be successful. David Grindle, Executive Director at United States Institute for Theatre Technology (USITT), comments that, "The first step in good relationship building is going to people, not making them come to you." This is known as MBWA . . . manage by walking around and is sage advice for the production manager.

According to Grindle,

> *Listening to the challenges of people is another. Most people simply want to be listened to. They will solve the issue or live with it, but they need their concerns heard. Conversely, after listening, you may not have the answer, but you may have another perspective. Departments are busy and don't always know what is going on in the other areas. A production manager does and can bring perspective. Lastly, be just in your decisions. Give reasons as answers, answering with reasons gives people perspective. It doesn't mean they will agree or will like it, but they will have an adult answer.*

Lee Milliken from the Canadian Opera Company says this about creating relationships: "I try to treat people with fairness, honesty and respect. I feel that sharing as much information as possible strengthens our team and helps to ensure that everyone is working together toward the same goal." This is an important step in the process of relationship building. Treating people with respect means that you are actually listening to them and are a willing participant in helping to achieve the productions goals. Listening is an essential objective for you to accomplish and should be a large part of your toolkit. "Understand what the person brings to the table and always listen to what the other person has to say" says David Stewart, Director of Production at the Guthrie Theater in Minneapolis. Good advice from someone who knows!

Understanding people is a big part of this process. Linda Cooper, former Production Manager at the La Jolla Playhouse, says, "I try to take a human approach. We're all human beings. Learning a little bit about them is always helpful to have a frame of reference. I also try to be honest and straight forward and build a foundation of trust so we can talk about the hard things." Having a "foundation of trust" from which to begin from shows the other person that you care about what they have to say, and that you will work hard at trying to help them achieve their goals. Rick Noble from CenterStage in Baltimore agrees with Cooper and states that "to build relationships I create trust—sometimes in a big hurry. To do this I answer questions with considered truth."

As you can start to see, the production manager is much more than just a budget manager or acquirer of goods and services. We are also part psychologist, as words like "trust" and "truth" starts to become part of our everyday vocabulary. In addition to being part psychologist, we have to be excellent communicators as well. Communication with others is essential and an additional way of creating and maintaining relationships with your production staff. Your team members want information in order to do their jobs correctly, and it is the production manager who has the responsibility to give them the tools they need to do their jobs effectively and efficiently. Abby Rodd, Production Manager from Glimmerglass Opera, says you must "communicate with people as much as humanly possible even if it is to say 'I don't know anything yet.' The more they are hearing from you the more they believe you are on their side and you've got their back."

As stated before, there is no one way to create and maintain relationships. Every production manager may have a different opinion on just how to do this, but the messaging seems to be the same; treat people with respect, treat people fairly and keep the lines of communication open. If you can do this successfully, you are on your way to becoming an effective production manager.

Creating and producing live performances and events requires the production manager to work on several important relationships at one time. Let's take a look at some specific relationships and why they are important.

THE PRODUCTION MANAGER AND THE ARTISTIC DIRECTOR

In the case of regional theatre, the artistic director may be the most important relationship to the production manager. Since artistic directors oversee and are involved in all of the shows, it is best for you as a production manager to try and get to know them as best as possible. Having insight into the way they think about such things as why each director is chosen, season planning, budgets, fundraising and designer choices will help you when it comes time to plan for your individual departments. David Holcombe is the Production Manager for Carnegie Mellon University and oversees a season of 16 shows. As far as relationships go, Holcombe says,

> I want to be most secure with my relationship to the artistic head of the organization. That is the person whose product you are charged with making sure gets onstage. That is the person whose opinion about the product matters the most.

THE PRODUCTION MANAGER AND THE DIRECTOR

An important relationship that is created and nurtured over the course of the production is with the director. Realizing the physical aspects of the imagined production as created by the director—and doing it within the resources allotted—is a challenging and rewarding job for the production manager. Directors don't always get what they want, and many times it is the production manager that has to be the bearer of the news that something can't be achieved or cannot be fully realized as originally intended. This can be for a variety of reasons, not just money. Time, space and labor, for instance, can also be contributing factors to directors not getting their vision achieved. It will be important for you to learn how to communicate these concerns without sounding too negative, and having a good relationship with your director makes having difficult conversations a little easier. (For more on communicating these conversations, see chapter 1.)

THE PRODUCTION MANAGER AND THE CREATIVE DESIGNER

The relationships a production manager has with the various creative designers (scenic, costumes, lighting, audio, video, décor, etc.) are also important ones to nurture. We have to work together to create the physical reality for the director or client, and all of us should have that same goal in mind. Strong relationships are vital for being able to negotiate the difficult paths that we may have to take to get to our goal. It is your job as the production manager to make sure that the design staff members have the tools that they need to create and do their work. Managing the designers' resources, such as time, budgets and physical space to work in, are all part of your purview and will need to be worked out in detail. At times, designers, their assistants and production managers are faced with challenges when it comes to dealing with limited resources such as money and labor. The production manager may have to be the bearer of such news, and the relationship can oftentimes help make the conversation a little easier. Having a strong relationship helps this process and helps to get the most dynamic and creative work from the designers. In addition to working on the physical part of the production with the designers, oftentimes, the production manager will also have to negotiate contracts and design fees, and having a strong working relationship with designers and their agents will prove helpful when dealing with these negotiations.

Anne E. McMills, author of *The Assistant Lighting Designer's Toolkit*, has this to say about the importance of the production manager / designer relationship:

> *The production manager and the designers must work as a team to make a production process a smooth one. The best decisions are made when these relationships are symbiotic. For example, the production manager's production calendar is most effective with heavy consultation and buy-in from the designers and rest of the production team: How many days will load-in take? How many hours are anticipated for moving light*

Figure 2.2
Credit: Image ©iStock

programming and focus? etc. And, in turn, the designers can rely heavily on the guidance and leadership of the production manager to help keep track of deadlines, navigate difficult scheduling or political issues, and help the production progress efficiently. This allows the designers to concentrate more fully on their designs rather than become mired in the details of the production process.

As we have stated earlier in this chapter, relationship building is a two-way street. Designers would like to have a great relationship with the production manager as much as the production manager would like to have a great relationship with the designers. McMills is in agreement and states, "I try to forge a strong partnership with the production manager based on mutual respect and trust. Production managers are the eyes and ears of the entire design and production team with an uncanny knack at solving problems much more quickly than me—who spends my time staring at the trees instead of the woods. Therefore, I rely on his or her strong leadership for guidance on the big picture. I try to return the favor by following my deadlines and schedules as closely as I can and consult with him or her when issues arise. I feel that it would be disrespectful of their work otherwise."

THE PRODUCTION MANAGER AND THE SHOP SUPERVISORS / PRODUCTION STAFF

"Everyone on the team is important."

- Lee Milliken, Production Manager at the Canadian Opera Company

Having a great relationship with your production shop supervisors such as the costume shop manager, technical director and scene shop heads, as well as assistant production managers and production assistants, is also a key to success. At times, when things get down to the wire and stress levels may rise, the niceties of conversation may get shortened, and it takes a really good working relationship to realize that things are not personal in the heat of the battle of getting a production mounted. Everyone on the team is important.

THE PRODUCTION MANAGER AND THE STAGE MANAGER

The production manager–stage manager relationship should be a close one. The production manager is overseeing the entire season and worrying about the bigger picture while the stage manager focuses on one specific production. The stage manager is the vital communication link between departments and is a crucial part of the production manager's team. Because the production manager is not in rehearsals every day (and shouldn't have to be) the stage manager is the production manager's "boots on the ground." Having a good working relationship with the stage manager will help make the process smoother and the goals become more achievable. Good stage managers are worth their weight in gold. You need to trust that your stage manager will keep you apprised of what you need to know. (Don't forget, trust is a two-way street!)

David Grindle agrees about the importance of the relationship: "The stage manager and production manager relationship is important in many ways. The stage manager acts as eyes and ears in the rehearsal hall. The information flowing from them allows the production manager to anticipate needs of one production from the administrative point of view. It also allows them to monitor budgets of time and money. Additionally, the production manager is the stage manager's advocate from an administrative side. Interfacing with other departments of the administration, the production manager can help insure the needs of rehearsal are being communicated throughout the company."

THE PRODUCTION MANAGER AND THE CREW

As a production manager, no one on your team should be overlooked as far as trying to create relationships and teamwork. While the production manager may not get personally involved in the crew selection (though on some occasions they do), it is important to make sure that you introduce yourself to the various crew positions and make the crew and other pertinent staff feel welcomed to the team. Empowering and showing trust in the show's crew from the first rehearsal is an important part of the relationship-building process. You wouldn't be able to have a show without your crew. You should make sure that they know that and that you appreciate their hard work. Kind words can go a long way when it comes time to motivate and encourage.

Rosie Cruz, Production Coordinator at Purchase College, says

> my crew and the people that I hire are the most important. These are the people that are going to work with me in order to make something great. They reflect on me and my work. They can make my life easier or harder. I can use their strengths and weaknesses to work to my advantage.

Make a point to get to know your crew. Say "thank you" at the end of a long tech day. Your life will be much more pleasant with a happy crew! Carolyn Satter, Production and Facilities Manager for the San Diego Theatres, has a few pointers as well for working with your crew.

> Random acts of kindness go a long way in maintaining relationships. If my crew needs something to do their job better, I will be the first one to make sure that they have the tools they need to do their work. Also, don't keep asking for favors from your crew without giving back. These relationships can't be a one-way street.

Figure 2.3   A hot meal on a long day is always appreciated!

Credit: Photo by Ryan Knapp

OTHER RELATIONSHIPS

There are a plethora of relationships that need to be constantly nurtured and maintained throughout the lifecycle of the show or event. Besides the relationships listed above, the production manager will also have, although perhaps not as close, a relationship with other departments within the organization. Marketing staff, box office management, development or fundraising departments and facilities management will all become part of your daily interaction and will need your time and attention.

Don't lose sight of the fact that everyone on the team is important. Neil Kutner, the Production Manager at the Brooklyn Academy of Music (BAM), says that "everyone who works for me or with me, I assume one day I'm going to work for them, and I treat them as such. I believe that everybody who works for me, if I've done my job right, is smarter than I am. I believe everybody who works with me has something to contribute that I can't contribute."

Most production managers around the United States have successfully created their production teams and have wonderful daily working relationships. But what relationship is the most important for the production manager? Not an easy question, and the answers may vary, but the bottom line is that *all* relationships matter, and you will need to put time and energy into them to make them work for both parties. Paul Horpedahl, Production Manager from Sante Fe Opera, agrees: "Everyone is important—the board member is as important as the director and as important as the janitor and the technical apprentice and the designers. We all work together to make the final product." Vinnie Feraudo from Seattle Opera adds, "It's all of them. It's just like parenting. You love each of your kids the same but the one in the room with you right now is the one you love the most."

Creating and nurturing relationships is an ongoing and daily part of the production manager's life. Having the skills necessary to do this will aid you greatly in becoming an efficient production manager. Practice making relationships work in your everyday life, and you will

Figure 2.4
Credit: Image ©iStock

begin to see how your work will start to get easier and easier each day. Here are a few tips for some quick relationship building:

- Manage by walking around. Stop in to see your production staff every so often. It means a lot to those who are working hard that the production manager takes notice of their work.

- Go out for coffee and have a "no agenda" meeting with one or more of your team members. Getting to know people on a personal level is an important step for building relationships.

- Make words such as "please" and "thank you" a regular part of your vocabulary. The words you speak are as important as the actions you take, and kind words really do go a long way.

- Go the extra mile to make everyone feel important and valued. Empowering your team is vital to success.

Using this chapter as a guide for relationship building should get you started in the right direction. Practice relationship building on a daily basis, and you will start to see these relationships blossom and flourish. James C. Humes, an author and former presidential speechwriter, puts it best: "Every time you have to speak, you are auditioning for leadership." Remember this and practice it regularly, and you will be on your way to creating and maintaining your own effective relationships.

CHAPTER 3

Management Techniques and Theory

The production manager works for the production. You work for the organization, and you work for your staff, as much as they work for you. To mount a show or an event requires an incredible amount of effort from an amazing amount of people. All of those various people must be able to work together. If you want to be a good manager, you must first be a good leader. A good leader must be:

- Adaptable: Each production will require something different from you. Each day, you will set out to accomplish a list of tasks, and the priorities will shift as a challenge arises. Each day, you will interact with a variety of personalities—some easy-going and some more challenging. You need to adapt as necessary to support the project and your team. "It is not the strongest of the species that survives; it is the one most adaptable to change." —Charles Darwin

- Calm/patient: No one wants to work with a stressed or angry production manager. If you can stay calm under great stress, you can inspire others to do the same.

- Collaborative: We do not do this job in a vacuum. Working well with others is vital to the success of a production. Sit down at the table with them and be a part of the team. You have a lot to contribute to the big picture.

- A good communicator: You need to be able to speak all languages (set design to the set designer, directing to the director, quick change to the wardrobe crew), and when two of those people can't figure out how to speak with each other, you need to intervene and interpret.

- A goal setter: Our goal is opening night. Often, other, smaller goals must be set in order to reach that main goal. The production manager must set goals and remind people about them to keep everyone focused and productive. Teams go astray when they lose sight of the goal.

- Organized: In thought, in paperwork and in action.

- Committed: The production manager should be the hardest-working person on the production team. No one should question their commitment to the project.

- Accountable: Trust is a huge factor in leadership. If your team cannot trust you will get something done, you are in trouble. You must also be willing to take the blame if things go wrong. Own your decisions—you are the one ultimately responsible for facilitating the production.

- A people person: Knowledge and interest in people, how they work and what motivates them is key. A good production manager does not sit behind a desk all day but interacts with everyone on the production constantly. Knowing and caring about those people makes that interaction much easier and meaningful for both you and them.

- Self-aware: Know when to act and know when to get out of the way. Understand how you best contribute to the project. Know your strengths and limitations.

- A good follower: The artistic leadership creates the vision of the production. You must be able to follow their lead and support their ideas. You may also need to explain this vision to others in order for them to be good followers, too.

- Informed: You need to know what is going on so you know how best to support the process. You need to know a little about every part of the project and every person working on it. You are not the master electrician or the props artisan, but you need to know how those people work and what they have to do to get their job done.

> "You need an open mind, patience and the ability to see things from multiple perspectives."
>
> - Dixie Uffleman, Production Manager at Northwestern University

FACILITATION

The production manager has a unique position in an organization and on a production. You advocate for the work of the creative team and for the work of the production staff. In an ideal world, those factions are aligned, but what happens when they are not? Oftentimes, the creative team will request a change or addition that the production staff might not be able to do or want to do. The production manager walks a fine line between art and practicality and must constantly find ways to keep everyone motivated and productive. The production manager is often the one who knows the most about what both sides need and want and therefore is the best equipped to make the final call. Often, sacrifices will need to be made; for example: "We can add the new platform to the set by the first day of tech, but we'll have to delay the installation of the backdrop until the following week."

> "A production manager has to be willing to be blamed for everything that goes wrong. It is my fault because I didn't provide enough resources, or time, or research, or budget. It's my fault no matter what went wrong. And what that does is free up everybody else to make bold decisions."
>
> - Neil Kutner, Director of Production at the Brooklyn Academy of Music

MANAGING THE SCHEDULE

The production manager makes sure things happen on time. When the curtain rises opening night, the show must be ready. But the path we take to get there can be rocky and winding. How do you insure that it will all eventually come together?

- Planning: Take the time well ahead of the project to lay out the ideal scenario. This may be one month to five years in advance, depending upon the complexity of the project. Think about the various stages that will need to occur (design, cost out, build, rehearsal, tech, previews, etc.) and how long each stage will take. If you are unsure of the process or necessities of time, then ask others or do some research. Each project will be different and might require new information.

- Communicate: Make sure everyone is on the same page with the plan. Share calendars, meet with groups and individuals and go over the plan so they understand both how we will reach our goals and why our goals are important.

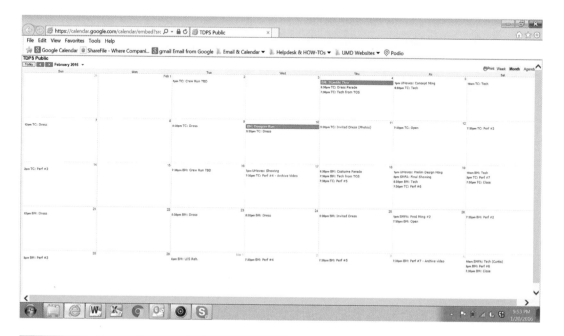

Figure 3.1 Online calendar example

- Be flexible: Things will go wrong. Even our best planning will be interrupted by a shipment delay or a last-minute design change. Look back at the plan and reevaluate. What parts of the process could be compressed to find additional time? What parties can work simultaneously to cut down on time? There are some things we can control and some we can't—flexibility means understanding the difference.

- Look at the budget: Money can often save time. Maybe something can be jobbed out instead of being built in-house. Many arts venues will allow items in their stock to be rented or borrowed: sometimes individual items, but in some cases entire sets or collections of costumes.

- Keep moving forward: Momentum can be stifled if you are not careful. Sometimes you need to assist with a decision or insist that one is made so things can progress.

> "A key attribute is decision making—sometimes you have to make a decision; it could be right or wrong depending upon the viewpoint. That can be the hardest part."
>
> - Linda Cooper, former Production Manager at the La Jolla Playhouse

Figure 3.2 "I stopped by the wig room to take a few process photos, and they really needed someone to test-fit wigs on, so I took a seat."—Ryan Knapp, Associate Director of Production and Instruction at the Clarice Smith Performing Arts Center.

Credit: Photo by Ryan Knapp

MANAGING BY WALKING AROUND

One of the best techniques for management is to be around your staff and their work as often as possible. Get up from your desk at least once a day, if not more, and walk around. These are not official meetings; there is no agenda. This is an opportunity for you to see how people are working. University of Oklahoma Production Manager Kasey Allee-Foreman says that walk-throughs are her favorite part of the day. "I love going and checking in, it makes me feel like I am in touch with the whole production. I love giving my staff and students an opportunity to show me what they have done, in their comfort zone." Be careful not to disrupt their work as you walk around. You don't want them to resent your presence by slowing down productivity.

> "A production manager must be exceedingly competent at the technical details and really good in the room with people. You have to be able to do both of those things to succeed."
>
> - David Holcombe, Production Manager at Carnegie Mellon University

MANAGING YOUR BOSS

Most production managers report directly to an artistic director, a managing director or an executive director or CEO (chief executive officer). Often, these people are artistically minded, without a background in production. One of the most difficult skills you must acquire is the ability to teach them about what you do without offending or upsetting them. You must also have an understanding of what is important to them, how they work and what they expect of you. Help them forward the mission of the organization or the project. Finally, you must appreciate the pressures they are under from those above them (often a board of directors or the like). Your boss may ask for a one-page budget summary not because they do not trust you but because they are expected to present a budget picture to the board of directors the next day.

> "You must have an artistic sensibility so you can understand where the artistic team is coming from and where they want to go. You have to have a passion for the work."
>
> - Vinnie Feraudo, Director of Production at Seattle Opera

> "You need to be really organized, good at communication, able to change priorities on a split-second notice, even tempered, and good at working with a vast array of people including artists, technicians and HVAC guys."
>
> - Deb Vandergrift, former Chief Production Officer at the Shakespeare Theatre Company

MOTIVATION

A good manager is able to motivate their staff toward a common goal. In our case, it is the presentation of a new project. One of the best things about working in this industry is our ability to tackle multiple projects and rarely do the same things twice! The result of this can often be challenging. Going through the same process multiple times each season can feel monotonous. How can you get your staff to break out of a perceived "rut"? The key is motivation.

In his book *Drive: The Surprising Truth About What Motivates Us*, author Daniel H. Pink dispels the rumor that motivation is caused by rewards such as money and recognition. He argues that true motivation is to allow people the opportunity to have:

- Autonomy: We all have the urge to direct our own lives. As a manager, you must know when to take a step back and allow your employees to work on their own. Guide instead of micro-managing, and they will achieve so much more!

- Mastery: Most people have the desire to improve themselves. Support your staff in professional development. You want them to stay current in an ever-changing technological world and get better at what they do. This will benefit your overall product.

- Purpose: We do what we do in service of something larger than ourselves. Most chose to go into the performing arts because we see the higher purpose in it. It's rarely for the paycheck! People in the performing arts work hard because they are members of a team and because they do not want to let their team down. Promote a team mentality in your work place, and much of the work will take care of itself.[1]

> "The technical stuff is easy to learn, and it's constantly changing anyway, so you will need to re-learn it. You are dealing with human beings. You have to have empathy for where everyone is coming from."
>
> - Perry Silvey, former Director of Production for the New York City Ballet

PRODUCTION MANAGER AS PSYCHOLOGIST

Any production manager will tell you that their office sometime feels like a psychiatric practice. Staff, designers, stage managers and even directors sometimes come to you with their problems (work or personal). All people want is to be listened to. To distinguish between the problem that is expressed (i.e., the set does not do what I thought it would) versus the underlying problem (i.e., I don't trust the set designer) can sometimes be the key to successfully solving the issue. To get to the root of the issue requires understanding what people need.

Psychologist Abraham H. Maslow's theory of the "Hierarchy of Needs"[2] does a great job of describing what people need. The theory states that all people have needs. If our needs are met, then we are happy. Our needs are constantly changing and are affected by outside factors. In Maslow's Hierarchy pyramid, the items at the bottom are the most crucial to basic survival. The items higher up cannot fully be achieved until the ones below it are fulfilled. It is believed

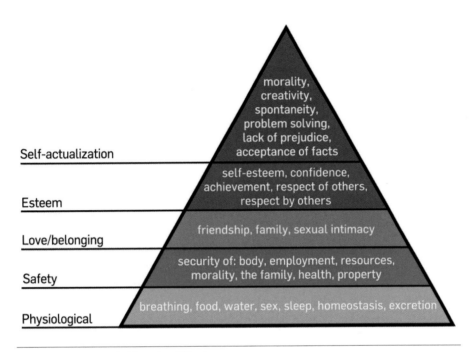

Figure 3.3 Maslow's Hierarchy of Needs

that to reach a point of true creative ability, one must achieve "Self-Actualization" (the top of the pyramid). This requires that all needs are fulfilled.

Many people cannot meet their needs alone and require outside influences to help them. As a manager, you can provide a great deal toward providing those needs. Here are some examples:

- *Physiological needs:* By insuring that people are paid on time, you do a great deal toward supporting their basic needs of food and shelter.

- *Safety needs:* Enforcing and maintaining a safe workplace is not only critical to physical safety, it supports the mental well-being of your staff as well. (See chapter 8 on safety).

- *Love and belongingness needs:* By creating a supportive and collaborative work environment where everyone's opinion is valued and considered, you build an artistic family where people can invest themselves. They feel they belong and their contribution matters.

- *Esteem needs:* Sometimes egos need a little stroking. What's wrong with that? Let your team know how much you appreciate them and how good they are at their work.

> **TIP**—Do not forget YOU in all this. Sometimes you need help, too. One production manager we interviewed said the most important relationship they had was with their own psychiatrist! We all need a release, especially if you spend all day hearing other people's woes and trying to solve their problems.

"You have to be able to have confidence in yourself and confidence in your team. Trust is a huge part of being successful as a production manager, and if you think it's all about you, we will fail."

- Kasey Allee-Foreman, Production Manager at
the University of Oklahoma

DELEGATING AND WORKING ON A TEAM

Many production managers (especially those early in their careers) find delegation very hard. Giving up a task to another can often feel like you are failing to get it done. In fact, the reverse can be true. By passing a task on to someone you trust, you can insure that it gets done while you can focus on something else. It takes time and practice, but good delegation is key to success as a production manager. If you struggle with this, it's best to start small. Test the waters by giving someone a small task that you could pick back up if you needed to. If it goes well, then increase the responsibility and try it again. Trust takes time to build; it is okay not to rush it.

In most organizations, production management is a lonely, one-person job. Larger institutions that produce large amounts of work choose to hire teams of production managers. If so, there is likely a lead production manager who oversees the other members of the team. The "associate" or "assistant" production managers are given specific tasks such as payroll, timesheets, purchase orders, contracts, calendars, etc. In some cases, they may be given their own shows to manage. In those teams, clear communication is vital. Who is doing what and when? Who is overwhelmed and needs help from another? The worst thing that can happen is when effort is duplicated or one member is overloaded in work. Regularly meeting as a team is essential to make sure everyone has what they need.

There are two distinct benefits to working on a PM team. The first is the ability to have team members cover for each other so no one person has to work all of the time. If you are in technical rehearsals for a week, chances are good you can share responsibilities and everyone can get a night (or day) off. Free time is good for morale. The second benefit is that more voices in the room offer opportunities to generate ideas. If you find team members you trust and respect, engage in conversations about the work and the challenges being faced. Two heads are always better than one. Having a partner or team that can see problems from differing angles is incredibly useful.

INCLUSION

Everyone wants to feel valued and a part of the team. Work hard to create an inclusive work environment where everyone feels comfortable sharing their thoughts and bringing issues to the table. This starts at the top. As production manager, you need to know that people look to you to set an example. If you show respect for others and their ideas, you will inspire others to do the same.

Figure 3.4   In his first few days, David "Dstew" Stewart, Director of Production for the Guthrie, checks out the flying system for the production of *A Christmas Carol*.

Credit: Photo courtesy of the Guthrie Theatre

Start by having an open door policy where everyone you work with knows they can come talk to you about anything at any time; it does not even need to be work related. You might even want to go a step further and hold open meetings or "town halls" where anyone can raise any issue they wish. When an issue is brought to the table, take it seriously and work hard with your team to address it and learn from it.

> "A good production manager understands quiet authority. Sit in the room and just shut the hell up and listen."
>
> - David Stewart, Director of Production at the Guthrie Theater

NEVER STOP LEARNING

Most of us have learned from a production manager whom we have worked with or who preceded us. Think back to what that person asked for or required from their team or specifically from you. Whether it was good or bad—learn from these memories. Sometimes, we learn great lessons of what not to do by watching someone struggle or fail with a project or a situation. Remember what you wanted from a production manager when you worked for or with them. Give that now to those who work for you. Take each project as an opportunity to learn something that you did not know and, by doing so, continue to grow. It will benefit you and your projects.

Sometime things will not go as planned. Even the best plans are sometimes thwarted by accident or on purpose. The best way to deal with a new problem is to be flexible and patient. The production manager is leading the charge. If you get upset, then it gives others permission to do the same. Review those essential qualities of a good production manager—adaptable, calm, organized, self-aware, collaborative, etc. When things go awry, go back to these key words and start again.

> "You need lateral thinking—seeing what the consequences of one thing means to everything else down the line."
>
> - Jesse Aasheim, Production Manager at Round House Theatre

You cannot think about management without thinking about leadership. Take guidance from this chapter and decide what type of leader you want to be. How will you guide your staff, your clients, or your creative team through the next project? What can you bring to the table? When should you get out of the way and let them work? Take pride in the leader you are and strive to be.

NOTES

1   Pink, Daniel H. *Drive: The Surprising Truth About What Motivates Us*. New York: Riverhead Books, 2009.
2   Maslow, A. H. "A Theory of Human Motivation." *Psychological Review*, 50 (1943), 370–96.

Planning and Scheduling

Shows and events do not come together overnight. They require special long-term planning and scheduling to make them successful. Depending upon the type of event, the planning may start six months to five years in advance. This chapter will help you through the steps of planning a single show/event or a whole season.

THE ROLE OF THE PRODUCTION MANAGER IN SEASON SELECTION

Every organization is different, and therefore their approach to selecting the work will also differ. Whether it is one performance or a series of events spanning a few months, there is likely a process by which those events are selected. If you are lucky, the organization values the input of the production manager and invites you to the season selection table. If such an invitation is offered, do not turn it down. If by chance you work for a producer who would rather shut their door and not open it again until the season has been chosen, then you might have your work cut out for you. Nevertheless, find a way to insert yourself into the process. The outcome can only benefit you, your staff and the organization as a whole.

By being a part of the season selection process, production managers have a chance to comprehend the ideas as they are developing. They can add production insight and start to prepare for how they will be produced. It is a wonderful way to connect with the artistic leadership of the organization by understanding what types of projects they want to do and why. You can bring a large amount of knowledge and forethought to the season consideration that many others cannot. Production managers have a special understanding for knowing how projects will come together and the resources necessary. If a project is being considered that is way outside the means of the organization, it is best to speak up early rather than coping later with a decision that is not implementable. This is not to say that the production manager's job here is to shoot ideas down; quite the opposite. Bringing challenges to the forefront allows them to be considered and hopefully solved. Perhaps a show requires more cast, crew and designers than any you have previously produced—that means more money. The solution could be that the overall season is reduced by one project to accommodate for these additional costs.

You must be an informed member of the season selection process, which means doing the work. This begins with reading the proposals or scripts, seeing performances elsewhere that are being considered, doing research on previous productions of these shows and talking to people about them. Careful consideration of each project is necessary. Here are some questions you should ask:

- How many people will this project take to produce (directors, designers, cast, crew, etc.)?
- Will this project fit into our standard production period? (Think about the time it will take to build, rehearse, tech, etc.)
- What are the design elements, and how large or small are they? (Will a unit set suffice or will the set need to show multiple locations? How many total costumes are required?)
- What is the time period of the show? (Finding and/or building period items can be more costly.)
- What special rehearsal requirements might be necessary? (Example: Does the cast need to learn to roller skate or play the banjo, or both?)
- Will the show have specific community outreach attached to it?

CREATING A SEASON

Often, seasons will be built around themes or ideas to connect them in a specific way. Some examples of this might be new work, current topics affecting the community, adaptations, etc. Sometimes the theme can just be an entry point for those choosing the season, and therefore it is not a consideration for marketing of the season. This is fine. Some organizations have a template for each season, so they know they are choosing two works from the company's repertoire, one new work, one workshop, etc. Some organizations choose their season based on what they think their audience wants. That may mean choosing crowd-pleasing titles or selecting shows that appeal to the demographics of their region.

VENUES

Along with the selection process, one must also consider where these projects will be presented. Different venues have different opportunities and challenges.

- *Proscenium theatre:* Since the 19th century, this has been the most typical location to produce a show. Most Broadway and regional theatres still use this type of venue. The benefits are plentiful—lots of options for backstage storage (be that in the wings, traps below the stage or fly loft), the audience location is predetermined and therefore does not require much attention (other than sightlines), lots of options for special effects, etc.

- *Flexible theatre:* A black box or other flexible theatre space does not have permanent seating, so they can be configured in any way of your choosing (as long as it meets the approval of your fire marshal; see chapter 8 on safety). You could choose a proscenium type configuration or maybe go with three-quarter thrust, arena or alley. One challenge to consider is labor and time, as it will take both to set up the venue as you wish.

- *Non-theatrical venue/found space:* Any space can become a performance venue—the lobby of a building, an art gallery, a hotel ballroom, a tent in someone's backyard. One big challenge with these venues is that none of the "normal" theatre areas or equipment exists and will need to be created—dressing rooms, backstage space, control booth, positions from which to hang lights and speakers, etc. You also need to give thought to the audience experience. Where do they enter/exit? Where do they sit? Or do they sit? Where do they go to the bathroom?

- *Outdoor venue:* Who says it has to be inside? Plenty of organizations produce outside in the summer months. Outdoor venues can vary from proscenium type theatres with permanent seating and a roof (or sometimes no roof) to a hillside or parking lot with nothing permanent other than what you choose to provide. The biggest challenge by far with outdoor venues is the weather. It is very unnerving to have this very large element of the experience completely out of your control. Contingency plans should be considered from the beginning of the project—what do we do if it's too hot, or too cold, or raining? Often, an alternate indoor location is a good back-up plan. Another big consideration with an

Figure 4.1 Liam Vincent and Danny Scheie in *The Mystery of Irma Vep* at the California Shakespeare Theatre

Credit: Photo by Jay Yamada

outdoor venue is the schedule. If you perform at night, then you will need to have technical rehearsals occur then as well. Some outdoor venues plan overnight electrics calls to get the lights focused.

Other important things to consider regarding venue:

- Does your organization own this venue? Do you already have approved access? Will you be required to rent it?
- Are you sharing this venue with others during any part of the process?
- How old is the venue? Has it been properly kept up?
- Is the venue already outfitted with seating, lights, sound equipment, etc., or will you need to provide those things?
- How much time will you need in the venue? (See Production Schedule later in this chapter.)

SCRIPT/PROJECT ANALYSIS

Once the project has been selected, it is helpful to do a detailed analysis. This allows you to understand everything this project will require and help you plan out the budget and schedule. If there is a script, that is the best place to start. Here is what to look for:

- People
  - Creative team requirements: director, choreographer, musical director/conductor, designers, writers
  - Support staff: fight choreographer, dialect/vocal coach, movement coach, accompanist
  - Stage management: stage manager (SM), assistant stage manager (ASM), production assistants
  - Cast requirements: gender, age, skillset
  - Production staff requirements: set, paint, props, costumes, lights, sound, projections, etc.
  - Crew requirements: backstage, wardrobe, lighting, sound, projections, etc.
- Design elements
  - Set/paint/props
  - Costumes
  - Lighting
  - Sound/music
  - Projections/video
- Special considerations
  - Effects: flying, fire, water, fog, haze
  - Children and/or animals

What if there is no script? Sometimes there is not, because it hasn't been written yet or the project will be devised. Maybe all you have is a list of characters and a synopsis, or maybe you don't even have that. The best thing to do here is assume the worst-case scenario—lots of people and lots of stuff. It's important to start having conversations with the playwright, director or choreographer as soon as possible so you can know the direction the show is headed. It's always best to stay ahead of the game, but sometimes you just have to keep up. For a project such as this, you might need to schedule yourself into the rehearsal room so you are part of the development process.

RIGHTS AND PERMISSIONS

Before deciding upon a specific show or project, it is important to find out if you can get the rights to produce it. Any published script will require permission from the publisher. Here are a few of the biggest theatrical rights houses at present: Dramatists Play Service (www.drama tists.com), Samuel French (www.samuelfrench.com), Tams-Whitmark (www.tamswitmark. com) and Musical Theatre International (www.mtishows.com). Their websites will walk you through the process of getting the rights to produce their shows. The rights houses will need you to provide information about your organization and your plans to produce the show. Common required information includes ticket prices, expected box office revenue, venue capacity, dates and number of performances.

If a show is not published, rights are often still necessary but need to be acquired directly from the playwright, librettist, composer or their representation—agent, lawyers, etc. If a show is being created by your organization, the question of rights will be determined by the content. If it is unique material generated by the company, then you do not need to gain any permission. If, however, it is based on an existing story or uses content from another source (song, movie, book, etc.), then permission is needed. These permissions will require you to track down the publisher, agent or other representative. A good way to start is an internet search of the title to see if you can find who owns the rights to the content. Then you will need to find the right contact person for that organization. It's best to start this process early, as you never know how long it will take. Your project is usually not a priority for them. You will need to ask early and often.

Once rights have been secured, you will be required to pay royalties. This could be a flat fee or a percentage of the box office or both. Every rights house is different, so it's best to do your homework when applying for the rights, so you are aware of costs and procedures for payment. The more popular the show, the more expensive the royalties. Musicals are notoriously expensive, sometimes costing thousands of dollars for just a few performances, whereas straight plays that have been in circulation for a few years might only cost a few hundred dollars. If you are working in an academic environment, the costs can sometimes be less, though not always.

Gaining the rights to produce a show does not allow you to do whatever you wish with it. Making changes to published material is not allowed without permission. If you wish to adapt the script or to cast it non-traditionally, it is best to ask permission first (not forgiveness later). Rights houses have been known to shut down a production when they discovered that these types of adjustments had been made without their knowledge. It is also illegal to photocopy a script without permission. Most rights houses will require you to purchase or rent the exact amount of scripts, librettos or scores you will require to produce the show. A rental package will need to be returned in the condition it was received, or fees will be charged.

Works that fall into the category of public domain do not require rights. Determining whether or not a work is part of the public domain is a complicated process, as there are many rules and laws about copyright, and most differ from country to country. Here are a few basic public domain rules:

- All works published in the United States before 1923 are in the public domain.
- Many works published in the United States from 1923 to 1963 are also in the public domain, as new laws about renewal went into effect after that time.
- Most countries follow an international copyright treaty known as the Berne Convention that was put into effect in 1886, which requires copyright protection on all works for at least fifty years after the author's death.

It's important to understand the Fair Use Privilege, as well, as it is another way to use materials without obtaining a copyright. This can be helpful if you are looking to use clips of video or songs, short length of text, etc., to make a larger and original artistic work. The challenge here is the vague nature of the law and how people may interpret it differently.

When Is Use a Fair Use?

The following four factors must be considered to determine whether an intended use of a copyrighted work is fair use:

- The purpose and character of the work
- The type of work involved
- The amount and importance of the materials used
- The effect of the use upon the market for the copyright work.

These factors are intended to be a highly flexible set of general guidelines. The courts do not apply them in a mechanical or numerical way. For example, not all factors are equally important to every case and it's up to the courts to decide what weight to give them. This makes determining whether a use is fair use a highly subjective and unpredictable exercise.

— Excerpt from Stephen Fishman's *The Public Domain: How to Find & Use Copyright-free Writings, Music, Art & More*[1]

TIP—When in doubt about copyright—talk to a lawyer!

SHOW TREATMENTS

Now that the season has been selected, the production staff will want to know more about the projects you will be producing. The production manager should plan to create "treatments" for each project that include the details that most people will want to know. These treatments should include the artistic lead on the production, casting, venue, dates, unique production challenges and, often, a synopsis, if it's not a well-known show.

Show treatment examples:

THE MATCHMAKER

by Thornton Wilder
Directed by Paul Allen
October 11–19 in the Trey Theatre

Setting: 1880's NYC
Cast size: 9 men, 7 women
Description: Old merchant hires a matchmaker to help find him a wife and ends up marrying her in the end

MOLIERE IMPROMPTU

Translated and adapted by Rinne Groff
Directed by R. Wilson Matthews
November 8–16 in the Cradle Theatre

Setting: Versailles, 1665
Cast size: 8 men, 5 women
Description: Moliere and his troupe in rehearsal are surprised by an unannounced visit by the King, who demands a performance. Done in Commedia dell'Arte style
Other items of note: Masks will be designed and built

CREATING THE SCHEDULE

The nice thing about producing shows and events is that there is no guessing the date when the project needs to be completed. Be it a single event or a show that runs for months, we all know that it needs to be ready by opening night. So in order to create the most effective schedule, you should start with the opening and work backwards. The next two questions to ask are about time: How much time do we need, and how much time do we have? If you are lucky enough, the answer to these two questions will match, but that is rarely the case. Due to budget or venue availability, you may have to make accommodations to make the schedule fit into a specific timeframe. A common shift recently in professional theatre has reduced the number of weeks of rehearsal from five down to four or sometimes even three weeks. This change has been made for monetary reasons and does prove challenging for the director and performers. Any sacrifice you make will affect someone. You, as production manager, will need to weigh the options and come up with the schedule that serves the overall production best.

DEADLINES

Lots of information will be required from individuals to make a production come together—scripts, designs, casting, etc. An important part of the beginning of the planning process is to determine the deadlines. It's best for the production manager to make the first draft of the deadlines based on what they know of the season, work load and time frame. Once the draft is done, it can be shared internally with the shop heads and, perhaps, artistic leadership for feedback. Once the deadlines are set, they need to be communicated to the people who are expected to meet them. Depending upon the items and the people involved, further negotiation might be necessary. However, once the deadlines are final, everyone needs to stick to them.

It's best to have multiple steps to the deadlines. Let's take a costume design as an example. Once the director and designer have met and discussed the concepts, a "preliminary" deadline should occur to allow everyone to touch base and check to see if their ideas are aligned. Often, there will be additional work on the part of the designer, and a "final" design conversation will need to take place. The next step is a "hand-off" deadline where the costume design package is handed over to the costume shop for work to begin. Typically, the shop will "cost out" the package (more on this in chapter 6), and if it is not achievable within a given budget, a "revision" of the package will also be requested. All of the phases (preliminary, final, hand-off and revisions) should have deadlines before the entire production process began. Further deadlines might be necessary, as well. If the costumes are being built, then certain fabrics and accessories will be due from the designer. If it's a new work and casting decisions are decided later in the process, you might need a deadline for final casting so the costumes can be completed on time. As you can see, it can be a complicated process, and deadlines help keep it on track.

Of course, unforeseen things happen; we need to remain flexible, and contingency plans may need to be developed. If, after a costume deadline, an unexpected script revision changes the necessities of the costumes (or any other aspect of the show), then we will have to make some hard choices. Do we make the changes and push back the final deadline? Do we choose not to accept the new script version because the changes requested are not possible? Or do we meet somewhere in the middle? The art of compromise should be one of the production manager's essential skills.

PRODUCTION MEETINGS

The best way to check in on the progress of the team and insure deadlines are met is to schedule production meetings around those deadlines. A production schedule can be extremely complex, so looking for moments of intersection can be very helpful. If you know a particularly challenging deadline is approaching, call a production meeting to check in with everyone and see how things are going. Perhaps challenges can be solved all together, or if not, at least you have a heads up that this deadline might not be met. (For more on production meetings, see chapter 5.)

REHEARSAL SCHEDULE

In most cases your stage manager and director will take on creating the rehearsal schedule. However, the stage manager might not start until a week before rehearsals begin, so you may need to have a hand in crafting the basic schedule until they join the project and fill in the details. The first thing to determine is when rehearsals will begin. You may need to decide how many weeks you can afford to hire your performers or, if they are volunteering their time, how much you can reasonably ask them to give you. Once the start date is set, you'll need to figure out what times rehearsals will occur and when there will be time off. If this is a union

A Midsummer Night's Dream   Rehearsal Calendar

Sunday	Monday	Tuesday	Wednesday	Thursday	Friday	Saturday
	SEPTEMBER					1
2 Rehearsal 10am-4pm	3 Labor Day ACTOR DAY OFF	4 Rehearsal 5:30pm-10pm	5 Rehearsal 5:30pm-10pm	6 Rehearsal 5:30pm-10pm	7 ACTOR DAY OFF	8 Rehearsal 10am-6pm
9 Rehearsal 10am-6pm	10 Rehearsal 6:30pm-10pm	11 Rehearsal 5:30pm-10pm	12 ACTOR DAY OFF	13 ACTOR DAY OFF	14 Rehearsal 5:30pm-10pm	15 Rehearsal (Stage) 10am-6pm
16 Rehearsal (Stage) 10am-6pm	17 Rehearsal (Stage) 5:30pm-10pm	18 Rehearsal (Stage) 5:30pm-10pm	19 ACTOR DAY OFF	20 Tech Rehearsal 5:30pm-10pm	21 Tech Rehearsal 5:30pm-10pm	22 Tech Rehearsal 10am-10pm
23 Tech Rehearsal 10am-8pm	24 ACTOR DAY OFF	25 Dress Run 5:30pm-10pm	26 Dress Run + Photos 5:30pm-10pm	27 Opening Night Show 7:30pm Reception	28 Show 8pm	29 Show 2pm Show 8pm
30 Closing Night Show 2pm	Notes: Only the fairies are required to attend **aerial** and **dance** rehearsals. Aerial rehearsals will be held at Joe's Movement Emporium					

Ruth Anne Watkins, Stage Manager   Updated: 8/4/2012 (RAW)

Figure 4.2 Rehearsal calendar example

show, there is guidance found in the union rules. The Actors' Equity Association (union of actors and stage managers in the United States) has very specific rules for how many hours per day can be rehearsed and how many hours there must be between the end of one rehearsal and the beginning of the next. One day off per week is the norm, and often this falls on Monday. The rehearsal venue might determine scheduling, as well. It might be that your rehearsal space is also a classroom used during the day, so it is only available in the evenings.

BUILD SCHEDULE

Trust in your shop heads to get the build schedule created. Your technical director, costume shop manager, master electrician, scenic charge, props master and other department heads will be able to advise the best course of action for their respective shops. The design of the show is the primary guide for the build schedule. Often, certain items will have to be created first, as other items build upon or relate to them. Labor is the next big determining factor. Working with the shop heads and/or crew chiefs to figure out how many people you have and how long it will take them to complete the necessary tasks is a complex puzzle. Finally, we need to know when the items need to be delivered to the stage so they can be used for technical rehearsals, or possibly even before.

Many production managers do not have their own staff and shops and are often required to bid out items to be built. A large number of commercial shops exist throughout the country. You will also find individual artisans willing to be hired for a single job or project—such is often the case in props and costumes. The advantage you have with these types of entities is that you get to determine the time and the money that can be allocated and then look for the right person who can deliver what you request. (More about bidding to outside vendors in chapter 7 on hiring.)

LOAD-IN SCHEDULE

The load-in schedule is one big puzzle. Each shop will need time to get their part of the show into the venue, and the production manager (with some careful consideration and knowledge) must orchestrate it all. Again, your shop heads will provide the most useful information about loading in, so trust them to give you guidance. It may sometimes be necessary for you to weigh in and advise or decide between competing priorities. The design of the space or show will be the best starting place for this schedule. One element might need to be installed first because another element may block access once it is installed. For example, it's often common to start with light hang in the theatre so the electricians have a clear stage to fly in the linesets used for electrics or maneuver ladders or lifts around the space without having to worry about the set. However, light focus cannot occur until the set is in place, so that will have to occur later in the schedule. Often, elements will cross over between departments and will require multiple steps and personnel, a TV monitor, for example, that lives attached to the wall of the set. The scene shop may need to install the wall first before the video department

Figure 4.3
Credit: Photo by Ryan Knapp

can install the monitor, but the scenic artist has to come back and finish the paint job once the monitor is in. The bottom line is that the elements in the venue should be complete by the time technical rehearsals occur.

TECH SCHEDULE

The tech schedule is best broken down into four phases—rehearsals onstage, technical rehearsals, dress rehearsals and notes periods.

- Rehearsals onstage: Whenever possible, try to give the performers and director and/or choreographer time in the space and on the set before tech begins. This time is invaluable and can save time later in tech. It's nice to begin the first rehearsal onstage with a walk-through guided by the technical director. This way, the performers get a chance to ask questions and understand how things were meant to be used. In an ideal world, the performers would have enough time onstage to space through the show, restage any necessary sections and get a full run-through in before tech.

- Tech rehearsals: This is where we add all the pieces together—lights, sound, costumes, automation, video, performers, etc. It is often described as the most inefficient and frustrating part of the process. Everyone is together in the room working on their aspect of the production. Everyone more than likely thinks their aspect is the most important. To determine how much time tech will take requires an understanding of all of the elements being put together. (A show with one set, no quick changes and no video will take a lot less time to tech than one with four sets, thirty quick changes and three projectors.) Another important element to understand is how the tech will be run. Will there be a paper tech, where the director, designers and stage manager sit down and talk through the whole show and all of its cues? Will it be a cue to cue, where each section of the production with a lighting, set or sound cue in it is worked, but then sections without cues are skipped? Will you dry tech everything first without performers and then attempt a run? Every show will require something different.

- Dress rehearsals: This is where the full show with all its elements is run through in order, preferably without stopping. Everyone learns a lot from doing the show in real time (stage managers, crew, performers, designers, directors/choreographers), so having at least a couple full dress runs before you have an audience is very important. Make sure there is time to do so in the schedule. Often, one of these dress rehearsals is when production photos are taken. It's important everyone knows this is coming so they can do their best to get everything completed in order to have the best photos possible.

- Notes period: This is the time the designers and shop staff take to refine the work and make fixes or changes based on what has been discovered during tech and dress. The notes period overlaps tech/dress, occurring at times when the venue and production elements are not in use for rehearsal. In the case of scenic, paint, lights, sound and video, these notes will need to take place in the venue, making for a complicated scheduling puzzle. Part of the production manager's job during the tech/dress period is to create a schedule for the next day based on the desires, needs and priorities of each person. It's important to understand who can work together and who needs the venue to themselves. Oftentimes, notes will not all get accomplished and will be pushed to the next day because time ran out.

STRIKE SCHEDULE

It's important to know in advance how much time you have in the venue following the final performance. This will not only help you plan the strike schedule but may also inform how much stuff you can put in the venue to begin with. If you only have four hours post-show for strike versus four days, that will drastically change the scope of the physical production. If the production has a long run, you can wait until after opening to begin the strike planning, but if it is a one-night event, you'll have to be thinking about strike at the same time as you are planning everything else. Similar to the load-in schedule, you will need to take guidance from your shop heads and crew to figure out the best way to get everything out. Some items might need to be struck first to ease the exit of others.

DOES THE SHOW HAVE A FUTURE?

Hopefully, you will know well in advance if the show will have future performances either at your venue or another. However, it is possible to find out after strike that the show will be remounted in a future season. In any case, preparation of show paperwork and proper archives is always necessary. In most cases, the stage manager for the show will be expected to turn in their production book, which contains all of the information about the show from the blocking to the cues. The production manager should make sure this book is turned over in a timely fashion and double-check that it includes all necessary elements. In addition to the info from the SM, it's important to collect all of the design paperwork (plans, renderings, lists, etc.) as well as any schedules, contact sheets and other paperwork you created. In the end, a full package of anything and everything to do with the show should be archived so as to help a future production.

If you know in advance that the show will be moved or remounted, then it's important to make sure the physical production remains intact, is properly stored, and is able to be transported. If the production move is happening shortly, it might fall to the production manager to plan for the storage as well as the transportation of the items. It's important to communicate the post-show plans to your team so that items can be engineered and built to come apart and be put back together easily as well as fit into the mode of transportation. Storage and transport cost money, so it's imperative that funds be allocated toward this as soon as possible. Finding the proper storage and transport can take time, so the sooner you know about this possibility the better!

MANAGING THE PHYSICAL RESOURCES

Whether it be lumber, tools, light boards, speakers, couches or petticoats, each item we use needs to be managed and cared for. This becomes doubly important if you have very few resources or an abundance of them. Creating a system where you can track what items you have is a critical step toward success. If you are lucky enough to have the money and space to house a large stock of properties, you should take the time to inventory and log what you have so items can be properly found and used when needed. If you don't know what you have, chances are good you'll buy something a second time without realizing it and waste money.

TIP—Another important thing to consider with physical resources is maintaining them. With tools like a table saw or a sewing machine, investing in their upkeep costs much less than constantly needing to replace them. Create a schedule where items are serviced and cleaned. Ideally, this would be in the off season, when the tools are not in use. Make sure you budget for this maintenance.

Figure 4.4   The College-Conservatory of Music at the University of Cincinnati

Photo by Adam Zeek, www.zeekcreative.com

Planning and scheduling are at the heart of what production managers do. Seeing a production from its inception all the way to completion can be a very fulfilling experience. Time, preparation and careful thought are the keys to success. It's never too early to begin to plan your next show or event. However, as with all things production management, stay flexible—your careful planning will often need to change. Keep those plan Bs (and Cs) in the back of your head in case they should be needed!

> "In any one five-minute period, you need to be thinking of what's happening now to the next five years . . ."
>
> - Perry Silvey, former Director of Production for the New York City Ballet

NOTE

1 Fishman, Stephen. *The Public Domain: How to Find & Use Copyright-free Writings, Music, Art & More.* 3rd ed. Berkeley, CA: Nolo, 2006.

CHAPTER 5

Meetings

Have you ever heard the phrase "death by meeting"? Well, it is true, or at least it can be. The true test of a production manager is how well they can facilitate a meeting. A good production manager can do it with a calm demeanor, in an acceptable amount of time, cover all that is necessary and keep everyone focused on the task at hand throughout. No one ever wants to feel that their time is being wasted or that their topic has not been given its proper attention. This is even more important at the end of a long day or week.

TYPES OF PRODUCTION MEETINGS

A production meeting is meant to be an opportunity to get all of the participants on a show or event in the room to discuss relevant topics that affect more than one or two people. Every production manager you speak to and every project you work on will have a different set of meetings that they require, so there is no definitive list. You will often see something resembling the following:

- A concept meeting: This is usually the first meeting where the director, choreographer or client explains their idea for the show or project.

- A preliminary design meeting: At this meeting, the designers or production staff present to the director or client what they propose based on the concept and their research of the subject matter. Often a discussion between the two parties will take place, hopefully resulting in a unified approach as the project continues.

- A final design meeting: The design is finished and approved by all involved. This meeting precedes the build process.

- A cost out meeting: Once the design is finished, we need to make sure it is affordable so the production staff will cost out each element, and, if we are over budget, a meeting might be necessary to make cuts or adjustments.

- A pre-rehearsal meeting: If you are working on a show that has a rehearsal period, it is always smart to meet as a group prior to the rehearsals to make sure everyone is on the same page. Oftentimes, this is the first meeting the stage manager will attend.

- A pre-tech meeting: Rehearsals are well under way, and the technical rehearsals will begin soon. Load-in is either about to start or in process, so this is a perfect time for another in-person connection.
- Post-tech meetings: After each and every tech and dress rehearsal, a production meeting takes place to wrap up the notes and activities of the day and then plan for the schedule and priorities of the next day.
- A post mortem meeting: Many projects will call a meeting after the show has been completed to reflect back on the process and learn from what occurred. This is common in an educational setting and also with events that will happen again.

SCHEDULING THE MEETING

Finding the perfect time for a meeting can be the most challenging part. Many production managers say they spend more than a quarter of their time getting the right people in the room for a conversation. Here are a few tips to ease this task:

- Acquire as many participants' schedules in advance as you can.
- Determine preferred meeting times for participants.
- Be flexible with your time. Move things around to accommodate others. There is a lot of good will that can come with that.
- Use technology! There are great, free online scheduling tools that are incredibly convenient and easy to use. The possible problem with using an online scheduling service is there will always be participants who cannot figure out how to use it. You will have to be patient while you work to accommodate those individuals.

Once you have the time set—communicate it! Send everyone the details of the meeting. If you are able to, create an online calendar appointment and invite everyone to it. Finally, send a reminder as the meeting approaches—at least one week before the meeting and then another reminder the day before.

HOW TO PREPARE

Adequate preparation for the meeting is extremely important. Production meetings tend to be filled with passionate people who often have radical ideas that require large agendas. With many passionate participants at the same meeting, you need to be prepared for wherever the conversation may go. It is impossible to be prepared for everything, but the more you attempt to be prepared, the easier and more productive the meetings will be.

There are two critical tasks that must occur before the meeting in order for the correct agenda to take shape. Step one is to have a generic agenda already pre-planned for your current point in the process.

If it's the first production meeting where the director presents his or her concept, the agenda might look something like this:

- Introductions
- Director presents concept to group
- Open conversation for questions/discussion
- Next steps
- Remind next meeting date
- Discuss what is due at that meeting

If it's the last production meeting before tech, it probably resembles something closer to this:

- Upcoming important dates
- Area updates
- Scenic
- Paint
- Props
- Costumes/hair/wigs/wardrobe
- Electrics
- Video
- Sound/music
- Stage operations
- Load-in/tech questions
- Review load-in/tech schedule
- Strike schedule

Once the generic agenda is complete, the next step is to take time to connect with every meeting participant to find out what topics they need on the agenda. This can be done via email or phone, but in person is always best. This helps you set the agenda as well as judge the emotional temperature of the soon to be face-to-face participants. Say, for example, that a big topic that will affect a large number of people is on the agenda. Who does this topic affect? What will their reactions be? Should this have come up before now, and will this frustrate people? Is this upcoming meeting the right forum for this conversation? Maybe not. It's perfectly within the production manager's right to hold off on bringing up a topic to the whole production team if they think it will cause unhelpful issues. The production manager should consider priming the conversation by talking with participants prior to the meeting so that they have more time to consider the issues before attending the meeting. Know the people you are working with; know what they need. Once the agenda is set, send it out to the meeting participants. This should happen ideally twenty-four hours in advance of the meeting. This is also a great last-minute reminder that the meeting is coming up!

Figure 5.1
Credit: Image ©iStock

PREPARING THE ROOM

This may seem a trivial task, but it is not. People have a physical and emotional reaction to spaces, how they are lit, how they are arranged, etc. Give yourself adequate time before the meeting to prepare the space. Are there enough chairs, and can they be arranged so that everyone can see everyone else? Is there a computer and projector set up for the agenda to be projected or to connect via video with a member of the team who cannot be physically present? Are the lights at a level that everyone can see? Is there a non-fluorescent option to provide? Where will you sit? Do we need documentation to refer to—schedules, set drawings, costume renderings, etc.?

FACILITATING THE MEETING

Start on time, and make it clear to everyone that you plan to do so. Respect other people's time and expect them to respect yours. If someone is late—call them and find out how soon they will arrive. Begin the meeting at the agreed-upon time even if you are missing people. You may have to jump around on the agenda to make sure not to cover items critical to the missing person. If someone arrives late, acknowledge it, quickly catch them up and move on.

If it is the first time this team is meeting, it is important to start with a round of introductions so people can put names to faces and understand everyone's role in the process. After introductions, clearly relate the agenda you will be following for this meeting. For example: "We will begin by checking in with each production shop, then discuss any outstanding notes from the rehearsal reports, review the tech schedule and then open the floor for any additional topics." Hopefully, participants will have already related to you what they hoped to see on the agenda, but at this time you should ask if there are any missing topics for the agenda. If participants add topics, you must quickly decide if they are to be inserted into this agenda or whether that topic should be set aside until you have had a chance to speak with this participant or for a more appropriate meeting to come.

Then the meeting takes off. The production manager's job is to keep things on track. There is an agenda for a reason.

- Stick to the agenda as much as you can, but also be flexible enough to recognize that an important topic may arise that needs to be allowed into the agenda immediately. Let new topics in, but don't let them monopolize the conversation.

- Dissuade side conversations that will inevitably come up. Remind people to stay focused on the main topic. You never know what comment or idea might affect someone else in another area. Make sure everyone is included in the conversation.

Figure 5.2
Credit: Image ©iStock

- Look for opportunities to suggest a breakout session after the meeting: "It seems that a new drawing of the scenery masking will be necessary. Let's plan to have the set designer, lighting designer, technical director and master electrician stick around after the meeting to discuss. If anyone else feels strongly about being a part of that conversation, you are welcome to stay."

- Keep an eye on the clock. If the meeting is scheduled for an hour—keep it to an hour, even if that means cutting a topic from the agenda. For example, maybe it would have been great to talk everyone through the tech schedule, but you are going to email it to everyone after the meeting is over, so, if necessary, we can remove it from the agenda. It is also okay to remind people how much time is left and to encourage the conversation to move on to other topics. In the event that the meeting needs to run long, give everyone as much warning as possible. You will need to gauge who can stay and who needs to go. Perhaps a participant only needs to make a quick phone call to arrange to stay later.

- Pay attention to the emotional temperature of the people in the room. Is everyone relaxed and joking, or is there tension in the air? What is their body language saying? What is causing that tension, and can it be resolved? Perhaps a director is being pushed to make a decision, and they are clearly not comfortable doing so right now. Yes, it would be ideal if we had the answer now, but it would be more ideal if the director did not erupt in anger. In this case, the phrase you should become familiar with is "I think we can table this decision right now. Can you get back to us tomorrow with your choice?"

WHEN SOMEONE ELSE FACILITATES THE MEETING

It is not a given that the production manager will always run the meeting. In some cases, a stage manager, producer or even director will step up to take that role. Taking a backseat is not a sign of weakness but, often, just the opposite. As long as you do not take a passive role in the meeting, you can still have a great impact. Regardless of the leader, it is still your responsibility to make sure notes are compiled, distributed and followed up on.

FOLLOWING UP

Someone should be taking notes at the meeting. These notes are as much for the people who could not be present as they are for those who were. It is possible that, three days later, the items we discussed will be forgotten. Ideally, the note taker is not the production manager who is running the meeting. You can run a meeting and take notes, but it is extremely difficult and should be avoided. The stage manager or assistant stage manager would be good options for note takers. An assistant production manager would be a great option, but you would have to be lucky enough to have one. After the meeting, the production manager should review the notes to make sure they are accurate and easy to read. Then the notes should be distributed to everyone.

Meeting notes should include the following:

- Who was in attendance at the meeting
- Where and when it took place
- Information about the next meeting (if known)
- Detailed notes of what was said (these notes should be organized by production area for easier referencing later). For example:

SCENIC

- Some of the elements are hopefully climbable.
- The director would like to use the set as a percussion instrument, possibly using microphones?

PROJECTIONS

- Each character having their own graffiti or written signature projected as each character is introduced to the audience.
- We'll need at least one actual television on stage, portraying the way so many people received information about the events.
- What are the rights surrounding the news video clips?

COSTUMES

- Police will wear gas masks, not necessarily all the same.
- Actors are barefoot for most of the show, at some point the police will put boots on.
- The director stressed the need for simplicity.

LIGHTS

- How comfortable is each character being in the spotlight? How are the spotlights different?
- Light will be used to create a foreground/background, telling the audience what to focus on, even if no one leaves the stage.

After the notes go out to the team, then the real follow up work begins. It would be great if, after sending out the notes, all the answers to questions magically happened, but this is unlikely. Continuously follow up with individuals to make sure that progress continues to be made. Make sure the director who promised a choice by tomorrow delivers. Hopefully, the follow up from the first meeting is done by the next meeting, but, if not, make sure those topics are top on the next agenda!

WHEN THE MEETING CANNOT BE IN PERSON

It is ALWAYS preferable to meet in person, but that is not always possible, and sometimes you need to sacrifice meeting in person in order to keep meetings timely. If someone cannot attend in person, the next best option is to meet with the rest of the team in person and have the missing person join remotely. If, however, no one can meet in person, as is often the case when working with out-of-town artists or people with demanding schedules, then embrace unfavorable circumstances and have everyone meet remotely.

MEETING VIA VIDEO CONFERENCE

Technology is amazing these days and getting better and more versatile every year. Only ten years previous to the creation of this book, there were no affordable and accessible videoconference options for theatres. Today, we have services such as Skype, Telepresence, FaceTime

Figure 5.3
Credit: Image ©iStock

and Google Hangout. Although these services are amazing in how they can create connectivity, they are only as effective as how they are used and the people who use them.

"I once did a series of Skype interviews to weed through a large group of potential candidates. I was shocked at how few of those being interviewed paid attention to how they presented themselves on screen. Everything from lights shining behind the person so they were in shadow the whole time to one person who Skyped from a phone and gave me an upward view of their face. Only one interviewee took the time to set up the shot. On top of that, she was three hours ahead of me and got up early so that for the 9 a.m. interview (6 a.m. her time) she was awake and prepared. For this, and for many other reasons, she got the job."

- Cary Gillett, Production Manager at the University of
Maryland, College Park

If a videoconference is necessary, make certain to give yourself adequate time to test the equipment. Can you actually get the remote person into the meeting effectively? If not, the meeting will likely be more effort than it is worth. Once the technology allows the person to join effectively, the meeting should be run as any other meeting. Special attention should be paid to make sure the remote person is able to understand what is being discussed, can see those speaking and has opportunities to comment when necessary. It can be surprisingly easy to forget that someone is in the conversation if they are not physically present in the room.

MEETING VIA CONFERENCE CALL

This is by far the most frustrating and ineffective way to meet, but yet it often needs to happen. Not being able to see the people you are speaking with is a major handicap to any effective meeting. There is no body language to read to know when someone has finished their point or if they are becoming agitated. Often, people on a conference call are multitasking (because they can, no one is looking at them) and their focus is not entirely on the call. One can hope that at least the multitasking is at a computer and not in the kitchen baking a pie. With phone conferencing, it is hard to know when to join the conversation, and people will inadvertently talk over each other. Although inadvisable, participants will call from their cars and will drop off the call when their cell signal is lost. When this happens, you may have to wait until they can rejoin the conversation again. All of this difficulty can waste time and feel ineffective. Even though there are difficulties with phone conferencing, when meeting this way, every attempt should be made to run the meeting with the same organization and leadership as if all the participants were meeting in person.

Figure 5.4   Scenery walk-through

Credit: Photo by Ryan Knapp

WALK-THROUGHS/SITE VISITS: "THE ROVING PRODUCTION MEETING"

Not all meetings happen in the comfort of a conference room. Many times, the production meeting may take the shape of a "roving" meeting. These types of walk-throughs are more common for corporate theatre and special events, but many times in theatre you may also have the need to move about the venue or shop. (For more details on the site visit for special events, see chapter 17.) The roving production meeting can be a good one for many, as physically seeing the space can help designers, technicians and event planners work more efficiently. Conduct this meeting like you would any other type of production meeting—keep an eye on the time and keep the agenda handy. Many times, as the group moves from place to place, side-bar conversations begin to happen without you realizing it. Before you know it, many people in the group are having private discussions that really should include everybody. As the production manager, you are responsible for keeping the side-bars to a minimum and keeping everyone focused.

Production management is a collaborative art, and meetings sustain the life of collaborations. Arranging and facilitating successful meetings is probably the most essential way to achieve project success. If you heed the advice described in this chapter, a successful meeting is yours for the taking.

Money and Budget

One of the key functions of the production manager is the creation and management of the production budget. Your immediate supervisor, whether it is a producer or client, will expect you to have intimate knowledge of the elements of the production and stay within the allocated funds for the project. This chapter will explain where funds come from and where they should go, as well as techniques for tracking money and managing changes.

INCOME SOURCES

Before you can decide how much money to spend on an event or production, you must first know how much you have. Funding for any performing arts organization comes from a variety of sources, and accounting for these funds is critical for effective budgeting. Organizations describe this income differently, but generally the presenting industry has titled these funds Earned Income and Unearned Income. Here are examples of both:

- Earned Income
  - Box office revenue: This is the money generated from ticket sales. In most cases, these funds only account for a portion of the amount needed to run an organization. Some box offices will add ticketing fees to cost of admission, which is also a revenue generator.
  - Concessions, gift shop sales: Some organizations have items for sale in their lobby before, during and after events. These are funding sources as well, though likely very minor to the overall financial health of the organization.
- Unearned Income
  - Grants: The two most typical types are grants from the government (local, state and federal) and private corporations. These funds typically require an extensive

application process, and you must report specifically on how the money was used. Many grants stipulate exactly how this money is to be spent.

- ○ Donations: Money can also come from private sources such as individuals or small companies. Unlike grants, there is no application process, but they require much work to secure. For this reason, organizations that need donations to operate will often need a staff of people to develop this income—hence, this staff is usually called the development team. The donor pool for any organization is an important one to foster. The funds they contribute can be critical to the success of the organization.
- ○ Fundraisers: The development team may also decide to hold large events for the sole purpose of raising money. These could be gala celebrations with a healthy ticket price and/or auctions where donated items are auctioned off and all proceeds go toward the organization.

> **TIP**—Don't underestimate the value and work of the development team. They raise the money! If they reach out to you for assistance in showing donors the production side of things—find a way to make it happen. Most people who donate to arts organizations don't know what is behind the scenes, and allowing them a peek can be a valuable move.

UNDERSTANDING THE OVERALL BUDGET

In most organizations, there are multiple budgets for the different departments, and the production manager will only be responsible for production's part of the budget. Take a producing opera, dance or theatre company, for example—they have multiple departments, all with their own budget—marketing/public relations, facilities, development, business, etc.

The person who decides the overall budget is most likely the producing or managing director of the organization, or client if it's a special event. They will likely begin the budget planning conversation in one of two ways—"What amount do you need to produce this season/show/event?" or "This is the amount we have allocated for you to produce this season/show/event." Let's look at each scenario in detail:

- When the overall budget is requested: If you are asked to provide your own overall budget, it's best to create a budget that is reasonable but achieves the shows/events you plan to be produce. If you request too little, you might get what you asked for and then find it challenging to work within a constrained budget. If you ask for too much, you might demonstrate that you are insensitive to the financial constraints of the organization and find it difficult having your budget requests fully funded in the future. Once you have submitted your request, be ready to justify your budget with specific data and artistic information to explain why you made certain budget choices.

- When the overall budget is prescribed: If you are given a specific budget amount, take that amount and make it work. However, it is in the best interest of the organization that the shows/events be successfully achieved. If the prescribed budget is too small, then you need to say something. It's possible a negotiation of more money or fewer projects might be necessary.

It's important to clearly understand what is expected to be in your budget rather than another budget within the organization. Here are a few examples of items that might shift between budgets depending upon the organization: Staff salaries and fringe benefits (health, pension, social security), professional development (training/classes for the staff), travel/transportation/vehicles, archival photography/videography and office supplies.

> "They are not my numbers, they are THE numbers. Don't get defensive."
>
> - Glenn Plott, Director of Production at Cincinnati Opera

CREATING THE PRODUCTION BUDGET

The truth is budgeting for shows/events is a catch-22. You need to create the budget before you create the show, sometimes before you even know what the show is going to be. All production managers are in this same boat, and, luckily, the more you do it, the easier it becomes. Here are some guidelines to help you if it's your first time through the process.

The production budget should include at minimum the following items:

- Artist fees: Directors, choreographers, musical director/conductors, performers, designers, assistants, etc.
- Union fees: Pension, health, etc.
- Producing rights costs: Royalties, scripts, music package rentals, etc.
- Supplies: Scenery, paint, props, costumes, lights, sound, video/projections, stage management (each area of production should get a budget line for each show/event)
- Overhire labor: Often you need to bring people in beyond any full-time staff to complete the work, or maybe you have no full-time staff, so you need only overhire workers. These people can be run crew, carpenters, electricians, costume stitchers, etc.
- Rentals: You might need to rent equipment or supplies from other people or companies to achieve the visions of the project.
- A contingency fund: The artistic process of creating productions and events is often complex and must plan for many variables. At least a small percentage of the budget (usually 5–10%) should be held for initially missed costs or emergencies.

How do you determine the budget amounts? This is the toughest part of the budgeting process and requires a significant amount of work. You need to do some in-depth research on the shows/projects/events that are planned and figure out what/who is required and what it's going to cost. Sometimes this information is easily found. If you are producing a show held by a major rights house, you can find out exactly how much you should budget for the rights (see chapter 4). Some large opera and ballet companies will rent an entire show package with scenery, props and costumes for a set fee.

Do not create budgets by yourself. Your production staff is a necessary resource for you, as they know exact material and labor costs, and they will know what needs to be built versus what can be purchased, rented or borrowed. Don't underestimate the value of your professional network, either. If you are producing a show that another theatre has recently done, call their production manager and inquire about their costs. If you are working with a new designer, find a production manager who has recently worked with that person. By doing so, you can learn how big (or small) they tend to design, and then, hopefully, you can anticipate their funding needs.

No matter how much research you do, however, sometimes you have to guess. Try to make those guesses as educated as possible, based off of what you know about the artistic process and what you have learned from your sources. It's also good if your guesses are based on some amount of historical fact. What was the total budget for your last big musical? That might be a good starting place for the one you are budgeting now.

> **TIP**—Trial and error is the reality of budgeting. You will learn so much about the process once you have been through it a few times. Learn from your mistakes—you will make them; we all do.

ARTIST FEES

A large challenge for any production manager is paying people what they are worth. Most of us did not choose this business to become rich, but we all hope to make a living. It's very easy to take advantage of people's desire to work on a specific project or with a certain company. It is true that some will agree to work for nothing or next to nothing, but that does not make it appropriate. A good production manager should try not to allow this. The smaller the theatre, the smaller the budget, and the more likely you will have to ask people to work for a small amount. If you are in this situation, own it and be honest with the people you hire. Work hard to give them compensation in other ways—comp tickets, travel support, good will, on-time payment, a reasonable work schedule, etc. And next time you hire them—try to give them a raise.

It you are working with unions, the artistic fees will be easy to determine, as they are based on the union minimums. The minimum is what you are required to pay each position. However, this does not preclude you from paying more. As people work their way up in this business, they expect more compensation, especially if they have worked at the same organization many times. You may be asked to budget before roles are cast and creative teams are put together. Start with the union minimums as your baseline, but it's a good idea to put in a little more money to give you some wiggle room for negotiating fees. Understanding the specifics in the labor agreements that you are working with is a huge asset. Do your homework (see chapter 7).

COMMUNICATING THE BUDGET

Once the budget is finalized, you will need to communicate it to your various production team members. At minimum, the budget needs to get to the creative team (the people making the ideas) and the production staff (the people implementing the ideas). It's best to communicate the budgets as soon as possible so everyone knows what framework they are working within. If the budget is not set before the conceptual process begins, make it known when the budget will be finalized and roughly what amounts they might be dealing with.

A clearly laid out and easy to read document is the best way to communicate the budget numbers. There is no prescribed or perfect format, so you have some creative license here. A spreadsheet format (such as Excel) can be a good option to consider.

MANAGING THE BUDGET

Once the budget is finalized, much of the work is just beginning. Hopefully, by this point in the book you realize that the work of the production manager is to manage the ever-changing demands of the production and to be flexible and considerate in finding solutions. In most situations, the budget is set before the project has begun, which means that the educated guesses you made will soon prove either right or wrong, and you will need to respond.

As the designers and director for a production complete their conceptual work, the discussion of money will need to arise. There are some designers that are good at designing within a budget, but others will design what they feel is best for the show and then make adjustments if necessary. At the completion of the design phase, your production staff will need to do what is called a "cost out" to determine what it will cost to achieve the production as designed. If it's over budget, you have a few choices—ask the designer to accept less expensive options, cut elements, change the design or find more money. This money could come from another show that was under budget, another budget line in the same show that is unneeded or your contingency fund. Before you work with your numbers this way, make sure it's something the organization is okay with. Many producers and clients are okay with "vertical budgeting," or moving funds from one budget line to another within the same project or season; however, some are not, and moving money requires approval from above.

Set expectations with those spending production funds (staff, designers, outside vendors) on what is an acceptable range for the final expenses. 10% under budget and 1% over budget is a good rule of thumb. If someone thinks they will be under or over more than that, they should be proactive and inform you as soon as possible. Being aware of financial problems early will allow more time to find better solutions. If scenery is forecasting being significantly under budget and costumes is forecasting an overage, then maybe shifting money from one budget line to another is a good course of action. You could also use your contingency here.

What if the budget you created is not sufficient for the production? Here is where a positive, respectful relationship with the producer or managing director will be beneficial, as you

	Show 1	Show 2	Show 3	Show 4	Show 5	Show 6	Show 7	Show 8	Show 9	Season Expenses	Total
Choreographer											0
Director											0
Musical Director											0
Performers											0
Stage Manager											0
Asst. Stage Manager											0
Costume Designer											0
Lighting Designer											0
Video Designer											0
Puppet/Mask Designer											0
Scenic Designer											0
Sound Designer											0
Make-up Artist											0
Wig Artist											0
Milliner											0
Fight Choreographer											0
Movement Coach											0
Text/Vocal Coach											0
Musicians											0
Accompanist											0
Run Crew											0
Artist Housing											0
Artist Travel											0
Subtotal Artistic Fees/Services	0	0	0	0	0	0	0	0	0	0	0
Royalties											0
											0

Scripts							0
Music Purchase/Rental							0
Subtotal Royalties/Scripts	0	0	0	0	0	0	0
Dramaturgy							0
Archive Video							0
Archive Photography							0
Subtotal Other Services/PR	0	0	0	0	0	0	0
Sets							0
Paints							0
Props							0
Costumes							0
Dry Cleaning							0
Hair/Makeup							0
Electrics							0
Puppet/Masks							0
Sound							0
Video							0
Stage Management							0
Other Supplies							0
Subtotal Supplies	0	0	0	0	0	0	0
Subtotal	0	0	0	0	0	0	0
Contingency 10%	0	0	0	0	0	0	0
Total Budget	0	0	0	0	0	0	0

Figure 6.1 Budget template

will need to approach them about additional funds. Requests for more money will likely be met with questions such as "why are we over budget?" or "how can you make sure this does not happen again in the future?" Come prepared with these answers. For example: "When we budgeted for the set last spring, the cost of steel was cheaper than it is now. We had no way of knowing it would climb so quickly. We can either add money to the budget to complete the show as designed or re-design the show. Though possible, a re-design at this point may cost us additional labor, as we're getting close to load-in, so my suggestion is we stick with the original plan and find the money for the more expensive steel. In the future, I have asked the scene shop to assume more expensive materials from the beginning to avoid this happening again."

> "Keep everything above board—no hidden agenda—don't play games with the budgets. My role is to achieve the greatest efficiency out of the resources that the theatre has for a given production. It should all be on the table."
>
> - Bronislaw Samler, Head of Production / Chair of the Technical Design and Production Department at the Yale School of Drama/Yale Repertory Theatre

TRACKING THE BUDGET

It is best to track the funds accurately as they are being used. Do not wait until the end to tally the receipts. You need to vigilantly monitor the budget on a daily basis to see how money is being spent and to help your staff from going over budget. Track each line separately for each show/event, rather than as one large production budget. Spreadsheet software can be your friend by providing an easy to read and easy to use table for your tracking needs. Be sure to know your spreadsheet software well enough to set it up correctly. Accounting errors will cause you incredible pain. Establish with those spending the money a schedule for reporting. Weekly is generally best. Once the updates have occurred, ask them to contact you to let you know it was completed and, possibly, to send you the updated ledger if you do not have access to it yourself.

Before you start spending funds, understand the required reporting rules for your organization. Will you need to file end-of-the-year fiscal reports? For many, the end of a season and the end of the fiscal year are the same. Make certain your production heads clearly report their spending, so your report can be easily and properly prepared. Some organizations choose to have a form filled out before and/or after each expense. This process may seem burdensome, but it can save time in the end when trying to track down expenses and how each expense should be properly categorized. The more money you have, the harder it is to keep track of it all, and the more organized you will have to be.

Tartuffe:: 2951940–3952						
Expenses	$ 7,223.76					
Allocation	$ 8,000.00					
under/(over)	$ 776.24					
date	merchant	item	what was it for	debit	credit	notes
7/27/2015	The Clarice	General Hardware		$ 727.77	$ —	
6/11/2015	A & M	MDF	Floor and Sculpture	$ 896.00	$ —	Split w/Large Storage Shelving
8/12/2015	1,000 Bulbs	6" and 12" Plastic Globes	Chandelier	$ 947.55	$ —	
7/28/2015	Amazon	3" White Plastic Globes	Deck	$ 17.87	$ —	Split
7/28/2015	Amazon	3" White Plastic Globes	Deck	$ 53.61	$ —	
7/28/2015	Vector Art 3D	Flourishes	Screens	$ 35.00	$ —	
7/29/2015	Home Depot	1/2" EMT and 1/2" ply	Chandelier	$ 566.40	$ —	Split w/ IA, Dance
8/5/2015	Fisher	Foam and Lu	Screens	$ 464.10	$ —	Split w/ APP
8/10/2015	Home Depot	Plywood	Shrine	$ 134.94	$ —	Split w. SS and IA
8/12/2015	Home Depot	Molding	Shrine	$ 50.70	$ —	
8/14/2015	Rosebrand	Muslin	Screens	$ 564.88	$ —	Split with Equip Purchase
8/17/15	1,000 bulbs	6" and 12" Plastic Globes	Chandelier	$ 380.00	$ —	
9/23/15	Foss Manufacturing	Black Damask Fabric	Black Damask	$ 805.00	$ —	
10/1/15	Theatre Services	Custom Curtains	Damask Curtains	$ 760.00	$ —	Split w/Equip Repair ($935.00)
9/10/2015	DS Pipe & Steel	1.5" tube	Chandelier	$ 225.12	$ —	
9/21/15	Amazon	Clear Ball Pit Balls	Chandelier	$ 116.39	$ —	To be returned
9/28/2015	Royal Designs Studio	Damask Stencil	Damask Stencil	$ 273.87	$ —	
9/30/2015	Royal Designs Studio	Damask Stencil Shipping	Damask Stencil Shipping	$ —	$ 74.07	
10/12/2015	1,000 Bulbs	6" White Plastic Globes	Deck	$ 190.20	$ —	
10/13/2015	Amazon	Credit for Clear Ball Pit Balls	Chandelier	$ —	$ 116.39	
9/30/2015	Amazon	Clear Plastic Ornaments	Chandelier	$ 159.90	$ —	
10/23/2015	McMaster	Magnets	Statue	$ 44.92	$ —	
				$ —	$ —	
				$ —	$ —	
				$ —	$ —	
			Sub TOTAL	$ 7,414.22	$ 190.46	

Figure 6.2 Budget-tracking document

PURCHASING

There are a few different ways in which money can be spent. Every person and organization will have their preferences. Any of these are valid:

- Accounts: If you purchase often from a distributor or manufacturer, it is a good idea to create an account with them so that your organization can get billed directly. This way, any staff can contact the company and make a purchase without having to make a direct payment. Accounts can sometimes come with a frequent buyer discount, which is always helpful!

DATE	VENDOR	ACCOUNT/SUB ACCOUNT	DESCRIPTION	AMOUNT	NOTES
7-Apr	Cosi	Hospitality/Crew & rehearsal	Lunch for rehearsal	$ 218.06	
14-Apr	Cosi	Hospitality/Crew & rehearsal	Lunch for rehearsal	$ 185.43	
21-Apr	Cosi	Hospitality/Monday lunch	Lunch for rehearsal	$ 420.41	
2-Apr	Men's Warehouse	Supplies/show costumes	Tuxedo rental	$ 40.00	deposit
19-Apr	Men's Warehouse	Supplies/show costumes	Tuxedo rental	$ 252.54	balance
18-Apr	FedEx Office	Supplies/production supplies	Script copies	$ 91.69	
16-Apr	Staples	Supplies/production supplies	Clipboards, card stock, spray mount	$ 96.70	
19-Apr	Giant	Hospitality/Production meetings	Bagels, fruit	$ 58.87	
19-Apr	Starbucks	Hospitality/Production meetings	Coffee	$ 31.69	
13-Apr	Wegmans	Hospitality/Crew & rehearsal	Water	$ 3.17	
21-Apr	CVS	Hospitality/Crew & rehearsal	Paper plates	$ 6.40	
20-Apr	Giant	Supplies/production supplies	Script card supplies	$ 26.40	
20-Apr	Giant	Hospitality/Crew & rehearsal	Drinks, snacks	$ 95.16	
21-Apr	FedEx Office	Supplies/production supplies	paper	$ 4.22	
			Total spent	$ 1,530.74	
			Original amount of petty cash	$ 1,650.00	
			Balance	$ 119.26	

Figure 6.3 Petty cash tracking

- Purchasing cards: Some organizations give staff charge cards. This can be an easy way to spend funds as it gets charged directly to the organization, and it does not need to be requested or reimbursed. Often cards such as these are only utilized by full-time staff. Part-time or seasonal staff might not have this option.

- Petty cash: Cash or a check can be given to an individual before they start spending organization funds, to avoid out-of-pocket expenses. You will need to anticipate the approximate amount that is needed so the petty cash allotment is appropriately sized. The individual who receives the petty cash will need to return receipts and/or cash that equals the amount they were given.

- Reimbursement: In some cases, petty cash is not possible, or it will take too long to process. Another option is to have individuals spend money out of pocket and be reimbursed. This is acceptable as long as the individual does not mind using their own money. If this type of purchasing is necessary, be sure receipts for reimbursement are submitted immediately. Processing of such reimbursements may take a while, and it is unfair to ask the individual to wait too long. Although necessary at many organizations, it has to be said that this type of purchasing is undesirable. Asking employees to make out-of-pocket purchases for organizational projects is basically asking an employee for a short-term, interest-free loan. There is also a terrible chance that the purchase might not be approved by the organization. This could leave your employee financially responsible for something that should be an organizational cost.

Not-for-profit organizations qualify for tax exemption on both a state and national level. This allows for purchases to be made without paying tax and helps your budget dollars to go further. Check to see if the organization you are working for has this exemption. If so, they will be able to provide you with a tax-exempt card and number which you (and others) will need to use while making purchases.

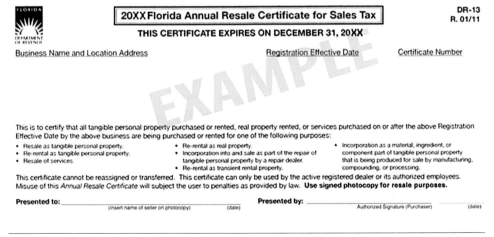

Figure 6.4 Tax-exempt certificate

A solid understanding of money and accounting is incredibly helpful for a production manager. If budget accounting is not your forte, you need not give up on production management; however, you should attempt to improve your skills. Take a class in accounting at your local community college or find an online course. The truth is, anyone can benefit from additional financial know-how.

CHAPTER 7

Hiring and Casting

Production managers are only as good as the people on their team. It's not always up to the production manager to hire everyone for a project, but when it is, it's imperative to get the right people for the job. This chapter will equip you with tools and techniques for hiring, as well as give you some tips about how to get hired as a production manager yourself!

WHO HIRES WHO?

Every organization is different. In some cases, the production manager will be expected to hire the shop staff and crew, while the responsibility for hiring positions like designers and performers will fall to someone like the general manager or company manager. When you accept a position as a production manager, you should learn quickly what is expected of you with respect to hiring. Some production managers choose to delegate the hiring of personnel for specific production areas to the heads of each area; for example, the technical director hires the carpenters. There is no right or wrong way to handle hiring as long as the end result is that the positions get filled and the best people get hired.

HIRING PROCESS

Depending upon your organization, the hiring process might be decided for you. In the case of a university or other large organization, the hiring process is decided by the human resources department or the like. If you find yourself working at an organization like this, the first important step is to research their process and understand how it works and where you as the "hiring authority" fit in.

   If you are creating your own hiring process, here are some important steps to follow:

- Writing the job description: It's important to create an honest and detailed job description to entice the right people for the job and lay out the job expectations. The job description should include the job functions, how it fits in the organizational reporting structure, the necessary skills (multitasking, good communication, specific computer applications, etc.), the minimum qualifications (college degree, three years of experience in the field, etc.) and any preferred qualifications that are not required but will be considered above the minimum requirements (i.e. master's degree, certifications). Be careful about overly inflating the requirements. This will limit the people who will consider applying for the job. If known, you should include the potential start date. You have an opportunity in the job description to present the organization to the job market and let them know not only what type of people you are looking for but also what type of people work there. For example, if your organization values diversity and inclusion, you can say something along the lines of "This is an inclusive workplace; applicants must be comfortable with diverse populations, backgrounds and languages." Make sure the job description also contains application instructions and what application materials are expected (resume, references, writing sample, etc.)

- Creating a search plan: A well-crafted job description is great, but if it doesn't reach the right people, you will likely not get the response you desire. Give thought to the type of people who might desire this job. Is it an entry-level position or internship? If so, then marketing this job to college students or recent grads might be the best course of action. You also want to make sure to market to a diverse crowd. By diverse, we don't just mean race, gender or sexual orientation. You should also look for diversity in areas such as the candidates' background, training, skills or artistic philosophy. Diversity can lead to a greater range of creative ideas.

- Publicizing the job posting: Once you've identified the populations you want to reach, get the word out! The job market can be a very competitive one, and you want to get your job posting out as soon as possible to catch the best pool of candidates. There are many ways to spread the news—listing it on your company's website, emailing it out to list serves and your own contacts, posting with trade organizations (United States Institute for Theatre Technology (USITT), Theatre Communications Group (TCG)/ArtSearch, etc.). Social media can be a huge help, as well. Postings can be easily shared among people even if you only post it once. Don't underestimate the power of word of mouth— start talking to every colleague you meet about your hiring needs; you never know who might be listening or who knows who.

- Putting together a search committee: As mentioned previously, a differing group of voices and opinions can lead to great success. This is certainly true in the hiring process. Many organizations do not utilize hiring committees, though it should be considered. Creating a group of people who will read resumes and conduct interviews allows for a varied response to the candidate pool. In addition to you, think about who in your organization will have the most contact with the new hire, and try to include representation from different areas of your organization. You don't want the committee to be too large, as it might be impossible to find consistent meeting times or come to a consensus.

- Reviewing the resumes and creating the short list: This should not be too hard if you have been specific about what you want in the job description. If candidates don't meet the

Position Title: Production Coordinator

Starting Date: Appointment begins June 2016

Position Description: The successful candidate will support the production effort for the Standard Theatre working alongside the Production Manager. Specific duties will include:

- Administering auditions.
- Assisting in supervising technical/dress rehearsals.
- Coordinating the travel and accommodations of guest artists.
- Coordinating between the production and marketing departments.
- Scheduling and staffing the rentals of rehearsal/performance venues.

Qualifications: Bachelor's degree is required. Also required: at least two years progressively responsible experience in performing arts management. Understanding of production process, good communication skills, good organizational skills, ability to multi-task, ability to prioritize and manage competing priorities are a plus. Degree in theatre or dance preferred. Theatre and dance experience preferred.

Application Deadline: April 25, 2016.

To Apply: Submit: a letter of application; resume; and the names, addresses, and telephone numbers to jobs@standardtheatre.org

The Standard Theatre actively subscribes to a policy of equal employment opportunity and will not discriminate against any employee or applicant because of race, age, sex, color, sexual orientation, physical or mental disability, religion, ancestry or national origin, marital status, genetic information or political affiliation. Minorities and women are encouraged to apply.

Figure 7.1   *Job posting example*

minimum qualifications, in fairness, they should be removed from the list. Sometimes, at this point, it is necessary to trust your instincts. If the candidate has potential because they are qualified and have appropriate work experience, put them on your short list. Meet with your search committee and get their opinions. They might differ from yours, and that is a good thing. Talk about each candidate, and together make the short list of people who will move on to the interview round. You may want to take a moment at this point in the process to talk with a few of the references of those on your short list to make sure they are the type of people you are looking for. See more on reference checking later in this chapter.

- Making an interview plan: If you have a few candidates on your short list (under four) then it's time for in-person interviews. However, if the short list is still a little long, perhaps a round of phone or web-conference interviews is the best next step. Once those are done, pare down the list again and set up the in-person interviews. You should consider what you plan to do with the candidate other than meet with them face-to-face. Perhaps a tour of your facilities and/or a meeting or lunch with others on your staff is a good idea. If you are hiring them to conduct a specific type of work, you may wish to see them complete this work or give a presentation. It's important to share the interview plan and schedule with the candidates so they come prepared.

- Preparing the interview questions: For best comparative data, you should ask every candidate the same set of questions. Devise the questions ahead of time, giving careful thought to what kind of information you need to know. Don't ask questions that can be answered by looking at a resume. Ask questions that give you insight as to how the candidate will work for and with you and your organization. You should be aware that it is not appropriate to ask questions of a personal nature that do not have bearing on the job. Topics such as religion, sexual orientation, family, child care, etc., are illegal to bring up and should be avoided.

- Conducting the interview: If you have thoroughly planned the interview experience and clearly prepared the candidates, the interview should run very smoothly. Make sure to have time for the candidate to ask you questions. They are interviewing you as much as you are interviewing them. The decision to take a new job, especially if it is a full-time job or a relocation, is a big decision. Make sure you take plenty of notes. After only a few interviews, the candidates can begin to run together. Though you should stick to your list of pre-determined questions, don't be afraid to ask follow-ups based on a person's response or work experience. Take time to get to know the candidate.

- Checking references: This is an important step that should not be skipped for any reason and could happen at any point in the hiring process, or at a few points. A good interview might only mean that the candidate is good at interviewing and telling you what you want to hear. Talking with people who have worked with and/or supervised the candidate is an important step to understanding how well they will fit in your organization. You should only contact the references they have listed. If you wish to speak with someone off their reference list, you must ask permission first. It's quite possible that the candidate has not told their current employer that they are searching for a new job. You don't want to put the candidate in a difficult position.

- Background checks and drug testing: Certain employers will require these to take place before someone is hired. It's important to make this clear to the applicants early in the process.

- Deciding who to hire: This can be the hardest step of them all. The final decision on whom to hire should be a careful consideration of all you have gathered about the person—their qualifications, previous work, attitude, personality, work ethic, etc. Again—trust your instincts. Hopefully, the decision will be clear, but if not, don't be afraid to give it some time, and maybe speak to the top candidates again or ask to speak to more references. Don't rush to hire. Not only is a bad hire a drain on your organization, a bad hire might require you to go back through this whole hiring process again! Once you have selected the person to hire, the process of negotiating the terms of their employment is the next step. More on that later in this chapter.

- Communicating with those not selected: With the success of one candidate comes the necessity of letting others know they were not chosen. If you have had personal connection with a candidate, it is proper to contact them directly to let them know of the choice that was made. Phone is usually best; email is to be avoided. It's important to be honest yet supportive, as this could be hard news for the candidate to receive. If the candidate asks for feedback on their interview or for reasons why they were not selected, be as honest as you feel comfortable being. It's best to keep these conversations short and sweet.

FULL-TIME VERSUS SEASONAL OR FREELANCE WORK

Many organizations do not have enough work to justify hiring full-time employees and choose instead to hire freelance seasonal or part-time employees when extra help is needed. You will see this most in organizations that work only one part of the year—summer stock theatre, for example. This is the same when hiring positions like designers, cast or crew who are needed for only one show or event.

Hiring freelance can be a different process. You are looking for the best person for the job, the one who can accomplish the tasks you need in the time you have allotted. "Fit" within the organization might not be as important, as this person is only expected to be with you for a short period of time. Of course, you want to hire trustworthy, honest people, and you do need to consider personalities that will work well together. However, it's not a long-term hire, so the stakes are different. It may be less important to vet these people in the same way as a full-time employee, with a search committee, presentation or staff interaction. At minimum, you should expect to see their resume, have a conversation with them (ideally in person) and speak to a reference (or references). Don't hire people if you don't know anything about them!

HIRING VENDORS AND INDEPENDENT CONTRACTORS

If you are a small company without a production staff or you have a large event or production that will require additional personnel, there are many companies that can provide services to you. There are commercial scene shops, as well as lighting, audio/video and labor companies. There are also individuals who are "jobbed-in" to build costumes, props and other specialty items. If you are located in a metropolitan area, chances are good there is help near you. Here are some helpful tips:

- Knowing who to select: Word-of-mouth is most helpful. Talk to your production management network and find out what companies they have used and if they received positive results.

- Asking for a bid/proposal: Regardless of whether you work for a large or small organization, it is recommended that you created a request for proposal (RFP). Creating an RFP will help you as you search for what you need from several companies or providers. The RFP details exactly what is needed and the time frame you will need it in. It also spells out who the vendor will report to at your organization and what communication and interaction between your company and the vendor is expected. If the service needed requires the building or installing of an item or system, you will want to include explicit details, which may include drawings or plans.

- Selecting the best vendor or contractor: Once the bids/proposals are in, you'll have to look at each very carefully. Are they able to do what you require in the time frame you need and for the amount you can afford to spend? This is another great opportunity to connect with your production management network and get opinions, especially if they have worked with this company or individual before.

- Following up: once the selection has been made and you have negotiated a contract, you will need to stay in touch with your selected vendor to make sure the work is progressing appropriately. It's likely the work may not happen on your premises, so find opportunities to connect with the vendor and see the progress of the work. You can do this by asking them to stop by with the items and paying a visit to where the service is occurring, or, at minimum, you could ask for photos of the work.

CASTING AND AUDITIONS

Not all production managers will be expected to oversee the audition and casting process. In some cases, it falls to a casting director or even a stage manager. However, it is important to know how they are organized and administered.

Here are the steps to a successful audition process:

- Identifying the type of auditions:
  ◦ Are these auditions for one event or for an entire season?
  ◦ Is it a dance concert, musical, opera or a play?
  ◦ What roles/types of performers are you looking for?
  ◦ Are the auditions open for anyone to attend or by appointment or invitation only?

- Creating the schedule:
  ◦ Who will be auditioning and when are they available?
  ◦ When are you likely to get the best attendance?
  ◦ What venue are you using for the auditions, and when is it available?

- Planning for audition format:
  ◦ Will the auditions be one-at-a-time, or will they be in groups?

- ◦ Should those auditioning come prepared with material or learn material at the auditions, or will there be cold readings?
- ◦ Will there be sides (selections from the script) provided?
- ◦ Are you auditioning for a musical or opera? Will you need to arrange for a piano accompanist?
- ◦ Will there be a dance component? Do you need mirrors in the room? Sound system? Ballet barre?

- Promoting the auditions: Once you have answered the questions above, you can begin to promote the audition. It's best to create an audition posting that includes all of the information—dates, times, location, expectations, details on the shows, etc. Also, make sure those auditioning know what to bring with them—headshot, resume, dance clothes, sheet music, etc. If there is a script they are expected to read, let them know where they can access it. Once the posting is made, you can begin to circulate it to places where performers will see it—email lists, casting websites, your organization's website, social media, newspapers, post fliers, etc.

> **TIP**—Take the time to make sure all of the postings are correct! It would be unfortunate if you were prepared for auditions on Saturday and the posting says Sunday. It would be equally challenging if your website says the audition started at 12 p.m. and you were planning for 2 p.m.

- Creating an audition form: You have an opportunity to gather quite a bit of information from those auditioning. Make a form for them to fill out that includes contact information, emergency information, personal information (hair, eyes, height, weight, allergies, do they wear glasses, personal limitations or challenges). This is also the best opportunity to ask about any conflicts they might have for the period of employment.

- Prepping the site for the audition: On the day of the auditions, you should take time before people start arriving to set up the space properly. Outside the audition room, there should be a place for people to check in and drop off their headshot and resume as well as a place for them to sit and fill out the audition form. Inside the room, things should be clean and tidy. There should be a place for those conducting the auditions to sit and perhaps a table at which to jot down notes. The table should be away from the entrance, so the auditionee can come right in and begin, as opposed to awkwardly crossing past the table to get to their audition spot. Finally, you need a place for those auditioning to perform—dance floor, open space for a monologue, etc.

- Running the audition: Someone needs to greet performers when they arrive, sign them in and make sure all the necessary paperwork is filled out and collected. This person should also act as time keeper to keep the auditions running on schedule. If you are running the audition, speak to the director, choreographer or whoever is judging the audition about how they would like to administrate the auditions and how best to stay on time.

SCHOOL OF THEATRE DANCE
PERFORMANCE STUDIES

SPRING 2015 THEATRE AUDITIONS

The Human Capacity

Written by Jennifer Barclay
Directed by Michael Dove

AUDITIONS: Sunday, September 21st, 12-3pm in Cafritz Foundation Theatre (2740)
Monday, September 22nd, 4-7pm in Cafritz Foundation Theatre (2740)
CALLBACKS: Wednesday, October 1st, 4-7pm Schoenbaum Rehearsal Room (3732)

Set in East Berlin, both before and after the fall of the Wall, *The Human Capacity* follows the journey of a Stasi officer as he seeks redemption from the woman whose life he shattered. Both torturer and victim find themselves caught in a struggle to reconcile the horrors of their past with their hopes for the future. The play is a searing look into a society and a family in turmoil, and an exploration of the human capacity for cruelty, perseverance and forgiveness.

Prepare:
- 2 minute dramatic monologue

Roles available for 7 performers – 4 Males & 3 Females
Performance Dates: May 2 – May 9, 2015 in the Kogod Theatre
First Rehearsal: March 23rd, 2015

Eligibility Requirements
In order to be eligible to audition for TDPS productions, students must meet the following criteria:
1. Maintain a minimum overall GPA of 2.7
2. Uphold the University Honor Code
3. Be in good academic standing with the University
Being a part of a TDPS production is a privilege, not a right. We trust each student to behave and act accordingly.

What to Bring: Resume and Headshot
Sign-up Sheets: Posted on 3rd floor callboard – across from Schoenbaum (3732)
Script are now on reserve at the Performing Arts Library

Please contact Cary Gillett with any questions or concerns

Figure 7.2 Audition posting example

- Holding callbacks: Often one round of auditions is not enough, and a second round of auditions, termed callbacks, is necessary. To set up the callback, repeat many of the steps above—determine the schedule, figure out what will occur at the callbacks, communicate the plan to those auditioning and judging, set up the room, etc.

- Deciding the cast: Once the artistic team has decided who they want to cast, the process of negotiating the terms of their employment is the next step.

AUDITION FORM

Name: _____

Address: _____

Phone: _____   Email: _____

Gender: _____   Ethnicity: _____

Union Affiliations: _____

Do you speak any other languages besides English? Yes ☐   No ☐

If so, what language? _____

Do you play a musical instrument? Yes ☐   No ☐

If so, what instrument? _____

Audition Selection: _____

_____

Medical Conditions/Allergies: _____

_____

Do you wear glasses? ☐   contacts? ☐

Are you right handed? ☐   left handed? ☐

Emergency Contact Information

Name: _____

Relationship: _____

Phone: _____

_____

Please list any conflicts you may have from August–October 2015:

_____

_____

_____

_____

Figure 7.3 Audition form example

• Archiving the audition material: When the auditions are over, don't lose track of the valuable information you collected. Headshots, resumes and auditions forms should be filed away for future reference. The director/choreographer might want copies of them, too.

NEGOTIATIONS

Once the right person for the job or role has been decided, the next step is to hire them. Often, it is the production manager who is responsible for contacting potential hires and negotiating salary and the terms of their contract. Negotiating can be a tricky thing, and some people feel uncomfortable doing it, but it is a normal part of the hiring process and should be embraced. As the future employer, it's important to understand what you have to offer in terms of money, benefits or incentives before you contact the potential hire. Members of unions (such as Actors' Equity Association) often have a minimum they must be paid and other fees such as health and pension contributions that are requirements. Do your homework and know what those requirements are before entering the negotiation process. (More on unions later in this chapter.)

The initial conversation with the future employee should include the exact details of the job they are being hired to do—schedule, expectations, outcome, salary offer and benefits (if applicable). Be prepared for the potential hire to not give you a decision immediately. The recipient might need to consider the offer and talk it over with friends or family. You should expect they will need some time, but you should offer a deadline for when you need a decision. Set a time a few days from the initial conversation when you will communicate again.

The next communication could play out in one of three ways—they accept the terms presented, they decline or they ask for different terms. If they are looking for different terms, it is usually because they wish to ask for more compensation. Now, it's your turn to decide. Is this person worth the money? Do you have the money to spend? You may need a day or two to make that decision and may have to speak to your collaborators or supervisors about the feasibility of the request. Don't let too much time pass before contacting the potential hire again. When you connect with them, there are the same three options—you agree to the request, you deny the request and choose not to hire them, or you give a counter offer. The counter offer should be above your original offer but not as high as their request. Usually, at this point, a decision between both parties can be made, but in some cases an additional round of negotiations is necessary.

If you are hiring artists, you might need to negotiate with an agent or other third party. If this is so, you will not talk directly to the artist; instead, the agent takes the role of the middle-man and will communicate with you and the artist separately. The negotiation process is essentially identical to what was previously described, but you will need to allow more time for the agent to contact the artist, talk over the terms and then get back to you. Be aware that an agent gets a percentage of the artist's compensation, so it behooves the agent to negotiate for as much money as possible. Don't be afraid to be honest when enough is enough and you have reached the top salary you have available. It's still quite possible that the artist will accept the job.

Money is not the only term that can be negotiated. If the person will have to relocate for this job (permanently or temporarily), then you should discuss such things as additional funds for travel, shipping of personal items, housing and per diem. You might also need to discuss other things such as vacation days, benefits, equipment (i.e. computers). Some artists will request special listing, or billing, in marketing materials and programs.

Favored Nations (or Most Favored Nations) is a somewhat common negotiation agreement in which artists request equal terms with any other similar artist on the same production. These terms can be money or other resources previously mentioned. According to the Actor's Equity Association website: "The Favored Nations rider has been utilized as a tool by an actor and his/her representative to ensure that no one else in the company (primarily, someone having the same stature or playing the same size role) was getting a better deal. It also became a means of allowing an actor who would normally command a large salary to work for a lower salary without cheapening that actor's value. For example, an experienced actor who would normally be paid higher than minimum might choose to do a role in a not-for-profit theatre which cannot afford to pay more than minimum, and by including the Favored Nations rider the actor, in essence, says to the commercial entertainment world: 'I still don't work for minimum, but in this particular situation I'm willing to as long as I know that no one else is being paid more than I am.'"[1] This clause can also be used by designers.

HIRING CHILDREN

Every state in the USA has different laws on hiring children. If you find yourself with a show or event that requires the use of someone under the age of 18, it's best to begin exploring the process as soon as possible. In most cases, you will need to file an application with the state government justifying why you need to use this person and how you plan to schedule their time and compensate them. The child will not be able to begin working until this application is approved and a permit is secured. Once it is approved, the permit must be kept on site wherever the child is working in case inquiries are made. Visit the US Department of Labor website for more information—www.dol.gov.

> **TIP**—In some cases, adults working with minors are required to undergo a background check to ensure safety for all involved.

Each state also has different views on the supervision of minors. In some cases, the parents will need to remain on site when the child is working. In other cases, they can be dropped off and left in the care of an employee. It's best to hire a "child guardian" if you are working with one, and especially more than one, child. This person's sole responsibility is to make sure the children do their job and remain safe and engaged. Their job begins where others' jobs end—stage management, company management, wardrobe, hair/makeup, etc. There is no pre-determined ratio of guardian to minors, but many camps require one adult for every five children, so that is a good rule of thumb to follow.

> On Broadway, it is a requirement to hire a child guardian for any show with one or more minors in the cast. These employees are members of Local 764— the wardrobe union. The collective bargaining agreement (CBE) took a year to negotiate and was put into effect in 2012.
>
> — From an interview with Jill Valentine,
> Child Guardian on Broadway

CONTRACTS AND RIDERS

Once the hiring process and negotiations are done, it's time to build the contract. If the person you are hiring is a member of a union (see more information about unions later in this chapter), you must use the contract provided by that union, which dictates what information you need to include. If the person is not a member of a union, you may create your own contract. Here are some items that should be included and some tips on how to craft the language:

- Information about the company and the person being hired: If your company has letterhead, it should be utilized. If not, make sure you list the organizational details such as name, address, phone numbers, etc. Also include the information of the person being hired. At minimum, you should include their name and address.

- Terms of service: Include what job they are being hired to do. If it's for a specific show, you should list the name of that show. If applicable, include a detailed list of their job duties. Include when they are expected to report to work for the first time and what other dates they should be onsite, as well as the end date when their services are to be completed. If this is not explicitly known, you can list a date range, but it's best to be specific about what is expected. Include what deliverables are expected of them. In the case of a designer, this might be drawings, renderings or a model. The more specific you can be with the contract, the more it can help you later if there is a dispute over the job expectations.

- Compensation: List the exact pay breakdown and a schedule for the delivery of payments. The schedule might be specific dates or when certain tasks are accomplished (such as one-third payment upon signing of this agreement, one-third payment upon first rehearsal and one-third payment upon closing of the production). Make sure to list compensated terms that were agreed on beyond fees, such as travel, housing, per diem, relocation expenses, etc. Make sure to include any other items that were negotiated beyond money, such as complimentary tickets, pension plans, health benefits, billing in publicity materials, etc.

- Future life of the project: If there is a chance that the project could continue past the timeline of the contract, many people will expect a clause called "right of first refusal." This states that if the project is remounted or reconceived, the signee has the right to be asked first to reprise their role/position before others are asked.

> The Actor's Equity Association's League of Resident Theatres (LORT) contract has a right of first refusal clause built in if there is a chance the production could move to Broadway. The contract dictates that if an offer to continue with the show is not made, that the actor will receive four weeks contractual salary. The Stage Director's and Choreographer's Society requires a payment of 50% of the original salary if right of first refusal is not offered.[2]

- Legal language: Many companies and individuals require or request language in the contract dealing with cancellation, arbitration, liability, force majeure, disputes and termination. All of this language is legalese for "protect your backside." No one wants things to go wrong, but sometimes they do, and you will want to agree up front how those challenges will be handled. With this and any other legal situation, it is best to speak with a lawyer before committing to anything or signing the contract.

• Expectation of when the contract should be completed: In most cases, you want the contract back immediately. If it stays unsigned for too long, that usually means something is wrong. It's best to request the contract back within one week. It's also useful to link the completion of the contract to the first payment, which often encourages its return.

• Signatures: As the creator of the contract, your company should sign first before it is sent off. By doing so, it is saying that you stand behind what is written on the contract and are ready to make a commitment. Make sure you know who in your organization has signing privileges for contracts. You might not have this authority; it could be a producer or artistic director or another person in upper management.

• Riders: A contract rider can be utilized if you need to make an addition to a standard union contract or if a contract has already been signed and something changes.

> The Actors' Equity Association requires riders if you are asking a performer to do something out of the ordinary such as perform nude, do stunts and/or move scenery. A rider can also be used to agree to additional compensation for situations such as use of personal clothing onstage or additional duties such as serving as dance or fight captain. Always check the union rulebook to identify what is worthy of a rider and how it should be formulated.

In some situations, you may be on the receiving end of a contract. This is sometimes the case if you employ a company to provide a service or if a particular individual has their own contract that they request to use. It's important to make sure all of the information mentioned previously is included; when in doubt, let your company's lawyer read it before signing it.

UNIONS

There are a number of unions that production managers may come into contact with as part of their job. Here are brief descriptions of the major ones.

• *Actor's Equity Association (AEA)* is the union of actors and stage managers in the United States. They focus on theatrical stage productions and, in some cases, corporate productions. There is also an Actor's Equity in England, but they are two separate unions. (www.actorsequity.org)

• *American Guild of Musical Artists (AGMA)* is the labor organization that represents opera singers, choral musicians and dancers, primarily ballet. (www.musicalartists.org)

• *Screen Actors Guild/American Federation of Television and Radio Artists (SAG/AFTRA)* is the union of performers and personalities in movies, TV and radio. (www.sagaftra.org)

- *Society of Stage Directors and Choreographers (SDC)* is what its title states, and is specific to stage performances. (www.sdcweb.org)

- *United Scenic Artists (USA)* is primarily a designer's union, though it does cover certain allied crafts people. Its members work in TV, film, industrials and special events in the United States. (www.usa829.org)

- *International Alliance of Theatrical Stage Employees (IATSE)* is the "behind the scenes" union and serves stage, TV and film productions. It covers positions such as stagehands, crafts people, board ops and wardrobe. As its title suggests, it is a worldwide union. (www.iatse.net)

- *American Federation of Musicians (AF of M)* covers professional musicians in the United States and Canada. (www.afm.org)

Each union has different rules about contracting, minimum payments, pensions and health contributions, travel and housing requirements, additional fees, etc. They also have various agreements about working conditions, length of workday and employment. You will need to research these unions if you foresee yourself working with any of them. Each has a very useful website that can be a great starting point. It's also not a bad idea to call and speak to someone from the union if you have questions. If your company is contracted to any of these organizations, the union contract should be available to you to have as a reference.

At the time this book was published, 25 of the 50 United States follow a "right to work" law that gives citizens the right to work for a living without having to join a union. Anyone is free to unionize, but there cannot be collective bargaining agreements and you do not need to join a union to be employed. In these states, some workers choose to join a union, as it offers health and pension benefits as well as a way into the business if they are new to the area. Some production managers say that the union labor is often more qualified, so they choose to spend the extra money, as they feel it is worth it. Often shows will be staffed with union and non-union members. Everyone on the backstage crew can work across departments (lights, sound, props, etc.), which is often not the case in a full union IATSE house. The venue can set its own rules about what is and is not acceptable, and you do not need to have a union crew present for every use of the space. For example, you would not need to bring in a union electrician simply to turn on the lights for a tour of the theatre.

PERSONNEL MANAGEMENT

The work of a manager is not done once the person is hired. Part of your management responsibility will require orienting, training and evaluating your hires, as well as supervising their compliance with employment expectations.

- Orientation and training: An efficient and friendly process for initiating employees will help your organization. Take the time to orient your new staff members to their surroundings. In the employee's first couple of weeks, schedule meetings, lunches and tours with people whom they will interact with in their position. Meet with new employees on a regular basis during their first few months on the job to talk about their transition. It may also be necessary to put new employees through training sessions. Training can happen right as someone starts or later in their tenure. Make a point to budget for employee training so you are ready to accommodate any need.

- Professional development: Many employees need development to get them to produce at their top potential. As employees grow and thrive in their positions, the overall organization benefits. Look for opportunities to help your employees grow. This could be skill-based classes, certifications, conference visits, etc. Professional development is best when it is encouraged organizationally and tailored to each employee. Include employees in deciding what kind of development opportunity they should engage in. In your budgeting process, make sure funds are available to support development—travel, housing, conference fees, class tuition, per diem, etc.

"To keep good artisans, you have to make sure they stay current. If anyone on our staff wants to take a class or brush up their skills, we work very hard to support them. We also partner with the union to train people on new equipment, like light boards. It's so important to invest in your local artists and crafts people."

- Tracy Utzmyers, Production Manager at The Muny in St. Louis

Figure 7.4 Production Manager Tracy Utzmyers and the production staff from The Muny in St. Louis.
Credit: Photo by Phil Hamer

- Performance reviews: Some organizations make it a requirement to meet with staff members at certain times in the year to discuss their job performance and to set goals for them in the future. Even if this is not your organization's policy, you should do it anyway. Producing shows and events is time-consuming work, and it is easy to get wrapped up in the tasks at hand. It's very important to take a moment to talk one-on-one with your staff members about how they are coping with their jobs. This is also a good time to share your impressions of their work and interactions with other employees. A great way to begin this conversation is to ask the employee to write a self-assessment. This way, you can see before the meeting what they think of their work and their role in the organization. This can often guide the conversation, especially if assessments differ.

- Resolving disputes: Let's face it. Not everyone will get along. There will be problems between people, and you will need to solve the dispute. It's important in situations like this to remain neutral and hear all sides. Sometimes, you will need to help resolve the dispute by making a decision. Other times, it might be best to get out of the way and encourage the two factions to solve their own problem. Conflict can be scary, and many people fear it. When working with human beings, conflict is unavoidable, so don't avoid it. If you are one who fears conflict, seek some professional development to help you address your concerns.

- Setting policies and procedures: If the positions you hire do the same type of work regularly, it may be important to establish policies and procedures for your company. This is even more important if you work with seasonal staff or have a lot of turnover, so that everyone working for you knows how things should operate. A policy is a course of action adopted firmly by your group—e.g., "we only use rigging equipment manufactured by these three companies." A procedure is a course of action that we follow—e.g., "we inspect all rigging to determine if it's safe and usable." Firmly setting these may be a group project with your staff. You will want guidance from experts on your staff, and policies and procedures are adhered to better when everyone is invested in their creation and feels that they are necessary. Once policies and procedures are established, you should document them, communicate them and post them where everyone has access. Nothing is worse than creating a policy and then finding out that it has not been followed because people were not aware of it.

- Comp time: The work we do is rarely 9-to-5. Full-time production staff members are often asked to work odd hours that fluctuate within any given week, depending upon the project and stage of development. The build of a show might be a 9 a.m. to 5 p.m., 40 hour-a-week situation, but technical rehearsals sometimes require up to 80 hours in a week. The concept of compensated time or "comp time" is one that allows employees to balance the time worked in those busy periods with not-so-busy periods. Some organizations establish an official policy on comp time—for example, an hour of overtime worked this week equals an hour you can take off at another point. Some organizations are less strict and consider requests of this nature on a case-by-case basis. Give some thought to how you will handle this with your staff, and clearly communicate any comp time policy.

- Labor laws: United States federal and state governments have workplace. The laws cover items such as safety, wages, benefits, protection, leave, etc. If you are unfamiliar with these laws, learn about them.

- Working the human resources department: Some production managers are lucky to work for an organization that has a human resources manager. Get to know this department well, as you can rely on them for personnel challenges or questions. They will become a necessary ally and invaluable resource for you. Make sure to document any performance reviews and/or disciplinary meetings with employees and file them with the HR department. They keep a file on every employee of the organization.

- Legal issues: If legal issues arise—talk to a lawyer! If topics such as sexual harassment or discrimination come up, or if there is a concern that laws are being broken, talk to a lawyer! You should not attempt to solve these problems on your own. As always, if you don't know something, find someone who does and ask questions.

HOW TO GET A JOB AS A PRODUCTION MANAGER

As with most jobs in the entertainment business, getting a job is often about whom you know and who knows you. Every production manager we spoke with for this book achieved their position by working their way up through other parts of the business. Many production managers got their start as stage managers, a few come through technical direction and there are also some from lighting and costumes. If this is a business you want to break into, you will have to do your time in other parts of the organization. Rarely, if ever, will you be trusted to run a production if you have not already participated at some level within the process, and people know you are knowledgeable and capable. People will need to trust in your abilities. Some of the larger theatres in the country hire interns or apprentices in production management. These positions are not plentiful, and the hiring process is competitive. However, if you can get an apprenticeship or internship, it is a great stepping-stone that might gain you access into the business.

"I started at the Denver Center Theatre Company as a stage management intern, which led to a season of work in stage management, at which point there was an opening for an assistant production manager, and I was encouraged to apply. I'm not sure I would have applied for the job if they had not reached out to me, as I didn't meet the requirements of the job posting. I spent five years in that position before moving to my current job."

- Rick Noble, Production Manager at Center Stage

Your cover letter is an important tool in the application process. It should be tailored specifically to the job you are applying for. Don't use a generic cover letter; it's a turn-off for employers. Make sure to include why you are applying for the job, why you think you are right for the job and what experience you have that backs up that statement. If you have a personal connection to the job or know someone at the organization, you should mention this here. It's all about relationships! Don't feel you need to list your entire job experience history; that's what your resume is for. Keep it short and sweet, though make your points and say what you need to. And always proofread!

When you apply for a job, make sure your resume is in top shape. Your resume should be:

- Easy to read: Don't make the reader search for the information.

- Pleasing to the eye: People are more likely to read a resume that is clearly laid out, nicely formatted and with a sense of style.

- Succinct: List the information that needs to be there, but keep it concise. This is what opens the door for you; if interviewed, you'll have more opportunities to elaborate on your skills and potential.

- Current: Make sure to update your resume with your most recent employment or training information. Weigh the importance of any credits/jobs and list the ones that show you off best. You may begin with a resume full of college experience, but once you have enough professional credits, remove the college credits.

- Specific to the job: Your resume should cater to the job for which you are applying. For example, if you are applying for a job in opera, make sure to list opera credits first.

- Without errors: Don't ever send a resume with a typo or incorrect data. It speaks badly about you.

- Truthful: Never lie; our world is too small

Your Name
Mailing Address/Email address/Phone Number

PROFESSIONAL EXPERIENCE –

2008–Present   Production Manager
                The Palace Theatre
- Supervise the production effort for ten shows per season.
- Coordinate the scheduling of performances, production meetings, rehearsals and technical rehearsals as well as pre-show and post-show events during performances.
- Work in association with the Producing Director to hire designers and production personnel.
- Maintain a production budget of $350,000.

| 2004–2008 | Production Manager |
| | Urban Theatre Project |

- Oversaw all production for three shows in repertory.
- Worked in association with the Artistic Director to hire all designers and production personnel. Allocated and maintained a production budget, requiring creative use of small funds.
- Supervised the student company, who served as the crew for all production aspects – set construction, set painting, light hang and focus, run crew.
- Coordinated the scheduling of production meetings, rehearsals and technical rehearsals as well as pre-show and post-show events during performances.

| 2002–2004 | Assistant Production Manager |
| | Round the Corner Theatre |

- Responsible for all payroll and bills for the production department.
- Facilitated the casting and hiring of actors, designers and production personnel, including negotiating with agents and generating union contracts.
- Assisted in scheduling production meetings, rehearsals and technical rehearsals.
- Maintained a production budget of $500,000.

SPECIAL SKILLS –

- Valid driver's license
- Fluent in American Sign Language
- Proficient at Vectorworks and Adobe Photoshop

EDUCATION –

Bachelor of Arts in Theatre from the Mid-Atlantic University, 2002

REFERENCES –

Anne White	Donald Wilson	Jamaal Mason
Producing Director	Former Managing Director	Production Manager
Urban Theatre project	The Palace Theatre	Round the Corner Theatre
Email/phone number	Email/Phone number	Email/Phone number

Figure 7.5 Resume example

Whether the employer requires it or not, you should list three references on your resume. These three people should be people you have worked with or worked for, not friends or family. Ideally, the three people would know you in different ways and in different situations. Three professors from the same school, for example, is not a smart choice. Some jobs require one or more letters of recommendation. Select this person wisely and, if possible, have a conversation with them about the job and why you think you are right for it. You want this letter to be personalized to you and speak to your strengths and possibilities.

TIP—always ask people if they are willing to serve as a reference for you. If you have used them in the past and plan to again—ask a second time, and maybe a third. Don't let it be a surprise when a potential employer calls a reference. You don't want them caught unaware. Also, make sure you ask your reference which phone number and/or email address they want you to list.

So you've gotten an interview—congratulations! Certainly, it's time to celebrate, but the job is not yours yet. Here are some things to consider for your interview:

- Do your homework: Know as much as you can about the organization, the people, the work, etc. Chances are good you might be asked about your thoughts on one or more of those subjects, and you want to be prepared.

- Dress the part: Make sure you dress one step above the people with which you are interviewing. Know that those working in the performing arts world rarely come to work in three-piece suits and tend to favor more casual attire, but a corporate theatre job could be the opposite. A good rule of thumb is to make sure you are comfortable climbing a ladder in what you are wearing. You never know when you might be offered a tour of the facility and need to do just that!

- Be ready to ask questions: Make sure you get the information you need to make the decision should you be offered the job. You are interviewing them as much as they are interviewing you. Some employers might expect questions as a sign of your job interest, your intelligence and your engagement. Questions can show that you have done your homework and you are serious about the position.

- Be on time: Make sure you know where to go and how long it's going to take to get there. If you have any concern, scope it out ahead of time. Don't be late! In fact, be early.

- Follow up: A small note or email to say "thank you" can show that you are serious and excited about the job. If you do not get the job, don't break the relationship. Maybe you were a close second choice, and maintaining a good relationship with the employer could mean a future job. The entertainment business is surprisingly small—don't burn any bridges if you can avoid it!

If you are offered the job, it's important to consider your own worth as well as the logistics of taking the job. For example, the job might offer good compensation, but the location of the work will require an expensive commute, which offsets your net pay. Make sure you are looking at the big picture. Can you afford to take this job? If it is important for your career, perhaps you can accept lower compensation for future success. You are the only person who can answer these questions. And don't forget—it's perfectly natural to negotiate. Many people, especially those young in their careers, feel odd about doing this. Most employers expect it. Don't be afraid of the process. Taking a new job is an important decision and should not be approached lightly.

The process of filling a position is clearly a lengthy and challenging one with lots of details and things to consider for both the employer and candidate. It should not be approached lightly. Whenever possible, take your time and make the best choices you can. Trust your instincts and maybe a few tips from this chapter!

NOTES

1   "Are You a Favored Nation?" *Actors Equity*. http://www.actorsequity.org/newsmedia/misc/FavoredNation.asp

2   "Actor's Equity Association League of Resident Theatre Agreement." *Actors Equity*. http://www.actorsequity.org/docs/rulebooks/LORT_Rulebook_13-17.pdf

Safety

> "No one should have to sacrifice their life for their livelihood, because a nation built on the dignity of work must provide safe working conditions for its people."
>
> - Secretary of Labor Thomas E. Perez
> Workers Memorial Day, Washington D.C., April 2014[1]

The safety, health and welfare of people engaged in work or employment is the responsibility of the organization in which they work. In performing arts and special events, it is often the production manager's responsibility to oversee this very important area. This doesn't mean it is solely the production manager's responsibility; everyone has a role in safety. Oftentimes, the technical director is involved, overseeing the safe construction of scenery or rigging installations, as well as writing and maintaining the shop manual for the safe use of tools. Other times, it can be a stage manager looking for hazards on and around the stage. The bottom line is that safety is *everyone's* responsibility, and this chapter will look at the various ways production managers can help keep people safe.

OCCUPATIONAL SAFETY

One of the main entities that you will have to contend with in regard to safety is the Occupational Safety and Health Administration (www.osha,gov).

Congress established a law and provided the Occupational Safety and Health Act of 1970. Known as the OSH Act, it was passed to prevent workers from being killed or seriously harmed at work, as workplace conditions were becoming overly dangerous. While it varies from state to state, most states follow the "General Industry Standards 1910" guidelines and you, as a production manager, should familiarize yourself with that, at the very least. Under this OSH Act of 1970, it is made clear that employers are responsible for safety and must provide a workplace that is free of hazards for the worker.

The act also created the Occupational Safety and Health Administration (OSHA), which sets and enforces protective workplace safety and health standards. Additionally, OSHA assures safe and healthful workplaces by setting and enforcing standards and by providing training, outreach, education and assistance. As an additional protection for employees, workers may file a complaint to have OSHA inspect their workplace if they believe that their employer is not following OSHA standards or that there are serious hazards. Employers must comply, *by law*, with all applicable OSHA standards. Employers must also comply with the General Duty Clause of the OSH Act, which requires employers to keep their workplace free of serious recognized hazards. So there are two acts of OSHA that are relevant here. One that says you must provide a workplace free of hazards (such as a theatre scenic unit with multiple levels) and one that says you will keep your workplace (like a scene shop or costume shop) free of hazards and perform regular training sessions for staff and employees.

The fact is that you can't possibly be responsible for keeping EVERYONE safe ALL the time. It is everyone's responsibility. It is also the responsibility of the individual to keep themselves safe by not performing unsafe tasks during the course of their time at work! The bottom line is that you, as a production manager, should do everything within your power to assure a safe and healthy working environment.

Figure 8.1

Credit: Image ©iStock

ASSESSING

"Assess everything so you know how to train."

- Nancy Mallette, Senior Manager—Occupational Health and
Safety for Cirque du Soleil

By assessing, you are documenting knowledge, skills, attitudes and beliefs of situations or circumstances ahead of time. By assessing, you also analyze procedures in place that keep people safe. Before you expose any artist to the workplace, the law requires that you assess hazards in advance. We shouldn't build a piece of scenery without knowing the risks involved to the actor or crew. That becomes part of the assessment and verification. (You can't wait for someone to get hurt and THEN evaluate whether or not the scenery was safe!) Bill Reynolds, Head of Safety at Yale School of Drama and Yale Repertory Theatre, agrees and says that

> by doing the safety inspection of scenery, rigging, etc. we are verifying that the safety concerns at hand have been properly addressed. It really is an ongoing risk assessment that has to happen with the technical director and the production manager or production stage manager.

Having these items assessed also gives you an opportunity to understand your staff's level of training in current safety standards. Proper staff training gives you the ability to have many

Figure 8.2 The College-Conservatory of Music at the University of Cincinnati

Credit: Photo by Adam Zeek, www.zeekcreative.com

sets of eyes looking at a particular circumstance. If someone sees a potential problem, we must train staff on how to *mitigate*, which means to lessen in force or intensity the situation at hand. The question becomes how to train, document, assess and mitigate and how to get staff to understand the importance of these tasks mentioned.

TRAINING

One of the biggest jeopardies in a workplace is the people (we CAN hurt each other); therefore, training becomes primary. Not just handing someone a manual but establishing a protocol for safety in all areas becomes the main focal point for the production manager. Having training sessions or discussions on one topic can oftentimes become the launching pad for other discussions on safety. For instance, a safety discussion on hanging scenery can quickly become a training session in using fall protection, or working on a man-lift, or proper ways to lift weights for the fly rail. A discussion of fire extinguishers can become a discussion about having an evacuation plan in place.

There is no single way to do safety training. It is based on the environment and the potential hazards or risks of that particular situation. Staff training in various life-saving techniques can also be a big plus toward achieving your goals with OSHA. Is your staff adequately trained in CPR, first aid or blood-borne pathogen response? What about your house managers? Your stage managers? Do you have a defibrillator in the lobby? Has the staff been trained to use a defibrillator? The list goes on, and, as you can see, it makes sense from a safety standpoint to have these leadership roles have some type of certification on their resume, especially those that are close to a large public gathering. Senior management should get involved, too, as safety is everyone's responsibility. They can help decide who gets trained where. Perhaps the technical director is well versed in first aid and addressing minor cuts and abrasions. Stage management would be best suited with CPR and first aid due to their proximity to the actors and crew. Every scenario will be different, and each circumstance will need to be individually addressed in order to best come up with that plan for OSHA. Plan on assessing your own situation, and decide what level of training might be necessary for your venue or company. If you are in an academic situation, perhaps it is time to consider this as part of the academic mission of your school. Discussions on safety can become an aspect of the educational environment. Reynolds states: "At Yale, the staff that is involved with the production process at the highest level possible should have the training of what is considered 'best practices in the industry.' Stage manager, production manager, producer . . . all should be trained in best practices of safety. It becomes part of the curriculum. We do shows as part of our academic mission. We should include safety as part of that. Safety isn't something 'in addition' to what we do. It IS what we do."

DOCUMENTATION

Documentation of training sessions becomes a key factor for the production manager. According to Nancy Mallette, Senior Manager—Occupational Health and Safety for Cirque du Soleil, it means everything: "I can't tell you enough how important it is to document what takes place in a training session. If you went over rigging, write down the day and date and what was covered. You should also document the name of the person doing the training and keep it all in a file in case you ever need it for reference."

You must also now document an injury if they ever happen under your watch. Performing art companies are no longer exempt from OSHA's record-keeping requirements, and companies with more than ten employees are now required to maintain an OSHA Form 300 (Injury & Illness Log). This is a recent law, and production managers must now contend with having additional, but very necessary, paperwork. Another change is about timely reporting (documenting) of work-related hospitalizations and fatalities. Lastly, new federal requirements make it so that you have to post an OSHA Form 300A every year from February 1 to April 30. While it may seem overwhelming at first, remember it is now law.

All of this documentation of work can and will become indispensable for you, especially in the case of an OSHA investigation of a work-related injury. Here is an example:

Let's say an actor slips off a step unit and breaks an ankle. OSHA gets involved and will begin an investigation, and you, the production manager, will become a prime candidate for questions. They may ask you something like: "When YOU investigated the accident, what were the findings of the root cause of the injury?" (If you didn't even investigate the accident, it will imply to OSHA that you don't take it seriously, which won't help your cause!) Another investigative question may be "when was the set last inspected, and how did you document that inspection?" Having the inspection reports available in your reference file becomes a huge factor in how OSHA will treat the situation. Mallette agrees and says that "the more documentation you have with someone's signature on it, the more OSHA understands that you are assuming the responsibility of keeping your staff safe."

If OSHA showed up, your documentation should include the following:

- Dates of when the set/stage platform was built
- Photos of the platform and photos of the step off the platform.
- Some documentation on how/why the technical director engineered and built the platform and step the way they did
- Dates of when you trained the actor how to safely step down off the platform
- Dates of when you rehearsed that part of the show (the step down off the platform)

This is a perfect example of why good, accurate information should be coming out of the stage management department in the form of rehearsal reports or accident reports. Have a discussion with stage management about the importance of documentation. This documentation also proves verification that issues have been discussed.

If you, as the production manager, have all of this information at your fingertips, your interview with OSHA will go better than if you do not. By doing the above minimums, you have shown a willful attempt that you, in advance, care about your actors and thought about their well-being. Remember, accidents do happen, but OSHA is looking for facts that reasonable precautions have been taken. It is in your power as the production manager to make that happen.

ASSESSING THE SHOPS

What other precautions can we take as production managers to help us show everyone, including OSHA, that you care about your employees? You should start with a self-guided tour. Go watch the costume shop use toxic dyes and other hazardous materials so that you really understand the possible risks involved. Look around when you do this. Is there personal protective equipment (PPE) in the shop? Are proper eye protection and breathing respirators available for the number of staff members involved with the project? What other common sense precautions can you come up with? How about fire extinguishers near the dye vat in case of an unforeseen fire or small chemical explosion? What about a chemical spill on the floor of the costume shop? As you can start to see, the questions you may be asked by OSHA are many.

Figure 8.3 Photo by David "Dstew" Stewart

Now take a walk around the scene shop and observe the use of power tools, among other activities taking place. Is there a first aid kit in the shop? Check their content to make sure they are properly stocked and that nothing has expired. Is there personal protective equipment (PPE) around the shop? How about eye protection for those using cutting and sanding tools, and is it being worn? Is hearing protection necessary for the use of the tool? If so, are there disposable foam ear plugs within reach of the tools? How about people working above ground? Do you know the rules of what height proper harnesses should be worn when working above ground? (Every state may be different, so check your OSHA website.)

The paint shop is another area that needs serious safety attention. OSHA regulations can be very strict with regard to paints and adhesives and other scenic materials. Have the brushes been cleaned or disposed of properly? Is paint being stored properly? What about eye protection and respiratory gear for the painters?

In some states, like California, merely leaving the lids off the paint can when done can trigger some severe monetary fines. No production manager ever wants to pay a fine to OSHA!

Figure 8.4

Credit: Image ©iStock

Once you have completed your shop tours, take a moment to reflect on all of the areas where you think you can make improvements to safety or in accident reduction. Work with your shop heads to make sure you have the proper equipment in place. If you don't already have a safety manual or "standard operating procedures" (SOP) manual, this may be your opportunity as a production manager to write one with your management staff. As mentioned earlier, safety is everyone's business, and everyone on the production team and in the act-ing / performing company should be encouraged and allowed to speak up and point out the possible unsafe situations. "See Something, Say Something" should be a standard operating procedure for all projects.

Did a light boom get put in place that wasn't on the ground plan? What about an added piece of masking that wasn't on the ground plan? Working closely with the other departments can help ensure that injuries can be kept to a minimum. You can also help alleviate the amount of questions asked in an OSHA interview by doing everything in your production manager super powers to advance the safety of the various working environments. If you haven't been that involved in safety before, now is your chance to take a leadership role in safety for your company or venue.

THE FIRE MARSHAL

A critical component for just about every project will be the relationship with the local fire marshal. The importance of maintaining a great relationship with this person cannot be over-stated. They have the authority to call off your event if they see a problem that would com-promise the safety of the workers or public audience. They have that power, and they will use it. That said, this relationship is not one to be scared of. You should be confident in your approach to the fire marshal, not scared OR intimidated. Always remember that their job is to protect people. That's it. Help them to do their job by doing a good job yourself. You should plan to meet your fire marshal, if at all possible. Take a meeting when you have a plan in place and are confident that your plan will pass the fire inspection or demonstration. However, if you don't have a plan in place, you can start to create and maintain this very important rela-tionship by using your fire marshal as an additional resource to help you develop it. Realize that the more you meet with your fire marshal, the more confidence they are building in you. They develop the confidence in your ability to do the right thing and your ability to follow through. They will learn to rely on this follow through, which only increases trust.

> "What grows out of transparency and truth is the ability to negotiate. We must be true to our word. If you can develop that relationship, it gives you the ability to do things that you might not have otherwise been able to achieve."
>
> - Bill Reynolds, Director of Theater Safety and Occupational Health for Yale School of Drama/Yale Repertory Theatre

Figure 8.5 Bill Reynolds

What are some of the things we can do as production managers to create a good working relationship with the fire marshal? The first thing is transparency. You need to let the fire marshal know what you are doing and have openness to the idea that the fire marshal can inspect your show. If the fire marshal is going to get involved with your effect, set, show, etc., at the very least, you should have the following at your disposal:

- Explanation/design of effect being used that triggered the fire marshal call
- Drawings, renderings, sketches of the effect or scenic piece
- Reports from your technical director on how the piece was engineered/built
- Documentation on training or training plan for employees

The same would be used for the permit to use open flame on a set, plus:

- Demonstrate that we know how to use the open flame effect safely
- Discuss and document what risks there are with using the open flame
- Discuss procedures in how we will deal with risks or emergencies
- Document that we have trained the staff or crew in proper use of flame and fire extinguishers

> Open flame is NEVER permitted onstage without the written consent of a fire marshal. You should always check with local fire department authorities in your area.

In some theatrical and special events, especially in hotel ballrooms, you may be required to provide what is called a "fire watch" staff person. Due to the use of haze or fog-producing products during an event, the fire alarm system may have to be turned off. This is an important item for the checklist, as it will oftentimes come with additional charges to the budget, especially if an actual fire department representative is needed during the entire event. This fire watch person is on hand to specifically watch for hazards and to report a fire, should one break out, as the fire alarms have been turned off.

By having these procedures in place, we can confidently tell the fire marshal, "if something goes wrong, we have a plan in place, and this is our plan." Don't look at the fire marshal as a burden to your creativity, but as -a resource. The more you get to know your local fire marshal, the more you will be put at ease that they are not there to interfere but to strictly reinforce standards and procedures that have been proven to save lives.

BUILDING SAFETY INTO THE SCHEDULE

As a production manager, we are usually the ones responsible for putting together the various schedules. Scenic load-in, light hang, video install, tech, dress . . . you name it, we schedule it. But how many of you build safety into the schedule? Has this ever been a part of your mind-set? If not, it should be. As the production manager, you're responsible for this happening. It is highly unlikely that anyone else will take the initiative to build safety into the schedule.

Take the time to guide your cast and crew on a tour of the theatre or performance space. (Oftentimes, it may not be a theatre!) Introduce everyone on the team, and describe to the performers and crew what their roles may be with regard to safety at the workplace. On the tour, you should point out where fire extinguishers or fire hoses are located. Also, indicate where the fire alarm "pulls" are in case anyone needs to immediately report a fire. We should then acclimate the performers and crew to the various exits, both emergency as well as regular exits. Make sure everyone knows how to get out in case of an issue needing immediate evacuation. While at the performance space, point out any step downs or platforms that may need to be navigated around. You should then conclude with a fire/evacuation drill. Perhaps it's just before a tech or a dress rehearsal, but you may want to practice to make sure everyone knows what their responsibilities are during an emergency.

TIP—If your performance venue has a sound attenuator (one that plays a pre-recorded voice or tone during an emergency) play it for the cast and crew so they know it is NOT a sound cue that is part of the show.

The emergency plan can be a very simple assignment list:

- Stage manager: Assess the situation and make God mic announcement of what to do
- Asst. stage manager: Call the fire department and report the incident giving EXACT location
- Stage crew chief: Begin evacuation of stage personnel—actors and crew
- Light board operator: Shut down power
- Costume crew chief: Make sure costume shop is evacuated or communicated with
- House manager: Begin safe, calm evacuation of the venue

You should have an emergency plan in place for everyone involved in the production. Even if that assignment is "get to an exit," EVERYONE involved has an assignment. You need to take the time to assign these positions and take this responsibility as seriously as making crew assignments for the running of the show. Again, every scenario will be different. You will need to assess your situation and make your own list according to your needs and resources.

You should build a mock evacuation into your schedule at least once during your tech/dress rehearsal week. (You should also ignore the sounds of despair coming from the director, who may think you are using valuable rehearsal time for mundane reasons!)

"Having the stage manager run the safety walkthrough / discussion sets the tone of who is in charge of not only the rehearsal, but the safety and well-being of the performers."

- Bill Reynolds, Director of Theater Safety and Occupational Health for Yale School of Drama/Yale Repertory Theatre

If you are willing to try and do this, it really could help alleviate panic during an actual emergency. If everyone knows, at the very least, where they need to be during a crisis, your chances of survival increase immensely. Reynolds agrees and says, "by doing this type of safety work, we are really setting a tone of awareness and shows that we have a well-defined process in place in case of an emergency. Make sure there is clarity in the room as to who is watching out for the safety items. Someone is watching the big picture."

Accidents and disasters can and are the result of improper planning and poor human judgement, and many accidents are preventable. Take the time to train, document, assess and mitigate each and every potentially dangerous situation. Take the lead on getting your staff up to date with the best industry practices in safety. By doing this, you will be on your way to becoming a very effective production manager (and a fire marshal's best friend!).

Figure 8.6   The College-Conservatory of Music at the University of Cincinnati

Credit: Photo by Adam Zeek, www.zeekcreative.com

CASE STUDY—STREET SCENE, SAN DIEGO, CALIFORNIA

CONTRIBUTOR: ZIP ZEMBENSKI—HEAD RIGGER

"The most dangerous part of a temporary stage roof move is when it's in transit, because you can't do anything about it."

- Zip Zembenski

This was about ten years ago. For years, I did Street Scene in San Diego as a production rigger for Kleege Industries. Street Scene is exactly what it sounds like—ten square blocks of downtown San Diego turned into one weekend of bands and festivities. Street Scene had many stages and many structures. This particular one, I later found out, was subcontracted from a company out of Los Angeles and was set up by the Los Angeles crew. It was your typical self-climbing, six-post rig that was 40 feet x 40 feet with sound wings. The rig was at head height. We had the motors in it, ready to raise up the rig when needed. The stage manager was flying in from San Francisco and was running late. In his absence, someone else from the production shouted "We need to get that roof up."

So I started to bump through the motors and found that the number 4 pole, the downstage right motor, was out of phase; so I had five motors in phase and one out of phase. I started to raise the roof and got it about fourteen feet off the ground when a huge wind came out of nowhere. (This was when Petco Park was still under construction.) The wind grabbed the structure, and the structure started to slide and kick backwards . . . upstage. At that point, I started to yell to everyone around to "get off the stage . . . get away from the stage" just yelling as loud as I could. People started jumping off the stage . . . . It was crazy. Simultaneously, I immediately hit the "down" buttons on the motor control pendant. The problem was, due to the motor phase problem I had, I now had five motors going "down" and one motor going "up," which in turn made the entire structure now start to skew in a radical shape. At that time, I noticed that the upstage posts were being supported and held up by very large 10,000 pound "K Rails". (A "K Rail" is a large concrete barrier often seen to spate roadways.) Thank God they were there. They were what kept the whole thing from falling over. I immediately stopped all motors and halted the structure from moving anymore. So, I'm standing there yelling "get a forklift and tie off the downstage guy wires and take tension!" I also called for traffic control and security to evacuate the immediate area.

Anytime you put down a structure with leveling screw jacks, you have to have a wood pad underneath the screw jack. This isn't for leveling, this is for friction. You must have friction when working with these types of structures. In this case, all of the screw jacks were on the concrete. No one bothered to put wood pads down, which meant there was no friction on the jacks that support the towers. Without friction, the structure posts started walking backwards with the wind.

Once I got the rig stabilized, we took the tension off with a forklift from the front and proceeded to try and level out the rig without anyone getting hurt. First—we needed wood pads fast. They were sent over within ten minutes. Now came time to fix our problem. With the tension off the rig, we had to take one tower at a time, with a load bar from the truck, slack the motor on it, lift it up, level it into place, put wood pads into place, re-level it, take tension on the motor, etc., and we had to do that for all six towers of the structure. Once we got it all stabilized, we were ready to take the roof structure up safely. Thankfully, no one was hurt and no damage happened to the rig. This all happened because someone decided to take a shortcut and not use twenty-four small wood pads under the tower legs. Ultimately, if it fell, it would have been my fault as the lead rigger. I made an assumption that the pads were underneath because I assumed my company, Kleege Industries, built the structure, and we would have never left the pads out. Not knowing that it was subcontracted was obviously an issue. The bottom line is that if you're in charge, you have to check everything . . . and I mean everything. Especially if someone's life can be endangered.

NOTE

1   Perez, Thomas E. "Workers Memorial Day Speech." *U.S. Department of Labor*. April 28, 2014. http://www.dol.gov/newsroom/speeches/20140428_Perez

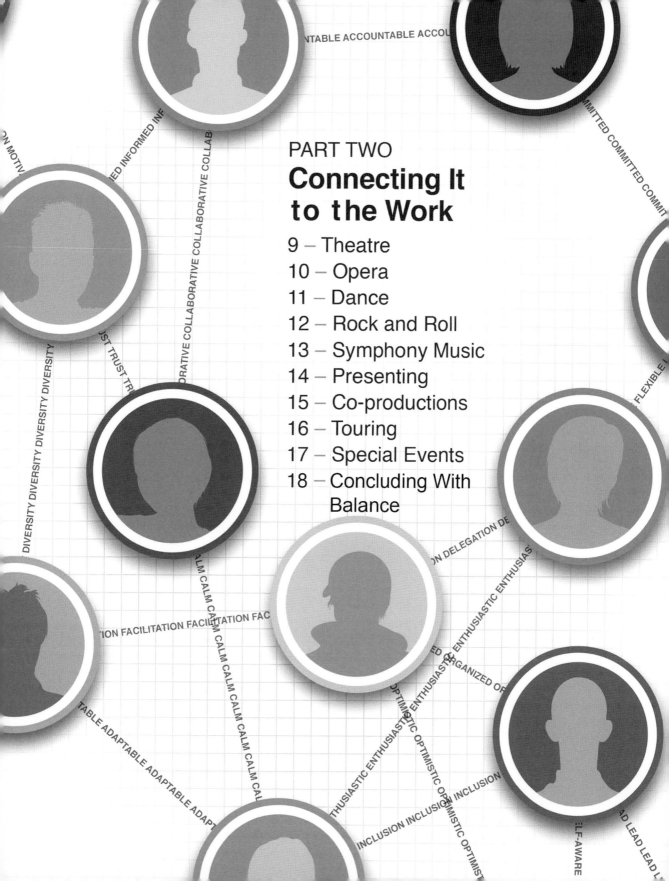

PART TWO
Connecting It to the Work

C H A P T E R   9

Theatre

There are a large variety of theatrical producing organizations in the United States. For the purposes of this chapter, we will focus specifically on regional theatre, Broadway and summer stock. There a quite a few differences between these three types of theatres, but the goals of the production manager are the same—produce the show on time, on budget, safely and, in the end, make sure everyone is still speaking to each other.

Figure 9.1 *The Price* (2015) at the Olney Theatre Center—set design by Jim Fouchard and properties by Rachael Erichsen

Credit: Photo by Stan Barouh

REGIONAL THEATRES

The largest amount of theatre in the United States is produced by regional theatre companies. These companies are often year-round or three-quarters of the year, and they produce multiple shows in one season. They usually own a theatre space or multiple spaces, and they employ production staff for their own shops. For regional theatre, the production manager is typically a full-time employee and a member of the senior staff. The production manager contributes toward the overall direction and future of the company. If the production manager has a good working relationship with the artistic director, the production manager might be a part of the season selection process and might have a larger say in choosing the creative team.

Regional theatres typically have various departments with which the production manager will need to collaborate. All your professional relationships are important and especially your fellow department heads. Some of these collaborators we previously mentioned in this text, but let us take another look:

> *Marketing/public relations:* This department is responsible for insuring the general public is aware of the theatre's offerings and of its mission. Marketing staff work with the local press to promote shows/events and to promote the organization through special interest stories. This department is responsible for attracting audiences, selling tickets and filling seats. Often, this department will need help from the production department for a photo shoot of an upcoming show (with actors, costumes and props) or perhaps coordinating an interview with a guest artist. No matter the request, it is important to be responsive to marketing requests and to work positively with marketing staff. A supportive relationship between the marketing and production departments benefits the entire organization.

> *Development:* This department houses the organization's money-finders. As explained in the Money and Budget chapter, it takes more than ticket sales to keep a theatre going. Unearned income from grants and donations keeps the organization financially successful.

> *Education:* Most regional theatres value education. By training the next generation of theatre professionals and educating current and future audiences, the education department can further the mission of the theatre. The production manager will need to work closely with the education department to schedule events such as student matinees and post-show discussions and may also provide needed information and/ or personnel for workshops and study guides. If your organization values education, they will likely have an internship or apprenticeship program. The production department will need to work closely with this program, as technical and management interns/apprentices will be supervised jointly by production staff and education staff.

"The single biggest communication success I had when I was at the Denver Center Theatre Company was repairing the relationship between production and marketing. Marketing was seen by the production department as annoying because they would constantly call asking for stuff. The big breakthrough was on a production of *Dracula*. Marketing had set up a relationship with a local newscaster who wanted to dress up like the traditional Bela Lugosi Dracula character for a local broadcast. Our costume shop manager and the crafts supervisor (who was also the designer of the show) were asked to help with the costume. They both got really annoyed, since that was not the costume we were using nor the type of show we were producing. I told them that the point of this was to show off what we do, not the specifics of what they asked us to do. What are we doing that would be interesting for them? A light bulb went off for the craftsperson and he said, 'I'm doing a fang fitting with some of the actors on Tuesday; why don't we have the newscaster come in, and I'll fit him for some fangs?' In the end, the newscaster got a much better story than he had asked for, and the costume shop got to show off their actual, very interesting work."

- Rick Noble, Production Manager at Center Stage

Figure 9.2 "This is a hilarious photo of me taken while I worked at Steppenwolf. It was at their big "Season Kickoff" event, where we lead tours all around the theater—I was in the wardrobe room giving a demonstration on how we have actors change in and out of false pregnancy bellies!"—Dixie Uffleman, Production Manager at Northwestern University

Credit: Photo by Kyle Flubacker

BROADWAY

A regional theatre and a Broadway theatre can produce the same play, but the process will be quite different. Unlike regional theatre, Broadway shows are produced one at a time and not as part of a season. The scale of the show is usually much larger than regional theatre, and budgets can often exceed a million dollars for a "basic" Broadway show. Broadway theatres are also very large, often holding upwards of 3,000 audience members. As you will learn in the chapter on presenting theatres, "four wall rental houses" are theatres used by producers and presenters and are available in most major U.S cities. Broadway shows are oftentimes produced in a "four wall" rental theatre, and the productions are brought in and designed especially for that particular theatre. There are generally no production managers on staff for a theatre. The staff will usually consist of a facilities manager and a house manager.

A group of producers will join together to put a play or musical on Broadway. Producers might develop, organize and produce the play on their own, or they may use a general management company to assist them. General management companies are brought on to manage the budget, find and negotiate with the theatre where the show will be produced and hire the staff and artists. The producer or general management company will hire a production company to provide production management services. The selection of the production company is usually based on a bidding system, but the contract doesn't always go to the lowest bidder. As is the case in every other facet of production management, relationships can play a big part of the selection process, as general managers tend to hire the same production companies as long as they can get the work done on time, on budget and in a friendly environment.

Production managers are among the few people on Broadway who have full-time employment. Directors, designers, stage managers, crew, etc., are brought on for a per-show contract. Production managers are employed by management companies that usually have multiple production managers, assistant production managers and interns on staff. There are a few freelance production managers on Broadway, but they are rare. A production manager might be hired anytime from one year to one month before a production opens. For a larger musical, it is likely the production manager will be hired at least a year from opening, because the larger the show, the more complicated the production process can be. If the show will transfer from another theatre, London's West End, for example, the production manager may not be brought on until a month before opening.

The production manager on Broadway also serves at the technical director. They are in charge of collaborating with the designers, shop crews and theatre facility staff to achieve the artistic goals for the show. They must supervise the builds, sign off on design drawings and oversee the production loading in and loading out. Unlike regional theatre, there are no in-house shops or equipment, so everything must be outsourced. Outside shops need to be contracted by the production manager to build scenery, props and costumes. Equipment such as lights, sound, video and automation will need to be bought or rented. Broadway theatres come empty, and each show supplies what they need. When the show closes, everything is removed, and the process starts again for the next show.

The production manager is onsite at the theatre facility from the first day of load-in through opening night. After opening, they remain with the show on a peripheral basis, troubleshooting and managing issues when they arise. Throughout the process, the production manager communicates regularly with the theatre's facilities manager and house manager to ensure that things run smoothly. When the show closes, the production manager will return to oversee the load-out. Most production managers will begin working on another show once the previous one opens.

One large part of a Broadway production manager's job is working with the International Alliance of Theatrical Stage Employees (IATSE). The theatre where the play or musical will be produced will have its own house crew consisting of a head carpenter, head props master and head electrician. This crew all belong to the New York IATSE local union, known as "Local 1." The rest of the crew needed to run the show will be hired by the production manager on what is known in New York as the "pink contract." This contract allows people who are not "Local 1" to work. They have to be IATSE members, but they can belong to another local, out of town, perhaps. The show crew is employed by the show, while the house crew is employed by the theatre. Everyone will need to work together, and it is the production manager's job to facilitate this relationship.

"We are there to realize the director and creative team's dream—from paper to reality, while being mindful of the production budget, just as it is in regional theatres across the country. How we get to their vision is perpetually evolving once we get into the theatre. The production side of Broadway is truly a family community. As we move from show to show post opening, while still continuing maintenance during the run of a show, quite often we find ourselves working with a fusion of the talented designers and crew members with whom we have worked on other shows over the years. It does not take long to realize that you are a member of the Broadway Box where everyone greets you in the streets with a nod while walking to the next theatre and working on their cell phone or with an empathetic hello while quickly grabbing a meal at the deli."

- Liza Luxenberg, Production Manager for Aurora Productions

SUMMER STOCK

A summer stock theatre will produce a full season of shows over the summer months. Shows within this short season will overlap with one show in performance while the next show is rehearsing. Builds and changeovers are likely to be only a few days, so there is little time to correct mistakes and make changes. Even more complicating is that many summer stock theaters are outdoor theatres, with challenges such as wisely using daylight, unfortunate weather and summer heat. As you can guess, most production staff for summer stock theatres are not year-round employees, which means that they will likely not come on board until right before the season begins.

The key to success for summer stock is careful preparation. Most companies employ a full-time production manager who will spend the off-months (September-April) preparing for the upcoming season. During this time, they locate and hire all seasonal artists and staff, designs are conceived, discussed and solidified, and schedules are set. Rehearsals tend to be quick—one to two weeks, including tech—so there is little time for discovery. Exact details of who is playing what role, how scene changes will occur, and other specifics must be figured out ahead of time. Once the season begins, it is full steam ahead. There is little time for discussion or to think things over. You have to make decisions as quickly as problems arise or "on the fly."

"Theatre is about compromise; we try to consider all requests. I don't make a decision in a vacuum. I'm surrounded by amazing people, and they all contribute. It's a collaboration.

"The more ideas in the pool, the better chance we can solve it the right way. I frequently tell people that I am not asking for perfection. We can't achieve perfect here at The Muny; there will always be flaws. What we can do is try our collective best and be proud of the results. If you are not striving for perfection, you can take a few calculated risks and try some new things, and that is exciting."

- Tracy Utzmyers, Production Manager for The Muny

Theatre organizations come in a variety of shapes and sizes, but, ultimately, the responsibilities of the production manager are the same—to support the vision of the creative team and make it a reality. The following case studies are great examples of when production managers were doing just that!

CASE STUDY—SYDNEY THEATRE COMPANY

CONTRIBUTOR: NEIL KUTNER—PRODUCTION MANAGER

I moved to Australia in 2006 when my wife was hired as the Director of Marketing and Development at the Sydney Opera House. Within a few months of arriving, I was lucky enough to get a job as Production manager at Sydney Theater Company, the largest theater company in the country. By the time I started working at STC, they had already designed the show that was to be the first directed by Cate Blanchett. Because of Cate's schedule, they had to design the show wildly in advance; it might have been a year. The show was to take place in STC's primary black box theater, Wharf 1. The design required the entire stage surface to be covered in water. Sitting in the middle would be a little island that's about a meter and a half by two meters,

Figure 9.3 Neil Kutner

where all the action would take place. They didn't have a production manager at the time that the design was submitted, so they hired an outside consultant to determine feasibility. The consultant said it couldn't be done for three reasons. One—the shop can't build a waterproof floor. Two—it's going to be too expensive. Three—the floor can't take the weight. I was handed that report and was told to call Cate and tell her we couldn't do it and she would have to start over. I thought there's no way that's the first conversation I am going have with Cate Blanchett.

What I did was begin to think about the problems that were presented and see if I could reduce them to bite-size amounts. The first thing I tackled was the assumption that the set could not be built watertight by the theatrical carpenters. I realized it might be true, but was probably not relevant. You don't want your carpenters to be waterproofers, you want them to be carpenters. So I asked myself 'who does waterproofing in the real world?' Roofers and tile layers! I started calling around and found a tile guy. I told him I needed to tile a bathroom and all I want him to do is lay the water-tight substrate. I didn't tell him that it was for a show. He doesn't know what theater is about. What he knows is tile. I told him I need a warranty. He said "no problem, I do a thirty-year warranty on all of my work. I guarantee it won't leak for thirty years." I said "I only need six weeks, but thirty years is good." He asked me how big the bathroom was and I told him it was 18 meters by 16 meters. There was a very long pause, and I'll remember this forever; he said, "Sure, okay." All the carpenters had to do was build a perfectly flat surface. This was right in their wheel house. I asked the tile guy to do an extra coat on every seam because I had money left over because he was so cheap. So I solved the leaking problem by hiring an expert, and I solved the money problem because the expert was cheaper.

Now there was the weight problem. The theater is on a wharf that has no structural drawings or engineered capacities. The consultant figured out how many tons of water it would be, and it sounded so heavy they decided we had a problem. But what I did was I converted 'tons of water' to 'numbers of people'. The average person weighs about 90 to 100 kilograms, so divided the weight by the number of people. I realized this really amounts to about 80 or 90 people. So I went to the Artistic Director and I asked if they had ever done a gala in this theater where they had people dancing on the stage? They said they'd had about 120 people in there. Since the water weight is equivalent to no more than 90 people and is to be perfectly evenly distributed and dancing people are a live load, people are a much larger stress on the structure. So the problem is solved and we didn't even need to hire an engineer.

Figure 9.4 A Kind of Alaska and Reunion at the Sydney Theatre Company's Wharf 1 Theatre
Credit: Photo by Neil Kutner

When I finally called up Cate and said, "Hi, I'm going to be your production manager for this show," she said "I know, I know, I have to get rid of the water." I said, "No, that's not why I called. I want to know how deep you want the water to be." That was the start of a beautiful relationship.

On the second day of tech, Cate asked me if the water level could rise at the end of the show to submerge the island.

CASE STUDY—CALIFORNIA SHAKESPEARE THEATRE

CONTRIBUTOR: JAMILA COBHAM—ASSISTANT PRODUCTION MANAGER

Figure 9.5 Jamila Cobham

During our season we produced four main stage shows: *Twelfth Night*, *Life Is a Dream*, *The Mystery of Irma Vep* and *King Lear*. The Director of Production, Tirzah Tyler, decided that we should share the lead on the shows; therefore, I was the lead production manager on two shows and she the other two. After only working at California Shakespeare Theater for one year, I was excited about being the lead production manager but also nervous because it meant more responsibility, and I was also slightly intimidated because I was generally younger than our designers, directors and production team. It was great for me to be asked for input by designers as to what would work well in the space. The hardest thing for me was that I only knew some of our limitations, not all. I had to be okay with saying "I don't know, let me check" and not feeling bad about that. It's okay not to know everything, and it's okay to be new and learning. Some things you can't learn until you go through the process.

We started design meetings for *Irma Vep* earlier than any other show. It was the third show (out of four) in our season and opened in August, and our first meeting was in November of the previous year. Our director was going on a sabbatical and was going to be unavailable for design meetings during our typical design process period, so we needed to get design prelims and budgeting confirmed earlier than usual. The play only has two actors, but the set and costume requirements are enormous, and it took a crew of eight backstage (four deck and four wardrobe) to make it happen. On the other hand, we weren't able to hold a design meeting for our first show until January due to everyone's conflicting schedules. Ideally, this would have occurred in November to allow a longer design and budgeting period.

One challenge for me was adjusting to every designer's process and method of submitting designs/drawings/sketches and accepting that deadlines usually fly by without a submission. For example, one of our designers preferred to supply an initial piece list rather than prelim sketches, which isn't preferable for the costume shop. Cutting elements in designs so that they were in budget was also an interesting process, because it seemed as though everything that could be cut eventually became "the most important element of the show."

Some of our shows were really too big for us to achieve. Each department went over budget a little bit. Materials were okay; it was labor that got us. Labor is always a challenge when you have such a tight turnover, and especially in the Bay Area, where we rely mainly on over hire crews. Our season begins in April, and the way our schedule lays out, we only have one dead week between shows one and two, and then after that it's a sprint to the end. It's a hard schedule on the staff. For example, on *Irma Vep*, we had four days of load-in, including focus. The previous show closed on Sunday, and we struck right after until midnight. On Monday, we finished the load-in so that lighting could start focus on Tuesday. By Thursday, we were starting tech, and all of the moving scenery and set "tricks" had to be ready. In reality, there were items that were not done by load-in, so we had to keep working on them in the mornings before tech and during the dinner breaks. This resulted in lots of overtime and double time. In the future, it might be best for that dead week to be before the biggest show to allow for everyone to get ready and have a breather before we hit tech.

We produce in an outdoor venue in the middle of the summer, so it can get hot during the days and then cold at night. Our tech days are usually 12:30 p.m. to 12:30 a.m., so we can take advantage of as much time when the sun goes down as possible. But you do end up working a lot of the day in the hot sun. That can really affect how people work. We have lots of cold packs and Gatorade on hand all the time to keep people cool and hydrated. We don't normally tech during the day with costumes because of the heat, but for *Irma Vep*, we could not avoid it. There were just too many quick changes to rehearse, and we needed all of our dark time for lighting.

Sadly, it does not rain much in California, but we still need to plan for it. We used a large painted ground cloth as our show deck. It was semi "water proof" and easy to clear off if it did rain. We also have a fantastic props department that pays close attention to providing things that can get wet. Of course, we always have a few things onstage that shouldn't really get wet but are critical for the show so have to be there. The crew knows to clear those first if it ever starts raining!

Figure 9.6   Liam Vincent and Danny Scheie in *The Mystery of Irma Vep* at the California Shake-speare Theatre

Credit: Photo by Kevin Berne

Personalities were also an interesting thing to navigate this season. There were some shows where either Tirzah or I was constantly putting out fires. People usually needed to vent, and I did my best to be there for them. There were times, however, when I really did not know what to do. I was so lucky to have my boss as someone I could turn to. The biggest lesson I learned was that I needed to embrace my inexperience.

CHAPTER 10

Opera

The major thing that differentiates opera from other disciplines is its scale. With opera, the production manager needs to manage a larger-than-average amount of people, things and, sometimes, even places. A large opera can have over 100 performers onstage, eighty musicians in the orchestra and sixty technicians behind the scenes. Though one can equate the day-to-day duties of an opera production manager to a theatre production manager, the jobs differentiate when one factors in the scale of the productions.

> "Opera is a large, expensive art form involving many people. Our production budget alone is larger than the entire operating budget of many small and medium-sized theatres, and there are regularly more than 100 people working as part of the production department to put on even a medium-sized show."
>
> - Lee Milliken, Director of Production at
> the Canadian Opera Company

The position of the production manager in opera grew from the technical director position, just as it has in other disciplines. Historically, the technical director was in charge of the opera production department, as it is in the European model, which still functions without a production manager in many cases. Opera in the United States closely follows a theatre model, so many companies have chosen to put a production manager in place in order to simplify communication and clarify who has the final word. Most opera production management positions were put in place in the mid-1990s but there are still American companies without a production manager position today. As with the European model, if there is no production manager, the technical director and/or the production stage manager takes responsibility of the production management duties described in this text.

Figure 10.1 *Silent Night*

Credit: Photo by Michal Daniel for Minnesota Opera

"My whole family has worked here at Glimmerglass. I can't remember a time when I did not know what a production manager did. I began as a technical director, and a lot of people started coming to me to get help solving challenges in other areas, and I decide that is what interested me the most."

- Abby Rodd, Director of Production at Glimmerglass Opera Company

The planning process for opera must occur very far in advance of the performances. There are some opera companies that select their seasons as early as five years out. The reasons for this length of planning are mostly based on the performers. Firstly, principal singers who are in demand are often hired early. In response to this, companies must rush to have seasons determined early enough to be able to contract the best performers. Secondly, it takes a long time for singers to learn the music and work with their vocal coaches prior to showing up for rehearsals. Unlike theatre, all opera performers are expected to arrive at the first rehearsals already knowing all the material. There are great benefits in having a long time to plan, such as having more time to construct a budget and resolve any special challenges before the work begins.

Most opera companies produce only one new opera a season. The remainder of the season will be dedicated to remounting previously performed operas that remain in the company's repertoire or renting operas from other companies. Co-productions are very common in opera. Often, two or more companies will produce a new opera together and then take turns presenting this new work at each of their venues. (See chapter 15 on co-productions.) It is common for opera companies to have large storage units filled with sets and costumes of productions that will be remounted or loaned out. Cutting down on costs is a necessity when taking into consideration the funds necessary to hire the multitude of personnel that opera demands.

Unlike theatre, the creative guidance of the production does not fall solely on the shoulders of the director. In opera, you will have two leads—a staging director and a musical director (or maestro/maestra) who often will conduct the orchestra in performance. You will often see the musical director taking charge, as it is primarily a musical art form, with the staging director working under them. It is also possible to see them work side by side and share the responsibility of leading the production.

With opera, technical rehearsals are accomplished at a somewhat quicker pace than in theatre. Because the timing of the show is based on the timing of the music, not the performers, elements such as lighting can be cued without the cast. Often, a tech day will begin with a long lighting session and then end with a run of the show with the full cast where cues are integrated but holds do not occur. Lighting fixes are done before the next run. This quick pace is necessary for the performers. Opera singers cannot be asked to rehearse for an eight- or ten-hour tech day; this could damage their voices.

Figure 10.2   The College-Conservatory of Music at the University of Cincinnati

Credit: Photo by Adam Zeek, www.zeekcreative.com

> **TIP**—You must be sensitive to the needs of your artists—an opera singer's body is their instrument, so be mindful of the conditions of the rehearsal studio, dressing rooms and theatre.

Most opera companies will begin singing with an orchestra only a few rehearsals prior to opening. This helps keep musician costs manageable. The integration of the orchestra usually occurs in the following way:

- Sitzprobe: a rehearsal with all singers and the full orchestra where the focus is on the music. The goal of this rehearsal is to integrate the singers with the orchestra by working through the entire score. It is essential there is this time for all the performers to get used to each other. This rehearsal is run by the musical director.

- Wandleprobe (pronounced with the W sounding like a V): Similar to a sitzprobe, but the singers are asked to do their blocking while continuing to integrate with the orchestra. Sometimes, the wandleprobe is utilized instead of a sitzprobe because there is limited time or the performers need the opportunity to review blocking.

All opera participants (performers, musicians and technicians) are usually union members. The exception is the chorus and non-singing roles called supernumeraries. Having such a large number of union members all working at the same time is incredibly expensive, hence the need to work certain people only when necessary. The most expensive rehearsals are the ones where everyone is there—cast, musicians and crew. Consider how expensive even a few minutes of overtime can be in this case. Proper scheduling and communication are vital.

> "Typically, you need to renegotiate with the unions every three to five years. I always advocate for a contract that is as long as possible. The unions respect that it is a drain on the whole company. The more time you spend on negotiations, the less time to have to do your work, and then more problems arise that are going to cause you to want to renegotiate. If you are well organized, good to your people and provide a safe work environment, then the union workers won't have a lot to bring to the table. We have labor meetings pretty regularly where we let everyone speak their mind. This way, they know they are being listened to and they can understand where you are coming from too."
>
> - Vinnie Feraudo, Director of Production at Seattle Opera

Opera remains a dominant art form throughout most of the world. As it began in Europe, it is not surprising that some of the most prestigious opera companies are European. It is not uncommon for American opera companies to work with individuals or companies from

Figure 10.3 Stage Manager Clare Burovac and Director of Production Vinnie Feraudo working at the production table during Seattle Opera's RING rehearsals

Credit: Photo by Bill Mohn

European countries, as well as companies throughout the rest of the world. Also, many operas are in languages other than English. As stressed repeatedly in this text, the ability to communicate clearly is of chief concern for the production manager. It is hard enough to be a communicator in one language, so one can imagine the extra challenge posed by multi-national and multi-lingual production teams. If production managing for opera is where you are heading, a basic understanding of various languages plus proficient non-verbal communication skills (body language and intonation) will be a valuable part of your production manager's toolkit.

"We work with a lot of people from France. Their command of English might not be the best, but neither is my French, per se. It's not so much the language but the intonation and limited vocabulary that can confuse and maybe upset an America staff. I once heard a French director tell a staff member something looked like shit. He did not understand what that phrase meant and did not realize it was an insult. He had just heard it used a lot, and if you add that to his tone of voice, it made it sound really bad, when all he was trying to say was that he did not like it."

- Paul Hordepdahl, Director of Production at Santa Fe Opera Company

OPERA America is the national service organization for opera dedicated to supporting the creation, presentation and enjoyment of opera. OPERA America draws on resources and expertise from within and beyond the opera field to advance a mutually beneficial agenda that serves and strengthens the field through programs in the following categories:

- Creation: Artistic services that help artists and companies increase the creativity and experience of opera productions, especially North American works;
- Presentation: Opera company services that address the specific needs of staff, trustees and volunteers;
- Enjoyment: Education, audience development and community services that increase all forms of opera appreciation.

The association provides members with an array of publications and online resources, regional workshops, an annual conference and network-specific services such as conference calls, listservs and direct contact with staff with expertise in opera production, administration and education. OPERA America provides members with tools to maximize the effectiveness of financial and human resources, expand the scope of repertoire and programs, and extend their reach to new and diverse audiences. Founded in 1970, OPERA America has an international membership that includes nearly 150 Professional Company Members, 300 Associate and Business Members, 2,000 Individual Members and over 16,000 subscribers to its electronic news service.

TECHNICAL/PRODUCTION FORUM

Twice a year, designers and technical/production professionals gather to share best practices and learn from one another about the demands of mounting new and existing productions, developing co-productions, and carrying out other tasks required by the art form.

Opera is a beautiful, complex art form and needs the same quality of production management merited by any other performing art. An understanding, compassionate and educated production manager will immensely benefit an opera company and their artists. Let us hear from one opera production manager who has mastered those skills.

CASE STUDY—*MORNING STAR*, CINCINNATI OPERA

CONTRIBUTOR: GLENN PLOTT—DIRECTOR OF PRODUCTION

Figure 10.4 Glenn Plott

Morning Star was a commissioned world premier that came out of our workshop program called "Opera Fusion: New Works" with the University of Cincinnati, College Conservatory of Music. In this program administered by Cincinnati Opera, with co-artistic direction from CCM, we take in new operas in development. The opera provides the creative team support and rehearsal space, and the school provides the performers. *Morning Star* got about ten days to find out if it sounded in real life how the composer imagined it sounding in his head. It was clear to us right away that this project had potential, and we had no time to lose; if we did not snatch it up, another company would have. I'm lucky that, in my company, I'm a part of that decision-making process with the artistic department; we have a very symbiotic relationship.

It took two years from the workshop to the fully staged production. It needed that long, as the opera was not fully written at the time of the workshop, and, on top of that, it needed to be fully orchestrated. We ended up supporting a second workshop along the way, as well. To make room for *Morning Star*, we kicked an opera out of the season, a co-production with another company, and moved it to the next season. It happens more frequently than many might think. You have to be opportunistic in this business. And we had to do it while the creative team was hot.

We are a summer company, and we know our start and end dates, which makes that part of the schedule process very easy. I create "rough guide" schedules at least five years in advance that have long run and short run options slated in. It's very formulaic, but it puts a stake in the ground and creates a place to start. I prefer to have a plan to present and then fine tune it from there with feedback from the rest of the company and the creative team. I had to make some adjustments for *Morning Star* to make sure my staff was not splitting themselves in two: piano tech for one opera during the day and an orchestra dress that evening for a different opera. Fortunately for us, we were opposite *Don Pasquale* (rented from Arizona Opera), which ended up being a technically simple show where everything fell into place.

My approach to budgeting begins with historical data—we know what size company we are, so I know quickly when something will not fit. I consider five main categories of factors with budgeting—programmatic issues (number of acts/ performers/locations/transitions), seasonal relations (how does this show overlap with others in the same season), support personnel (who beyond my standard staff and crew does this show need?), equipment and plant (trucks/power/special effects) and regulatory (safety/insurance/inspection/customs).

New shows are generally more expensive than rentals or co-productions, but, for an opera *Morning Star* was relatively cheap. It was still being written as we began the design process, so I created "allowances" for materials and designers. I needed to make and keep room for the art to happen. It was also being presented in a second venue, so that had to be taken into consideration as well. Luckily, it was a venue I am familiar with.

About a year before the production, I was told to cut 15% of the cost. This was because budget projections from other departments were not lining up. In the end, *Morning Star* ran over budget. Because the piece was still unfinished, the designs were all coming in late, so we had to build it in a very big hurry, which was costly. Some of the items we built were never seen by the audience due to cuts, rewrites and tweaks in the opera. I've developed Plott's rules on opera over my career, and one of them states that the amount of time and money you spend creating something is inversely proportionate to how much it will actually be seen on stage. In the case of *Morning Star*, I allowed certain areas to go over budget, knowing that I had three more operas in the season that could help me out. If I'm going to make a mistake, then I'm going to make it to the benefit of the production.

I planned for lots of extra time in the theatre for things like projections and script changes. I'm glad I did, because the script changed up until opening night. Props changed up until the last minute, too, but it kept getting pared down, which in my opinion is the sign of a good director. I can always tell when a director is in trouble— they add more props: a technical solution to a non-technical problem.

Figure 10.5 *Morning Star*

Credit: Photo by Phil Groshong for the Cincinnati Opera

We had to deal with four unions on *Morning Star* and every production, which makes each venture anything but ordinary. They all have different regulations, and none of them ever align. AGMA can work six hours a day and thirty-six hours a week, the musicians can only work twenty hours a week, and I have two IATSE locals—stagehands and wardrobe. When I have all four unions, I adjust my priority to the service we're performing. Here are two examples: If we are doing a sitzprobe, then I'll focus primarily on orchestra and performers; the consequences to the stage crew will be just what they have to be. If we are doing a stage orchestra technical rehearsal, I can let the musicians play up to the very last second, but I'll shut down the technical systems at five minutes before to allow the technicians to walk out the door at the published end time. A lot of directors don't like it when I shut down their lights five minutes before the end of rehearsal, but that's a very expensive five minutes if it means I have to buy an additional half-hour to have it. I'd never shut down on an orchestra dress; in that case, they go until they are done. When you consider that I can burn $4,000 to $5,000 an hour when everyone is in the theatre, that five minutes gets placed into perspective.

Every plan we made for *Morning Star* needed to exist in a state of change. I operate with a lot of custom budget-tracking documents built from years and years of producing operas. I was grateful I had these good, solid tools on *Morning Star* so I could easily track the changes and anticipate how these changes would affect cost and schedule in the rest of the process and know the consequences right away. The truth is, you need to roll with the changes as best you can. The key thing is to be open and honest with everyone (director, design, technician, department head) about what resources we still had and how they were changing and constantly asking what we still needed to accomplish. I manage by walking around—I put the questions out there, then walk away and come back later once they've had time to think about it. My job is to empower and enable everyone with the information they need to see the big picture and the authority to act on it.

We're incredibly lucky to have a relationship with the Cincinnati Symphony Orchestra that dates back ninety-five years. We engage them as an entity, which means we get their managers and music librarians. Not only is the sound coming out of the pit amazing, but there is a top-line organization behind it, which not all opera companies can say they have. They play for the ballet as well—it's a very strong three-company relationship. A lot of people in our community see the value in shared services and as the future of the industry. I know the musicians and have been passing them in the halls for eighteen years. I know all of our cast members, too. They know I'm there, and they know I'm working for them. Those relationships are vital to what we do.

I certainly hope this production has a future. I love to see my production go out on rental, but what I really hope happens is that another company decides to reimagine it. That has been a big focus of Opera America—to get shows produced a second time. That's the thing about new operas; they are not successful until they are done again.

Dance

To understand the duties of the production manager in dance, we need to understand the discipline, the reasoning for the work and how it all comes together. The unique part of this art form is that its driving force lies within the movement. The story, the themes or even, sometimes, the music take a secondary role to the movement of bodies in space. "Dance" is an all-encompassing art that contains many styles, but for the purposes of this chapter, we will focus on two types of dance—ballet and modern/contemporary.

BALLET

"At the second performance of *The Daughter of the Snows*, this change turned into a complete fiasco. The wings, as well as the set at the back, cracked, toppled over, and broke in pieces. The machinist at that time was Legat, a relative of the Legat family of ballet dancers. The disastrous incident of the scenery so affected him, that he lost his reason right there on the stage."[1]

- From the memories of Marius Petipa, choreographer (1818–1900)

This quote leads us to understand that there was a technical supervisor as part of ballet even as far back as the 19th century. This machinist is no doubt the technical director as we now know it. As technology progressed and electricity became a part of ballet, the technical director began to take on the role of lighting, as well. And as productions became more and more complicated to achieve, the stage manager joined the team. The position of production manager in ballet grew out of the need for one person to wrangle the various technical elements, budget and schedule. The job of the production manager in dance is very similar to other performing art forms. The difference lies in handling the unique nature of the discipline.

Figure 11.1 The College-Conservatory of Music at the University of Cincinnati

Credit: Photo by Adam Zeek, www.zeekcreative.com

The origins of ballet date back to the 15th century, when European nobility were entertained by and often participated in dances as part of large celebrations such as weddings and coronations. In the 1600s, ballet existed mostly as a component of opera until the 19th century, when it emerged as an independent entertainment. Most of the classic ballets that we know today began in this period—*Coppélia, Swan Lake, Giselle*. This is also where the dancers first began dancing on pointe shoes and tutus first made an appearance.

The modern ballet world exists as part of what some term the elite arts—a highly specialized and honored form of dance that people often pay a great ticket price to attend. The lavish production elements and skilled dancers, whose training often begins as children, make it a challenging and often costly performance to mount.

Ballet companies are similar to other large producing entities in that they have departments such as marketing/public relations, development, business and production. Dissimilarly, they have departments and personnel unique to this art form.

- Ballet master/mistress: This person (or persons, in some larger companies) is in charge of the upkeep of the company of dancers by leading a daily conditioning class during rehearsals and performances. They are also tasked with leading rehearsals to reinforce the choreographer's work. They may also be able to re-stage or "set" classical works on the company in lieu of the choreographer.

- Lighting: One of the most important production elements of any ballet is lighting. In some cases, it may be the only design element. For that reason, many companies choose to hire a full-time resident designer. Some companies may choose to have a lighting director who might serve as both designer and master electrician.

- Music administration: Almost as important as the movement in many ballets companies is the music. Most ballets are performed with live orchestras, so the synthesis of the music and the orchestra is important to a successful production. The head of the music department is the conductor or maestro/maestra. This person selects and rehearses the musicians and then conducts the orchestra during the performance. The maestro often will have support staff, including a librarian and a music manager. The librarian is tasked with making sure the correct sheet music is distributed and archived for later productions, and the manager schedules and contracts the musicians. There is often a full-time rehearsal pianist as well who plays for all of the rehearsals and company classes.

- Health and wellness: Ballet is hard on the body. Most dancers have only a few years in their prime before the art form begins to take its toll. Injuries are very common, so the need for a physical therapist, masseuse and other health and wellness professionals is common. Many large companies have these positions on staff or have on-call relationships with local health care professionals.

- Education and training: Many ballet companies incorporate a school with the goal of training the next generation of ballet dancers. Often, the head of the school and the teachers are former or current dancers in the company. Students in the school might serve as extras in large ballet—very common in productions of *The Nutcracker*.

The season of a ballet company is likely to include a few different types of performances. A *narrative/story ballet* is a two or three act long ballet with a plot and characters, such as *Sleeping Beauty* or *Romeo and Juliet*. These ballets might be presented with the choreography of the original creator, or they might be reimaged by a new choreographer. A *repertory program* is an evening made up of more than one ballet, sometimes as many as five or six, that are short in length, usually based on a theme or idea, and often do not include a plot or characters. The program might be connected by the works of one choreographer, composer or a common theme. Many ballet companies also include local, national or even international tours as part of their season. (More on touring in chapter 16.)

Some productions, such as the story ballets, might include a variety of production elements— scenery depicting multiple locations, costume changes for each scene, etc. Some, however, might be very simple, with only one costume per dancer and no scenery other than black side masking and a blue scrim backdrop, commonly referred to as a "black and blue." Most repertory programs require simple production needs, so you can easily transition between works without having to take a lengthy break or intermission for changing scenery. Many ballet companies do not own a theatre, so they must find road houses that will allow them to present their productions. The cost of renting the theatre and paying for the union stagehands is high, so most companies choose to perform only a few shows over one or two weekends. The exception to that is *The Nutcracker*. This popular show, with its holiday theme, attracts large audiences and is a sure money maker for a company. For this reason, it is usually performed multiple times over weeks or sometimes months.

Figure 11.2   The College-Conservatory of Music at the University of Cincinnati

Credit: Photo by Adam Zeek, www.zeekcreative.com

Some ballet companies have productions in their "repertoire," meaning that they have someone on staff who can stage the choreography and they have the production elements in storage, with set pieces and costumes that can easily be reused. Not having to start from scratch results in a major cost savings. Companies who hold onto these production elements for their repertoire can generate revenue by allowing these production packages to be rented by other ballet companies. The production manager of the company that owns the production will work closely with the production manager of the company renting the package to negotiate the fees, shipping and return.

Some companies choose to create new work, or "premieres." Creating new work follows a similar timeline to other new performing arts productions. With premieres, the production manager facilitates the choreographer and designers through conceptual and design processes, similar to theatre productions. The process will result in executing production elements. Rehearsals are necessary for all ballets, but the rehearsal process will most likely be much longer than if existing choreography was used. It generally takes about one year from conception to performance for a new ballet.

Ballet companies produce new work less often; therefore, the need for full-time production artisans is unlikely. The exceptions are that most ballet companies employ a full-time lighting person, and it is also common for there to be a small costume staff. This costume staff of at least one or two workers fits and maintains costume inventories and facilitates the process of renting costumes to other companies. When it is necessary to build scenery and props, the production managers for ballet companies often contract with independent shops or hire individuals for show-by-show needs.

Perry Silvey, former Director of Production for the New York City Ballet, sums up the work of the ballet production manager best: "There is not much that is absolutely necessary for ballet. A dancer can dance on a beach on the sand if they wish, but as soon as you come into the theatre, you have to prioritize for them. They have to have the floor, it's the first thing. Then you go from there and add every layer that is appropriate—music, masking, lighting, etc."

CASE STUDY—NYC BALLET IN ST. PETERSBURG (PART ONE)

CONTRIBUTOR: PERRY SILVEY, FORMER DIRECTOR OF PRODUCTION

The Mariinsky stage in St. Petersburg, Russia, used both for opera and ballet, is rather hard, not ideal for the muscles and joints of the dancers. In other theatres with hard stages, we bring and install our portable wooden resilient floor. We were unable to bring this floor to Russia because of the cost and the schedule, so we were prepared for a week of extra aches and pains for the dancers, but, almost by accident, we found a solution to this problem. The Royal Ballet (who was there performing before us) had brought their resilient floor, and I was talking to one of their technical staff and joked with him, "how about leaving your wooden floor for us to dance on?" He took me seriously enough to mention it to his boss, and the upshot was that they graciously loaned us the floor.

Valery Gergiev, the artistic director of the Mariinsky, head of the Kirov Opera and Ballet, was to conduct on opening night, and we did not know him or what his tempos would be. At 2 p.m. the orchestra rehearsal was scheduled to begin, and around 2:05 we were told that Gergiev was not there yet. In every kind of theatre, being late is considered unprofessional, but we knew that he had traveled the night before, so we waited. He arrived around 2:15 and, without apology, he took the podium. We began the rehearsal of Tchaikovsky's *Serenade*, and it went well. There were a few tempo notes, which Gergiev accepted graciously, and, by the end, we were breathing a bit easier.

The *Symphony in Three* rehearsal went well, but when it was over, and time to break and change over for the third ballet, *Symphony in C*, Gergiev continued to rehearse the orchestra. I mentioned to him that we needed to go on, assuming that the orchestra needed a break before the last ballet, but he said he needed fifteen, perhaps eighteen minutes more, that the orchestra would not break but go right on after he was finished. That seemed strange, but fit into our schedule, so we agreed. Fifteen minutes turned into almost twenty-five, but Andrea took the podium, the orchestra played on without a break, we rehearsed *Symphony in C* and were as ready as we could be for opening night.

The house was full on Wednesday evening, and Gergiev took the podium for *Serenade*. Hearing Tchaikovsky played from the same pit that had held so many of the premieres of his great ballets was a thrill, and there were many who reported goose bumps after the performance. The dancers were wonderful, overcoming their fatigue to dance with great energy. The audience responded enthusiastically, and the curtain fell to cheers and rhythmic clapping.

The intermission change was a simple one for us, and as the dancers gathered on stage for the beginning of *Symphony in Three Movements*, we had a feeling that we were well launched. A few moments before we were to begin, however, we received word that Gergiev needed fifteen more minutes. Without mentioning it to us, he had taken the orchestra upstairs to a rehearsal room. Peter Martins (artistic director) and I asked Gergiev's messenger to report to him that we wanted the orchestra in the pit right away so we could continue. We were greeted by a fearful blank stare and told, "We cannot tell him anything. If you want to say something, you must tell him yourself." I arrived in the rehearsal room to find the maestro working with the orchestra and asked him to stop and send them back to the pit, as the dancers were ready and the intermission had already been over twenty minutes. He replied that he needed more time, and that the audience could wait. ("They are hot and need a longer break," he said, "and we never have twenty-minute intermissions anyway, and besides they haven't rung the last bells." This last was true because he had specifically told the stage manager not to do so.) I insisted that even if all that was true the dancers were warmed up and ready, and it was not right to make them wait. He waved off my objections, told me that he would rehearse for five more minutes, then would give the orchestra another five minutes to get to the pit, and then we could begin. There wasn't much we could do except fume, so I went back to the stage and forced the stage manager to resume ringing the audience back in. The intermission ended up over thirty-six minutes long, and the audience was booing and clapping for us to begin for the last five or so.

The whole flap could have been easily avoided, of course. If Gergiev had mentioned to us that he needed a longer intermission, we could have warned the dancers and the audience, and there would have been little problem. This lack of communication was a theme for the whole week, occurring in many different forms and from many different departments. We had meetings to determine a schedule or to request some action on their part, a plan would be agreed on, then something else would actually happen. Or a change would be instituted by them but not mentioned to us till too late.

Figure 11.3 *Symphony in Three Movements*—choreography by George Balanchine, copyright the George Balanchine trust

Credit: Photo by Paul Kolnik

"The dancers were ready and on their chalk mark, but as you know, we all kept waiting for the orchestra to return. I had ample time to photograph the dancers, literally from an onstage position. This was only able to happen due to the bizarre circumstances of an 'orchestra rehearsal' occurring during the intermission. The taking of this photograph is perhaps the one good thing that happened because of the delay."

- Paul Kolnik, photographer

One of the weirdest scenarios that I was involved with during our time in St. Petersburg concerned the two grand pianos that we had requested (and written into our contract) for *Hallelujah Junction*. For this ballet, there are two grand pianos on four-foot high platforms placed upstage of the dancers, with a black scrim in front of the pianos, and the visual effect is of two pianists floating above and behind the dance. The technical department of the Mariinsky had built the platforms to our specifications, and we loaded them in and set them up on Thursday. I asked when the pianos would arrive, when we could place them on top of the platforms, and was sent to the office of a gentleman whose name I choose to forget. He hemmed and hawed and explained that they did not have two grand pianos, and that even though I had requested them, and the contract called for them, and the platforms had been built for them, he had only heard of them an hour before, and anyway the memo he received must have had some problems in translation from the contract, because it did not exactly call for concert grands, but only for grand pianos, and that meant smaller pianos here in Russia. He continued his tap dance with the plea that he was only a bureaucrat, and that it was now important to find out who was to blame. I tried to insist that we should just try to find pianos instead of blame, but to little avail. When we finally performed *Hallelujah Junction*, there were two large platforms holding two small pianos—and no one to blame.

Our second program consisted of three Jerome Robbins ballets: *Interplay*, *Dances at a Gathering*, and *Glass Pieces*. The first two are fairly straightforward technically, while *Glass* is a bit more complicated, using white legs and borders, a plastic drop painted with a grid pattern, and several lighting cues that require specially focused lights. As we perform it in New York, the second movement calls for two bridge follow spots, small spots run from the downstage lighting bridge above the dancers, pointing almost straight down. The Mariinsky had a bridge in the right position, but no provision for spots, so it took some ingenuity and effort on the part of our lighting team, as well as the cooperation of the local electricians, to rig what we needed. Our crew came up with a system, and for both performances of *Glass* they climbed out onto a rickety walkway, strapped themselves to the bridge for safety and, through difficult contortions, managed to follow the two principal dancers, making a huge difference in the look of the ballet.

The carpenters were having their own troubles with *Glass Pieces*, as each time we set it up, the white borders would end up a little higher or lower than where they had been trimmed. In our theater, where most of the pipes are raised and lowered by hand, trimming involves putting a piece of tape around the rope, marking exactly how high or low the scenery should end up for the performance. The Mariinsky has a motorized fly system, and after several tries at finding repeatable trims, I approached the head carpenter, airing my frustration over spending forty-five minutes on what should have taken five. He explained that the fly system was installed in 1947, that it was old and cranky and difficult, and shrugged his shoulders. My reply was that I was also born in 1947, that I was old and cranky and difficult too, and that we would find a way. Eventually, we tied black strings to the ends of the border pipes, trimmed the borders again, then tied knots where the strings touched the floor. It was primitive, but it worked.

The pause after *Concerto Barocco* was a tricky one for us, as we had to strike the plastic used for *Barocco*, fly in and set the special legs for *Hallelujah*, move the piano platforms into position and check a few specially focused lights. I had guessed that it would take us five to eight minutes, and we had warned all the stagehands to be ready for a quick pause, as we didn't want the audience to wait too long. On Monday night it went very well, and we started *Hallelujah Junction* just six minutes after the end of the *Barocco* bows. On Tuesday, however, there was a new shift of carpenters, and, despite our warnings, the chiefs had not prepared their men for the work to be done. They moved the piano platforms too quickly and too far and ripped our linoleum. They missed the marks on the legs, attached one instead of two clamps to each one, and by the time Gary Justesen, our carpenter, and I had gone around the stage re-doing almost everything they had done, the pause was over ten minutes long. I don't think I would have minded so much if Peter Martins had not asked me, just before the performance, if we would be able to keep the pause as short as the night before, and of course I had answered in the affirmative.

After our load-out, I stayed another two hours to supervise the loading of the Royal Ballet's floor. In order to secure their permission to keep the floor, I had signed a paper absolving them of blame in case of injury, taking responsibility for proper care and promising to see that the floor was loaded correctly so as to arrive in good shape. When the last piece was on the container, I felt such relief that my sigh might have been heard for many miles.

MODERN/CONTEMPORARY DANCE

Modern dance is an all-encompassing term that can mean any dance that is not ballet, tap or world dance (indigenous cultural dances from certain countries). Legendary choreographers such as Isadora Duncan, Martha Graham and Merce Cunningham contributed to the modern dance movement, each bringing new perspective and evolving the art form with new styles and techniques.

Figure 11.4 Tiffanie Carson and Ellie van Bever in *De-Generate* (2012), choreographed by Christopher K. Morgan

Credit: Photo by Brianne Bland

Modern dance today is commonly called "contemporary dance," which accepts inspiration from all forms of dance, creating new performance experiences. This form of dance can be challenging to understand and watch, as it does not often lend itself to a clear story or idea. Choreographer Christopher K. Morgan explains that "there is no mysterious language that only dancers and choreographers speak. Each viewer's own experiences and knowledge that they bring to viewing the dance are all that are needed. Trust that. And know that your viewing of these dances is a valuable part of the choreographic process."

Contemporary dance can be performed and experienced in a variety of venues ranging from traditional theatres to non-theatrical settings (also termed a site specific work). Contemporary dance might be performed as a solo program, a shared program or in a festival. Let's look at each iteration:

WORKING IN A THEATRE

There are dance-specific theatres throughout the country or flexible-use theatres that can present dance among other art forms such as theatre or opera. Similar to ballet, the type of floor is very important. Many dancers prefer a vinyl floor (often called a Marley floor, named for a company that used to produce them), while others prefer a bare wooden floor. Regardless of the surface, the floor needs to be a "sprung floor," which means that the top wooden layer should have space directly under it to allow the floor give. Dancing on floors that are not sprung (concrete, linoleum, etc.) can be very harmful to dancers, resulting in injuries. As production manager, you will also have to plan for many of the same technical elements as you would for a theatrical presentation, such as masking, lighting, sound, costumes and sometimes scenery and projections. The production manager of the company presenting the work will need to work closely with the production manager at the venue to ensure clear communication and accommodation. (See chapter 14 on Presenting.)

SITE SPECIFIC WORK

An increasingly popular choice for contemporary dance is to move the performance beyond the walls of a traditional theatre and create choreography using a non-traditional space. Site specific work is so named as it uses the location as the inspiration for the movement, patterns and emotional qualities of the dance. The site specific movement grew out of visual art installations that similarly used space as inspiration. The site can be anywhere—the lobby of a theatre, a stairwell, a city street. Not utilizing a theatre space can be extremely challenging for the production manager, especially when planning how to incorporate, acquire and utilize elements such as lights and sound. Also one must carefully consider many factors that we take for granted within theatre spaces, such as permits to use the space, creating a "backstage" and, if performing outside, the weather. There is also the question of the audience experience—are they seated, and, if so, where, or are they encouraged to move amongst the performers. In

Figure 11.5 *Visible Seams*, created by Erin Crawley Woods in the Clarice Smith Performing Arts Center

Credit: Photo by Zachary Z. Handler

general, audiences are expecting to sit and watch, so if something else is required of them, it's best to prepare them ahead of time and/or use performers to help them know where to go and what to do.

SOLO CONCERT VERSUS SHARED PROGRAM

Many choreographers aspire to produce or be presented in a solo show, meaning they are the only choreographer on the program. If this is the case, then complete control of all elements resides with the choreographer. The light plot, masking, projector placement and so on are as the choreographer and their design team desires. However, if it is a shared program with one or more choreographers, then compromise is necessary. Shared programs are common in contemporary dance. Often, dance works are short in length, which lends to a concert with multiple components. Shared concerts can also be more economical, especially if the choreographers are required to find and rent their own venue.

DANCE FESTIVALS

Dance festivals occur throughout the United States, bringing together multiple choreographers to present work. Presenting in the festival format often means collaborating on a predetermined physical set up of the stage and light plot. Because there are many works being brought together in one theatre space, there is usually a strict time limit for technical preparation and for striking after the performance. There may also be a time limit for each dance performance. Most dance festivals will employ a production manager to oversee the entire festival and make sure things run efficiently. The creation of the tech and performance schedule is a complicated task for the production manager, as these festivals may have 10 choreographers or more within a short period of time.

Unlike ballet, there are fewer contemporary dance *companies*. There are some successful companies, such as Doug Varone and Dancers, Susan Marshall and Company and Camille A. Brown and Dancers. As you can tell from their names, they are based around a founding choreographer. Rarely, if ever, do these companies perform the works of different choreographers, though many collaborate with their company dancers to create the themes and movement of their performances. Most choreographers do not have the financial resources to assemble a company of dancers and support a full season. It is more likely that choreographers assemble a group of dancers for a single performance opportunity. In these instances, the dancers might not be paid or are paid a percentage of the box office receipts. For these less-funded single performances, the choreographer might have to take on the production management functions as well.

CASE STUDY—AMERICAN COLLEGE DANCE ASSOCIATION

CONTRIBUTOR: REBECCA WOLF—PRODUCTION MANAGER, TOWSON UNIVERSITY'S DEPARTMENT OF DANCE

The American College Dance Association (ACDA) produces multiple festivals around the country each year. The festivals are by geographic area and are hosted by colleges or universities. When Towson University (in Baltimore, MD) considered hosting the Mid-Atlantic festival, I was quickly brought into the conversation. We began the discussion about two years out. The first consideration before we made a commitment was—did we have the space to do it? The second was—could we actually afford to do it? And the third—could we create a good support team to carry it out? I remember the chair of our department asking me before we went ahead—did I think this was possible and was I up for it? I gave an enthusiastic YES!

The support we were given from ACDA was pretty great. At one point in the process, we were calling them daily. We learned that we did not have to take things at face value. It was okay to ask questions that were out of the ordinary. Just because this festival had been done a certain way before did not mean that we had to do it that way.

The actual schedule of our department's productions changed to accommodate the festival. That was very insightful on my chair's behalf, and I very much appreciated

Figure 11.6 Rebecca Wolf

Credit: Photo by Neal Golden

that. We merged two shows into one big show for the fall semester to open up space in spring, when we planned to host the festival. We started detailing the festival schedule ten months out. Once we had more details about the specific classes that would be offered, things went into full gear, because we knew what we were working with. Planning in the beginning was difficult because we were working with approximate numbers of 400–500 people for the festival. Those numbers were not confirmed until two months out. It was really, really late. It was the epitome of hurry up and wait. We were waiting, then we were really hurrying.

The scheduling of tech and performances for the various concerts in the festival was really tricky. We were struggling with how much time to allot for tech versus how many hours there were in the day. We divided tech into chunks of available time whenever we could. Sometimes we'd only have an hour, and we'd try to get three to four pieces teched in that time. Everyone in the adjudicated concerts needed to have the same amount of tech time, or we had to say something to the adjudicators so the participants were not penalized. That actually worked in our favor. It made it easier, at times, to push people along. It was also really frustrating because not all projects were equal, and it would have been nice to give some of the more complicated ones more time. However, if anything seemed unsafe, we always made sure that they had an adequate amount of time to hash it out. We were hoping to build in some wiggle room in between each tech, but, in the end, that was not possible. I fought hard for that, and it was hard to let it go. If you are working with people who have never been in your space before and really want to shine, you are going to want that extra time to talk through things with them, and we couldn't put that into the actual schedule. Five minutes between techs when you are teching twenty pieces in a day, which adds up to a lot of time. Plus, we were teching out of order, so even to take a moment and think about what was coming before or after this work in the actual concert would have been nice. People kept saying dancers are quick—we don't need much time. But I knew that things would come up.

ACDA 2105 Tech Schedule

Friday, March 6: Tech A1 (8 pieces)

Tech Start Time:	Tech End Time:	Institution	Title	Length	# of Dancers	Program Order:	
9:00am	9:20am	Comm College of Baltimore County	*Laempana Sinua*	11:00	7	A	2
9:20am	9:40am	Goucher College	*With Grace"d*	11:45	14	A	3
9:40am	10:00am	Goucher College	*Dissonance*	7:45	9	A	10
10:00am	10:20am	Univ of MD Baltimore County	*Ebb & Flow*	10:00	4	A	5
10:20am	10:40am	Univ of MD Baltimore County	*Swans in an Ugly Duckling World*	11:00	4	A	8
10:40am	11:00am	Univ of MD College Park	*Say Something*	6:30	1	A	7
11:00am	11:20am	Univ of MD College Park	*Drape*	7:30	2	A	9
11:20am	11:40pm	American University	*Jazz Is . . . (redux)*	9:00	9	A	6

Friday, March 6: Tech A2 (4 pieces)

Tech Start Time:	Tech End Time:	Institution	Title	Length	# of Dancers	Program Order:	
1:00pm	1:20pm	Ann Arundel Comm. College	*Perspectives*	8:07	15	A	11
1:20pm	1:40pm	Ann Arundel Comm. College	*Don't look back*	3:25	1	A	4
1:40pm	2:00pm	Coppin State	*Territories*	7:00	5	A	1
2:00pm	2:20pm	Coppin State				A	12

Friday, March 6: Tech B1 (3 pieces)

Tech Start Time:	Tech End Time:	Institution	Title	Length	# of Dancers	Program Order:	
8:45pm	9:05pm	Towson University	*The Way We Do It*	6:58	1	B	5

Figure 11.7 Continued

ACDA 2105 Tech Schedule							
9:05pm	9:25pm	Towson University	*Babble*	7:10	6	B	1
9:25pm	9:45pm	West Virginia University	*Perception With Moving Minds*	6:00	4	B	3
Saturday March 7: Tech B2 (9 pieces) & C1 (5 pieces) & D1 (1 piece)							
Tech Start Time:	Tech End Time:	Institution	Title	Length	# of Dancers	Program Order:	
1:00pm	1:20pm	East Carolina State	*Hearts Are Young*	11:45	7	B	4
1:20pm	1:40pm	East Carolina State	*What You See Ain't All I Got Darlin*	11:50	5	B	6
1:40pm	2:00pm	James Madison University	*Still I Rise*	4:45	1	B	11
2:00pm	2:20pm	James Madison University	*We Interrupt This Program*	5:30	5	B	9
2:20pm	2:40pm	Old Dominion University	*Tie Shopping With My Father*	10:00	9	B	8
2:40pm	3:00pm	North Carolina State	*Waking, Finding You Here*	10:30	2	B	10
3:00pm	3:20pm	North Carolina State	*Between Life And Art . . .*	5:06	4	B	7
3:20pm	3:40pm	Shenandoah University	*Quartetto*	7:43	4	B	12
3:40pm	4:00pm	Shenandoah University	*Homines In Machina*	10:20	10	B	2
4:00pm	4:20pm	Salem College	*Sovereign Ablution*	6:00	7	C	4
4:20pm	4:40pm	Salem College	*Djealor Revisited*	12:00	7	C	10
4:40pm	5:00pm	Radford University	*Zwitterion*	6:38	8	C	3
5:00pm	5:20pm	Lynchburg University				C	1
5:20pm	5:40pm	Meredith University	*Fantasia on Break-Ups*	12:00	11	C	5
5:40pm	6:00pm	University of Delaware	*See No, Speak No, Hear No Evil*	8:15	12	D	3

Figure 11.7   Continued

ACDA 2105 Tech Schedule							
Sunday March 8: Tech C2 (7 pieces) & D2 (2 pieces)							
Tech Start Time:	Tech End Time:	Institution	Title	Length	# of Dancers	Program Order:	
8:00am	8:20am	George Mason University	*Fourth Shift*	8:00	4	C	7
8:20am	8:40am	George Mason University	*Toxic Infatuation*	5:00	5	C	12
8:40am	9:00am	Sweet Briar College	*Under Construction*	4:30	1	C	2
9:00am	9:20am	Sweet Briar College	*Inner Moment Out*	5:30	1	C	9
9:20am	9:40am	St. Mary's College	*Blue Lily Red Lotus*	7:00	1	C	8
9:40am	10:00am	St. Mary's College	*Milieu*	7:00	2	C	11
10:00am	10:20am	Frostburg University	*Fortunate Son*	3:41	8	C	6
10:20am	10:40am	University of Richmond	*Turn & Turn*	8:00	7	D	1
10:40am	11:00am	University of Richmond	*Into the Dark*	6:33	5	D	10

Figure 11.7   ACDA tech schedule for adjudicated concerts

We had a serious amount of snow on the first day of the festival. Our school delayed opening until noon, and no one was able to get to us on time, even the local schools. I was on my phone nonstop with people calling to say they would be late or even miss their tech time. We lost half a day. To make up for it, I ended up taking away tech time for the non-adjudicated pieces and only giving them enough time to walk the space. That miraculously ended up being just enough time. It's interesting what your brain comes up with in a pinch.

Most places who have hosted the festival before were able to make a profit. We had trouble seeing that ahead of time and knowing if that was possible. The parts of the budget that I was responsible for were production labor and food for the crew. We knew that would take up a big part of our budget. Each person we hired came at a different rate, so that was tricky. I always over budget for labor, and that helped me here.

It's hard to find adequate crew in our area, and we just did not have enough people. We wanted to have two crews each at eight-hour days, but that just wasn't possible. We ended up working people eighteen hour days. We were very lucky that the people we did find were willing and able to work those hours, of course they were paid for them. I was adamant that the staff and volunteers were fed, since they were working so hard and for long hours, sometimes with only short breaks for meals. I've worked so many shows where the production manager does not think about breaks and food, and all I kept thinking was—I'm not going to be that person! You have got to take care of your crew. People often forget about human sustainability. Over the course of doing this for a lifetime, if people make it that long, we work crazy hours, and it's not fair of us to ask them to work without breaks and good food.

I really appreciated the participants who planned ahead and reached out to me to ask questions. One project had a drone that flew onstage with the performers. That was really great to know ahead of time. We even had one local school that came by weeks in advance to test out a projection idea; they even brought their own projector. We had the time, so we were able to brainstorm and make it work for them. It was nice to stay one step ahead. There were also people who had hosted this festival before who participated, and they were so patient and supportive and really kind.

I had worked many different types of festivals before, but this one was totally different. When we began planning, I reached out to the Production Manager's Forum to see if anyone had resources or advice for producing a festival. I got an email from someone in California with a scheduling document that ended up saving my life. It was great to see what someone else had used before, and it was easy to change to serve our needs. I don't even know if that person realizes how much they helped me.

Production managing for dance can be a challenging yet rewarding undertaking. If you love dance and are inspired by the creative process, you will certainly enjoy this work. Many of the challenges come from working with dance professionals—choreographers and dancers, specifically. These artists have rarely had training in technical theatre and production management aspects of the performing arts. Unlike most undergraduate theatre programs, dance programs rarely require their students to take technical/production courses. Some choreographers, who are accustomed to producing their own concerts, might find it difficult giving over responsibility to a production manager. Others might be grateful to finally allow someone else to handle the logistics so they can simply create!

NOTE

1   Petipa, Marius. *Russian Ballet Master; the Memoirs of Marius Petipa*. London: A. & C. Black, 1958.

Rock and Roll

"An organized show is not hard to achieve as long as you are on top of the details. Pay attention and do what needs to be done ahead of time, and then your show day should be seamless and organized. Remember that *Proper Prior Planning Prevents Poor Performance*"

- Michael Richter, Production Manager for REO Speedwagon / Richter Entertainment Group

The glamorous world of rock and roll and the touring music business is another artistic genre that requires a reliable and competent production manager at the helm. Whether on the road and touring or having a staff job as a venue's production manager, the job of the production manager is fast paced and has many moving parts that need careful management on a regular basis. Much like production managers in other artistic disciplines, flexibility and patience are top attributes of a production manager in the music business. John Sanders, a top production touring professional whose recent credits include Sting, Paul Simon, KISS, Def Leppard and The Eagles, agrees and says,

> On a typical show day, a production manager could have any number of people coming at them in a very short amount of time. For instance, the first thing prior to load-in, venue personnel will want to see stage placement and dressing room assignments, the truck drivers will want to know parking and order of trucks unloading, and the bus drivers will want to know where to park. While all of this is happening, crew members will want to know about the location of catering and laundry, riggers will want to see a tickets-sold map for an audio hang, and the list goes on . . . and all of this within the first ten minutes of walking into a venue. It can be overwhelming, and having a great deal of patience and flexibility are strong qualities of a good production manager. These attributes will get you through event days while maintaining a cordial and professional

Figure 12.1
Credit: Image © iStock

> *demeanor. All of this takes discipline. If you cannot discipline yourself, you won't be a good production manager.*

Being flexible refers to dealing both with people and with situations. Dealing with the physical needs of the production requires quick and flexible thinking on the part of the production managers, as each venue has its own quirks, both good and bad. As Sanders notes,

> *some venues have truck docks, some don't; some venues have plenty of dressing rooms, some never have enough; some venues have great local crews, some have poor labor crews; some venues can get a show up in four or five, some venues may take eight hours for the same shows; some venues can hang your entire show, some venues can hang 50% of your show.*

As you can see, the production managers need to be flexible and work together to seek out solutions to the challenges they face to make a concert happen.

TOURING NEEDS VS. VENUE CAPABILITIES

What are the similarities and differences between the TOURING production manager and the VENUE production manager? Both have goals that they need to attain, with the main goal being to safely load a show into and out of a venue in the most efficient manner using the resources available.

When it comes to the differences between the two jobs, Sanders says,

a venue production manager and a touring production manager are different in what they are experts of. A venue production manager is (or should be) an expert as it relates to the capabilities of their venue and should be able to communicate those capabilities to the touring production manager. They do not need to be an expert in the details of a show but only how their venue capabilities can provide for the show's needs. A touring production manager is (or should be) an expert as it relates to the needs of the performance and should be able to communicate those needs to the venue production manager. If both the venue and touring production managers maintain the same   urse of action to achieve their goals as noted above, then they will be successful in s⌄ ly loading the show in and out in the shortest amount of time, in the most efficient manner and with minimal or no issues.

With regard to touring, one may think that it's an easy life "on the road," but there are some challenges. The production manager in the touring aspect has a few more hurdles to jump over compared to the venue production manager. The first and most obvious is the fact that 80% of the world's tours will travel on tour buses. This will include the band and band's staff, including the production manager. Learning to live with up to ten other crew members in a single bus can be a challenge. Sleeping quarters are approximately 8 feet x 3 feet, generally there are

Figure 12.2 Load in for "Feeding America Concert"
Credit: Image © Jay Sheehan

Figure 12.3 Setting out the truss line

Credit: Image © Jay Sheehan

Figure 12.4 Adding the shade roof

Credit: Image © Jay Sheehan

Figure 12.5 Posts are in

Credit: Image © Jay Sheehan

Figure 12.6 Ready for sound check

Credit: Image © Jay Sheehan

Figure 12.7   "Feeding America Concert" featuring Chicago
Credit: Image © Jay Sheehan

no showers on the bus, groceries are often shared (or fought over!) and the main living quarters on the bus are shared with your fellow travelers. Getting along is essential to a happy tour!

Living on the road has its other issues, as well, such as eating healthy meals, getting enough rest and keeping proper hygiene. Schedules for crew oftentimes find them eating at abnormal hours or late at night. Exercise is challenging while on tour, and special attention needs to be paid to personal well-being. All of this adds up to some real stresses for people on tour, and the production manager must always be at the ready to deal with these added challenges.

That's not to say that the production manager that has a venue job doesn't have some of the same challenges. Early load-ins, bad catering and cranky stagehands can certainly be found in non-touring applications as well. Either way, the rock and roll production manager must be flexible and adapt to the ever-changing environments for themselves and their staff.

"VENUE" PRODUCTION MANAGEMENT

Large venues will usually have a staff venue production manager to represent the venue. They will handle the "advance of a show" (more on that later) and communicate the needs of the touring show to the venue's staff and vendors. This is the primary job of the venue production manager, and like in the other artistic disciplines, this information needs to be collected and disseminated. When representing the venue, the production manager must always have the best interest of the venue in mind. This can, at times, cause some distress between the venue and touring production managers, but the art of compromise and negotiation are essential components of the production manager's toolkit. Each entity is working for their own agenda, their own set of bosses and their own budgets needing to be met. Venue production managers may be trying to find ways to save money for the venue or local promoter while the touring production manager is asking for more labor to help his touring crew get the show in. It is a constant negotiation between the two parties, each trying to get the most out of their resources.

> "A good thorough 'advance' is important so the day goes seamlessly. In my opinion, there is no reason everything can't be in order from the start of the day to the end of the day if both the touring production manager and the venue production manager pay attention to all the details given during the advance."
>
> - Michel Richter, Production Manager for
> the Richter Entertainment Group

ADVANCING A SHOW

The first step when planning a large music event for the venue is the dissemination of information from the band's contract and rider. Usually, this document contains everything that the in-house production manager will need to know to get the show "advanced" with the touring production manager. "Advancing the show" will be a very common term you will hear when working as a production manager in the music business. *Advancing* means getting and disseminating as much detailed information as possible to all parties in advance of the shows arrival.

Figure 12.8

Credit: Image © iStock

THE CONTRACT AND TECHNICAL RIDER

The contract not only contains the artist salary, or band fee, but it will also contain all of the technical needs that the tour will either be bringing with them or will need locally sourced from the in-house production manager. Technical needs, labor needs, hospitality and catering needs (those items put in the band's dressing rooms), and security calls, are all part of this sometimes cumbersome and detailed document. Once the venue production manager receives the rider from the touring production manager or agent, the actual "advance" can begin. As you begin to read contracts and riders in your career, you will start to understand what items will affect you the most. Usually, there are many pages at the beginning that are the mandatory legal jargon (such as cancellation policies, insurance needs, etc.), and, while this is important information to have and to understand, the integral parts of the rider that affect the production manager are the technical needs and hospitality.

It is prudent to ask the touring personnel if you are working from the most current rider. It is not uncommon to see outdated riders while working as a production manager, and you must stay on top of making sure you have the most current rider.

TECHNICAL NEEDS

Bands that are "carrying production" mean that the tour or artist is providing the show with the equipment and it is travelling with it on the trucks. Lighting, audio, video, automation and special effects are all items of the touring production gear list. On many tours, an entire truck can be dedicated to wardrobe or other items that make the artist feel at home. (The Rolling Stones used to carry two trucks filled with video arcade games for the band and their back-stage guests to play while waiting for the show to start!)

The tech rider will let you know if the band is carrying production or partial production or if you will need to rent out or provide "local sound," "local lights" and "local video," as some of the smaller or newer touring bands may not have the capacity or resources to carry their own production. The rider will indicate what you will need to acquire. It is not uncommon to see specific requests for audio gear, such as a certain brand of speaker or make and model of the front of house audio console. Specialized lighting is often asked for, with several various brands and models of moving lights and lighting consoles. Special effects are often discussed in this section of the rider as well; requests for CO_2 tanks for confetti cannons or pyrotechnics are not uncommon.

With regard to audio, as mentioned above, some artists may ask for a particular brand or make of audio speakers for the main PA (PA is still a term used in rock and roll and stands for public address). The monitor board may also be a specific brand request. Some artists and audio engineers are very particular (and SENSITIVE) about specific brands of gear, so be sure you read and understand their requests.

Figure 12.9 Rock and roll stage
Credit: Image © Jay Sheehan

Another important portion of the technical rider is called the audio input list. This is especially important for your sound crew to have, as it contains all of the instrumentation and audio channel assignments going into the main audio console. Additionally, this list will contain microphone types used and even what type of microphone stand is used.

The last important piece of the rider puzzle is the stage plot. The stage plot is the equivalent of the ground plan and will be a valuable source of information for the production manager. This document will (or should!) have the placement of all equipment that goes on stage. Audio monitors, drum riser, microphone placement, keyboard placement and space for the technicians to work in are all part of the stage plot. Having the plot ahead of time will help expedite the load-in. If you don't see one, ask the production manager. Much like keeping and maintaining a prompt script in theatre, the technical rider is a document you want close to you at all times, so keep it handy either in your binder or on a tablet so that you are prepared to answer (and ask!) as many questions as possible when it comes to advancing the show.

TIP—As in many of the performing arts, most music tours today will have a light plot indicating what is being used or what needs to be outsourced locally. If you don't see it in the rider, make sure you ask for one from the touring production manager. The light plot is especially important if you need to acquire lighting from your local lighting equipment provider, as they will use this document to prepare the light rig in the shop and send it to the venue.

Figure 12.10

Credit: Image © iStock

LABOR NEEDS

The massive amount of equipment in the trucks requires a great number of people to unload and set up. Typically, tours will carry department heads, such as a stage manager, lighting director, audio engineers, automation and video technicians, etc., but will need local crew to supplement the rider in order to get the equipment set up in a timely manner. It is not unheard of for bands like U2, Lady Gaga or Madonna to call up to 100 local crew members to get their shows loaded in. A previous Lady Gaga tour incorporated close to forty 53-foot trucks and needed a virtual army of crew to get the job done. The 2015 One Direction tour used similar numbers. It is the venue's production manager who must secure the labor needs as presented in the rider. The good news is that most major cities with large concert venues also have a local stagehand staffing office, and the in-house production manager simply calls the labor office to ask for the amount of crew needed. It is imperative that the local production manager has a good working relationship with the local stagehand labor provider. The local production manager will always expect top-notch labor, and having a close relationship with the labor company helps to ensure that the touring stagehands are appropriately supported.

Labor numbers are clearly indicated in the rider, and it will usually look something like this:

Load in: 9 a.m.

Four truck loaders

```
                         Four lighting crew
                         Four audio crew
                         Four video crew
                         Two backline crew
                         One up rigger
                         One down rigger
                         One electrician


*******************************************************************


Show Call:   6 p.m.
                         Four stagehands
                         Two follow spot operators
                         One wardrobe


*******************************************************************


Load-out:   11 p.m.
                         Four truck loaders
                         Six lighting crew
                         Six audio crew
                         Four video crew
                         Two backline crew
                         One up rigger
                         One down rigger
                         One electrician
```

It is not uncommon to see crew numbers get increased for load-out, as the touring production manager has one goal in mind at the end of the night, and that is to get all the equipment taken down in a safe and efficient manner, as the next stop may be several hours away. Having a good local crew helps get this accomplished and gets the band and crew headed toward their next stop.

HOSPITALITY

Touring personnel usually have two goals in mind when first getting off the bus in the morning: a hot shower and good breakfast! This is where the artist catering and hospitality rider will come into play. Made famous by Van Halen's 1982 contractual demand that brown M&Ms be plucked from the group's candy bowl, the catering and hospitality rider often reflects the delightful or difficult nature of the individual artists. (More about the brown M&Ms later.)

The local production manager should take careful note of the hospitality rider and start to make arrangements with the local caterer to procure the items needed for the day. Like with the labor company, most if not all of the major cities around the globe have a local catering company that will handle this for you. It is not the production manager's job to go and shop for food. Your local caterer will take care of that. It is the production manager's job to make sure that the rider is fulfilled. This hospitality rider will not only include a guide for breakfast, lunch and dinner, but will also contain the food requests for after the show, dressing rooms, stage coolers, the production office, bus stock and towels for showers. It is not unusual for the artist to request a specific type of meal on Monday, Wednesday and Friday, etc. This assures some variance to meals and guarantees that the touring personnel won't be eating hotdogs and burgers seven nights a week!

The hospitality rider is a living, breathing document, ever changing, as artist needs can change on a daily basis. Make sure that you have the most recent hospitality rider prior to advancing your show. You can get the most updated rider by contacting the band's production or tour manager or the band's agency. You may also get a copy of the contract from the producer if you are working with these bands in a "corporate special event." There is no one person to ask for the rider; ask away at all your contacts until you find it. Having an up-to-date rider will make your day go by much better if the correct rider requirements are fulfilled. A well-fed artist and crew mean a happy artist and crew. (Most times!)

Touring riders will oftentimes have items requested that may seem strange or difficult to get. Don't get discouraged or caught up in the idea of why the artists need these items; just do your best to get them and make it happen for the touring personnel. It is not unusual to be asked to cover dressing room walls with drape, have special lighting (not fluorescent!) in the dressing rooms or provide any other creature comforts of home. Again, always remember that the artist and crew are living on the road and not in their own homes. It is the job of the local production manager to make the tour members feel at home. If you or your venue gets this reputation of taking care of the artist and crew, generally speaking, the good word will get out to the other tours travelling around the country. Like theatre, the touring world of the music business is a small one, and touring personnel talk to each other. Being on the good side of the tours will always be a bonus for the local production manager and for the venue. No one wants to be known as the venue that doesn't do their job or, worse yet, doesn't care about the touring group.

So what exactly do they ask for in their dressing rooms? As you read the following, try to read with a sense of humor and not a sense of "are you kidding me?"

The rider of a popular artist (who will go unnamed!) required the performer's dressing room (which has to be draped in cream or soft pink) to be outfitted with two cream-colored egg chairs, one of which should have a footstool. A coffee table needs to be "Perspex modern style." A pair of floor lamps should be in "French ornate style," and the singer's refrigerator must come with a glass door. As for the dressing room's flower arrangement, she wants "White and purple hydrangeas, pink & white roses and peonies." If those flowers are not available, she will settle for a "selection of seasonal white flowers to include white orchids." However, promoters are advised, *"ABSOLUTELY* NO CARNATIONS.*"* That warning is, of course, underlined.

When it comes to hotel provisions, this artist requires a "1 bedroom presidential suite" in a "5 star property." And free internet service and a complimentary breakfast must be provided to the performer and her touring party. Chauffeurs, the rider notes, are not allowed to "start a conversation with the client." They also are directed not to stare at the backseat through the rear view mirror. Drivers should also not "ask for autographs or pictures, and especially not while driving!" Finally, her ride should be outfitted with "four water bottles."

A second example comes from another popular woman. On this tour rider, the singer required promoters to stock her backstage roost with "Cristal champagne," which she consumed via "bendy straws." Next, she asked for a $200 bottle of cabernet sauvignon and her dressing room "outfitted with two dozen white roses and vanilla aromatherapy candles." As for the furniture in her "living room space," she wants "no busy patterns; black, dark grey, cream, dark pink are all fine." The room "should be about 75 degrees," and a "lamp or clip light" should be provided so that "harsh lighting may be turned off" in her backstage bathroom.

All of the crazy requests are not just from the women of the music business. The men get involved as well. When this unnamed artist headlined at a local university, he banked a $750,000 payday for his performance. But this chart-topping performer did not get every perk requested in his concert rider, since the school does not provide artists with alcohol, tobacco or $400,000 luxury vehicles. This male artist demanded that promoters provide him with ground transportation while he is in town performing. Specifically, this star requires a late-model black Maybach (either the '57 or '62 model) with tinted windows. The dressing room (72 degrees, please) must be stocked with Sapporo beer, vodka, tequila and two bottles of $300 champagne. This performer also needs two bottles (at $200 apiece) of 2004 Sassicaia, which his rider helpfully describes as a "Red, Italian Wine from Bolgheri Region." Additionally, he requires "good quality" peanut butter and jelly, one martini shaker, twelve shot glasses and a pack of Marlboro Lights.

It can often seem like a chore to get all of those items for the dressing rooms or stage, and sometime the requests can be a little challenging. But all of these items are put in the rider for a reason, and that is to assure a happy and top-notch performance by the talent. While we may think some of these dressing room or technical equipment requests to be strange or petty, it is important to remember that the touring artists and crew don't have the luxury of waking up in their own home every day. They live in a bus, live out of a suitcase and generally don't have the comforts of home. The rider requests help to close that gap a bit and to help create a feeling of home for those who work on the road. You shouldn't look at the rider as anything more than that—a document that will help the day go by smoother and could help everyone get along a little better.

All this being said, dressing room riders can be funny or frustrating for the local production manager. Take it in stride and do your best to get it fulfilled. Once you get the hospitality rider, it is always fair game for the local production manager to ask the touring production manager if they can make any cuts to the rider in order to not waste product or labor or money. Most times the answer is "No—get me what's on the rider." That is the easy way out, and some touring production managers don't want to deal with changes or don't want to deal with an upset artist if the "bendy straws" aren't there to sip the champagne. Fair enough. On the flip side, there are artists and production managers who do not want to see wasted food or beverages and will make cuts to the rider based on what is actually needed that day. Perhaps the artist won't want that "cheese platter for six" or "deli tray for ten." It is worth asking the band's production manager, at the very least.

And about those brown M&Ms in Van Halen's dressing rooms? This famous story comes from the fact that David Lee Roth, the famous front man for the band, always demanded brown M&Ms be removed from the candy bowl in his dressing room. He did this not because he hated the brown M&Ms but because he wanted to see if the venue production manager and catering company actually read the rider. If the brown M&Ms were in the bowl, legend has it that the management would get an earful from Mr. Roth!

> **TIP**—Make sure that when you ask about making cuts to the rider, you ask with a tone of "trying to save wasted product" and not about trying to save the promoter or producer money.

SECURITY

As a venue production manager, you will be asked to provide backstage security for the various positions around the artist and their entourage. The rider should clearly indicate the various positions needed, but it is up to the venue production manager to communicate those needs to the security company or operations manager of the venue.

> A typical security call in the rider may look something like this:
> - Two (2) persons to be available at all times from the time the crew arrives to ensure the security of equipment, crew members, their vehicles and personal property throughout the day.
> - A minimum of two (2) additional persons (dependent on the integrity of the backstage area) to be available from 2:30 p.m. to ensure the safety and security of the band upon their arrival at the facility, until their departure from the facility.
> - From thirty (30) minutes prior to doors opening to the public, until all the public have left after the performance:
> - One (1) person at each access point to the backstage area.
> - Two (2) persons for the dressing room area.
> - Four (4) persons (two on each side of the stage) at the base of the stage access stairs or access points, whichever is applicable.
> - Eight (8) persons to be positioned in front of the stage, behind the barricade.
> - Two (2) persons to be placed to secure the front of house mix position.

The security meeting, usually held about an hour before the doors to the venue open, is one of the most important meetings of the day. During that meeting, the tour manager or tour security director will go over the day's "pass sheet." The pass sheet is a visual look at all of the backstage and tour passes issued for that day's event. Usually color coded and dated by city, the pass sheet clearly indicates what areas are accessible to those pass holders on that given day. It is not uncommon to have five to six different colored passes, all indicating a different level of security access.

> While backstage passes are cool to have and to give out, remember that the backstage area is a workplace and that guests should not be permitted to wander around without an escort. Historically speaking, the backstage party was indeed that, but in these modern times, the backstage area is becoming more of a place of business and less of a party hangout.

VENUE TECHNICAL PACKET & ADVANCE CHECKLISTS

While the rider should contain everything you need to know to produce the show, unfortunately, there are those riders or touring production managers that miss the mark, and you, as the venue production manager, will need to seek out additional information. Having a "venue technical packet" and an "advance checklist" are important tools for you to use during your advance with the touring production manager and should be used every time you advance a show.

VENUE TECHNICAL PACKET

If you find yourself in the role of the venue production manager, you should have a venue technical packet ready to send to the touring production manager. The technical packet should contain all relevant information about the venue's physical and technical layout. This is information that the touring production manager will need in order to do his or her job efficiently.

Here are some examples of what should go into the venue's technical specifications packet:

- Venue address—with written directions (not everyone own a GPS yet!)
- Shipping address
- Venue capacity
- Curfew times, if applicable
- Decibel limits, if applicable
- Contact information on important people at the venue, i.e., production manager's cell, operations managers, general manager, box office, production office phones, transportation company, audio head, lighting head, etc.
- Contact number for person responsible for ticketing and production holds
- Contact number for whoever is paying the band at the end of the night (also known as settling)
- Stage dimensions

- Size of rigging grid
- Front of house mix position dimensions
- Distance from front of house position to the stage (important for audio and lighting crew to determine cable lengths needed)
- Power available for lighting, audio, video, buses, etc.
- Load-in information/loading dock info
- Dressing room layouts

You will note that many of these questions are going to be asked of you during your advance call or when you are required to fill out the production questionnaire. While you have done your due diligence in creating and disseminating the venue technical packet, don't assume that the touring production manager will always read it. Many times, the touring production manager will be seeing your technical packet for the first time when they first contact you.

> **TIP**—Don't get discouraged or ask yourself "didn't they read my technical packet?" All the information is in there! Just answer the questions that the touring production manager presents to you.

ADVANCE CHECKLIST

The advance checklist is the document that the venue production manager should keep ready when preparing to talk to the touring production manager. This list will assist you in ensuring all questions are answered prior to the band's arrival on show day.

Here are some examples of items that you will need to know and should have on your advance checklist.

- Get contact information of everyone important on the tour. This will include the tour manager, production manager, lighting designer, audio head of department, artist agency and catering, and merchandise seller contacts.
- What are the labor calls?
- Is a production "runner" needed? (A production runner is someone locally who has a car and can go out and get items needed at the last minute. Usually an entry level position for those trying to break into the business.)
- What are the lighting and sound needs?
- What are the power requirements needed for the show?
- Is there open flame or other special effects?
- What are the catering and hospitality requirements?
- How many buses and trucks are you traveling in?
- What are the dressing room layouts ?

- How many towels are needed for showers for crew?

- Will the band need local ground transportation, such as vans or limousines?

- Does the artist need stair access from stage to house?

- Will merchandise such as tee shirts, hats, etc., be sold during the event?

- How many backstage passes will be used?

- Will we or can we release any ticket production holds? (More on that later)

The above list of questions should be answered during the advance of the show. As mentioned earlier in this chapter, the advance of the show will be your main responsibility during the pre-planning stages. A proper advance will save you a lot of time on show day if you know everything that's going to happen. Of course, the unplanned will always happen, but having your show advanced well may help prevent many other additional challenges come show day.

TOURING ADVANCE CHECKLIST

While the above points are important information and questions to ask the touring production manager, there are even more questions the touring production manager will have for you about your venue and its operations. These questions will often be delivered in the form of the "venue advance checklist." This checklist should be filled out by the venue production manager and sent back to the tour as soon as possible. This information will then be used by the touring production manager to create the itinerary documents for the touring personnel.

Here are just a few examples of some questions that may be asked of you during the advance:

- Stage size/wing space size of your venue

- Dimensions of riggable grid area above the stage

- Dimensions of riggable grid area down stage of the proscenium

- Number of trucks that can park at the loading dock

- Number of buses that can park backstage

- Is shore power available for buses? (Shore power is power that buses connect into so they do not have to run their generators. Using shore power saves generator gas along with eliminating gas fumes and excessive noise. When an option, always use shore power.)

- Is a forklift on site?

- Do you have in-house follow spots? If so, what type, amount and location?

- What power is available onstage or backstage for lighting and sound equipment? (Remember that lighting and audio should always use separate power services. When needed, video can often share with others if separate video power is not available.)

As you can see, a sizeable amount of information needs to be exchanged between the touring production manager and the venues production manager. Having proper checklists and venue technical packets helps to ensure that the correct information is being conveyed to the necessary staff on the tour.

Figure 12.11

Credit: Image © iStock

PUTTING ON THE SHOW

Once the show has been advanced by phone between the two production managers, you will have an opportunity to start preparing your venue and vendors for the band's arrival. Security, lighting, audio, video and stagehand providers can all be contacted now. Most likely, you will be contacting your local stagehand company to secure the additional stage crew needed to get the show loaded in. The next vendor you will contact will be your catering and dressing room hospitality company. At this point, you should have made any cuts or changes to the rider and can confidently pass on that information. Make sure you have accurate counts for the meals for band, crew and guests.

> **TIP**—Don't forget to ask about the venue's staff meals that need to be ordered. Oftentimes, key staff members will need to be included in the meal count numbers, as they don't get a chance to get away for a meal.

Lastly, get in contact with your lighting, audio, and video company (if using local gear). Prepare them for the show by relaying information provided for you or have them contact the tours department heads directly. Oftentimes, the touring audio head will want to have a direct conversation with the venue's audio head. This ensures effective communication about the audio needs of the show.

TICKET HOLDS / PRODUCTION KILLS

One area you will want to pay attention to when working in a venue will be to inquire about any production holds or "kills" needed to support the production. It is not unusual to kill or hold seats for front of house mix position or the "mix shadow" (the mix shadow is the area directly behind the front of house mix position, usually having obstructed views of the stage.) Other production holds could be for cameras, camera platforms, follow spots, follow spot platforms or any other piece of equipment that may take up seating. Having this information early and getting to the box office manager is a critical step in getting the show to run properly. There really isn't anything worse for ticket holders than to show up only to find their seat has been taken up by a camera and riser. Having the proper box office advance helps to save the patron from having to deal with this type of situation and potentially ruining a great night. Make sure you ask about any production holds and get that information to your box office manager during the advance. Also, make sure you have a copy of the venue seating map with the production holds, as you may have the ability to release some tickets back to the box office after loading in.

> **TIP**—Temporary stairs leading from the stage to the house can also create a need for production holds. Make sure you confirm this during your advance!

Not every seating diagram will be perfect, and not every production manager will have the exact seating kills held correctly. During load-in, make sure that you check the seats affected by the production and keep the box office informed of any changes or additional seats that need to be held. In some instances, the seats may have already been sold, but the production still needs the seats for equipment. This will result in the relocating of the ticketed guest. "Re-Lo's" are another term you may hear when dealing with box office in the music industry. Having a minimal number of guests affected by the production is one of your main goals, so stay on top of this very important area.

Once all of these other duties have been completed, you sit and wait for the show trucks and buses to arrive. Show day is an exciting day for both the touring and local production managers. Because you are usually the first to greet each other, this is an opportunity for you to make a good first impression. Give the touring production manager a tour of the backstage areas. Catering, dressing rooms, production offices and any other backstage amenities should be pointed out. You don't get a second chance to make a first impression, so make sure your venue is in good shape for your guests. Next, the stage manager will want to know about power locations and stagehands. Point out where everything is located and introduce the stage manager to the local crew chief or venue stage manager. Unlike the theatre stage manager, who calls cues, the rock and roll stage manager is more of a stage manager of people and equipment. Your last order of business first thing in the morning should be to attend the "chalk out" session with the touring production manager and rigger. Much like taping out the ground plan in theatre, the chalk out session is simply marking on the stage the various "rigging points" needed to get the show flown off the grid. An accurate chalk out session ensures that the production will hang safely and properly.

During the advance, you may be asked to provide a production runner who knows the area and can get the touring personnel items needed at the last minute to get the show on. Introduce this runner as soon as possible in the morning and get the day started.

> **TIP**—Good production runners are essential to the overall success of the event. Having someone that knows the local area and can get items on the fly or last minute can be a valuable asset to both the production and you, the venue production manager. This is also a great entry level position for those interested in being a part of the concert event excitement.

If you have done a proper and complete advance, then the rest of your day should be about making sure tasks are handled on an as-needed basis. Putting out theoretical fires and attending to the needs of the touring production personnel become part of your task list. While the tours are fairly self-sufficient, attention must be paid to the details to make sure that the tasks are being completed in a timely manner.

The rest of the day will consist of sound checks for both the headliner and for any support acts that are either on the tour or acquired locally. If a local support act is needed, make sure you check with the touring audio head to assure that the local act can be accommodated on the tour's front of house board.

> **TIP**—Many times, the touring act CANNOT accommodate the opening act, and a second front of house board must be brought it. If this is the case, make sure you have ample room and power at the front of house mix position. If you don't, you might have to kill some seats to accommodate the second front of house board.

After sound check, and as mentioned earlier, there will most likely be a security meeting that takes place in the production office. This will be the chance for the tour's security director to go over the pass sheet, general rules about photography and eviction policies of the venue, should fans get out of hand. The production manager, along with the venue's operations manager, should attend this meeting to ensure all security policies are understood and adhered to.

After the security meeting, the next step is to open the doors to the venue. You should check with the house manager or operations manager to assure that they are ready. Security and ushers should be properly placed. The touring production manager will want to know that security and ushers are ready and that the stage barricade (if used) is staffed properly with the correct amount of security guards. Once you have clear indications that the staffing is correct and ready, ask the touring production manager if they are ready to open the doors to the venue.

Once you have the green light, let the house manager know that you have the all clear from the stage to open the house.

As you get closer to show time, there is less for you to do as the venue PM, as the touring PM really runs the show at this point. The touring PM will get the artist ready and communicate with the tour manager, touring stage manager and crew about the start of the show.

> **TIP**—Don't expect concerts to always start on time. Many factors will contribute to the late start, such as traffic or parking problems, issues at the box office or, at times, because the artist isn't ready. Perhaps there aren't enough people in the seats yet for the artist's ego to start. (Yes, this happens.) The reasons run the gamut, but make sure, as best as you can, that you and your front of house staff know when the show will start.

The show will then tend to run its course. The opening act will go on, usually followed by a fifteen-minute change over and intermission. Once the headliner is set and onstage, "settlement" (paying the band) and the load-out planning can begin. The touring stage manager will usually get with the venue production manager and start discussing crew strategies for an effective load-out. Meanwhile, you may also be planning an after-show meal or bus shopping trip with your runner.

The end of the show brings with it another load-out and packing of the trucks for the next stop.

CASE STUDY—ROCK AND ROLL STAGE FAILURE

CONTRIBUTOR: JOHN SANDERS—TOURING PROFESSIONAL

It was late spring 2011, and we had just finished four fly dates, St. Petersburg-Moscow-Beirut-Rabat, in seven days. We were flying to Barcelona, Spain, to begin a five-stadium show run in the next seven days. The same day our flight arrived in Barcelona, we immediately went to the stadium to begin production load-in for our show the same night. Sleep was not something we were going to get much of over the next several days.

Barcelona went off without a hitch. The stage and venue were ready upon our arrival. All we needed to do was to get our production loaded onto the stage . . . something we had done for eighty-four shows thus far on the tour. No problem.

After the Barcelona show, we went straight into another stadium show in Valencia the next day. Again, nothing eventful transpired. Everything was ready upon our arrival, and we loaded in the show for the eighty-fifth time. Our crew was definitely on their game, and our local promoter staff was a godsend, as they had everything ready for our arrival in every city.

The crew finally got a day of well-deserved rest before our third stadium show in Almeria. We arrived there the day before the show and got some time to walk around this scenic little beach-side city and take in the great weather and culture.

Going into our eighty-sixth show of the world tour, and our third stadium show in four days, we were expecting the day to be as uneventful as any one of the previous two shows in Spain. We were going to load in the same production onto the same locally provided stage that we had seen many times before when in Spain. We were four or five hours into our load-in, with most of the audio, lighting and video floating, and we were working on building the set on deck. What could go wrong? Then . . . CRUNCH!!!

I was in my show office reviewing expenses for the forthcoming show when we all heard a very loud and awful sound coming from the stage. It was one of those sounds you just did not want to hear at a stadium show—metal fracture. What immediately happened next were crew members yelling for everyone to clear the stage. The radios went crazy with chatter about the major stage failure and requesting everyone clear the deck in case of a catastrophic collapse.

What the heck just happened? It turns out there was truss failure in the upstage left corner of the stage. Several load-bearing cross-members of the main roof-carrying truss failed, and the roof dropped 12 to 18 inches in that corner. Well, this day just got a whole lot more interesting. Was this fixable? We had about six hours before doors opened. Could we rig a crane to help support the weight of the roof and continue loading in? Could we bring in welders to install safety cross-members to help support the weight? Could we have a show that night?

A call was made to the owner of the stage. He happened to be less than an hour flight away and took the next available flight to Almeria to check out the damage personally. Because of our high concern for safety, all work under the roof ceased. We were at a stand-still on stage . . . we could not and did not want to do anything until we had the expert assess the damage. We did everything we could off of the stage—finish setting front of house, spotlights, chairs, dressing rooms, anything and everything else we could do in the event we could still have a show that night.

Meanwhile, I was alerting everyone on my end of the stage failure and advising them of our plan of action. Nearly all of the folks on my contact list were on the U.S. west or east coasts . . . what a nice email to wake-up to. There were a few people in London who I put on the email chain as well. People on my list included upper-level management, bookers, operations staff, legal counsel, ticketing and marketing.

If our show was going to cancel, each of those persons on the email chain had an immediate responsibility to act. Tickets sales were to be suspended; bookers and management would check schedules and venue available and try to reschedule; legal would advise of and handle cancellation insurance claims; marketing, in conjunction with artist management, would generate a press release regarding the cancellation/reschedule. And all of this had to happen in a matter of an hour or two if the show did indeed cancel.

The stage's owner arrived on site about 3 p.m. and began to assess the damage. After about thirty minutes of inspection, he came down, and we set up a meeting with all heads of the artist touring party (tour manager, production manager, stage manager, head rigger and tour accountant) and touring promoter party (i.e., me). The stage owner went into some detail of the cause of the fracture, and in his professional opinion, with the help of an on-site crane, the truss and roof would support the weight of the show, and he advised the show could go on. The artist tour manager, a very experienced tour professional, asked a very direct question of the stage owner, "Would you put your family on stage during the show?" He answered, "Yes!"

As an engineering major in college, I had some experience with statics and dynamics in trusses and truss systems. I understood his descriptions of the failure and his resulting conclusions, but I still wasn't convinced it was 100% safe. There was more weight to be added, as we didn't have the entire production floated yet; there would be stage vibrations brought on by the PA when run at show levels; there were moving parts of the lights and video during the show; there were outside factors such as wind and weather; there were people and equipment that would need to be moved about on stage before, during and after the show. I didn't think any of these things were taken into account when he came up with his final assessment. And . . . his family was not in Almeria, so they weren't going to be on the stage during the show.

After the meeting, I met privately with the artist tour and production managers and discussed their assessments as well. We all came to the same conclusion. But before we could do anything, I had to relay our consensus to my folks across the Pond, as it is ultimately their financial responsibility for the show, and they had to give me the go-ahead to proceed with or to cancel the show. The response was almost immediate—cancel the show. There was no way they were going to let the show happen if their "boots-on-the-ground" advised them it was not 100% safe.

The next ball was immediately put in motion. Ticketing folks suspended all ticket sales; booking and management folks could not find an available date in the tour schedule to reschedule the date so marketing folks worked on and sent out a press release notifying ticketholders of the canceled show; legal counsel took my summary of expenses and backup documents and submitted a claim for costs to our cancellation insurance provider; operations staff provided support and guidance through the entire process. By 4:30 p.m., the press release was sent out notifying ticketholders of the cancellation and where they could receive refunds. A crane was brought in and rigged to the roof to provide a safe environment to load-out our equipment, as we had our fourth show in Madrid two days after Almeria. I began collecting all show expenses and backup documents available at the time and began preparing my settlement for the cancellation insurance claim, and, by 9 p.m., we were on our way to Madrid to begin loading in our eighty-seventh show of the tour.

Just another day in the world of rock 'n roll touring . . .

C H A P T E R   1 3

Symphony Music

Production management is a necessary component that supports the different musical genres and large variety of special events and projects. As we have seen, production managers play an integral role in the artistic process, and the same tools and training are required in the world of production managing for symphony orchestras.

Most major national and international cites have a large, multi-million dollar budget symphony orchestra and, depending on the season, can perform up to 50 weeks a year. The Los Angeles Philharmonic, the San Diego Symphony and the San Francisco Symphony are just a few organizations on the West Coast that employ full-time production managers and have a very busy production team.

When we think of production management for an orchestra, you may think "how much is there to do? Don't the musicians just sit there and play music?" The answer may surprise you. The production manager (typically part of orchestra operations) is an invaluable asset to the team and must be heavily relied on throughout the production process. Like in the other genres of art forms, production managers must also rely on their organization and communication skill sets in order to be effective. Jennifer Ringle, Production Manager for the San Diego Symphony, uses her vast set of skills on a daily basis:

> Because an orchestra is so different than theatre or rock and roll, you really have to think globally and be more sensitive to the orchestra musicians. Instruments (age and value!) tunings, concert programming, lighting, audio, air-conditioning/ heating issues (it can't be too hot or too cold in the venue—this can cause great harm to instruments), and union regulations are all a big part of the daily life of a production manager.

Ringle also says, "It's not just about working with the department heads to produce a concert. It's about getting into the heads of the musicians as well." As mentioned above, you may not see actors on stage, but the different art forms share production components including lighting, staging, audio and video components—all of which must work together to ensure the highest-quality final product.

Figure 13.1 Dekelboum Concert Hall in the Clarice Smith Performing Arts Center at the University of Maryland, College Park

Credit: Photo by Ryan Knapp

The orchestra production manager must rely heavily on their tools in the toolkit to be successful at their job. Communication in the orchestra world is no different than that found in theatre or special events. Production managers must communicate clearly, effectively and efficiently. "Advance notice, advance notice, advance notice," says Ringle. "Orchestras are the slowest moving trains in the industry. If you want anything done, you'd better have lots of patience and plan ahead—at times, three years ahead."

One of the most important tools production managers have is their ability to build and preserve relationships with those involved in the project. "You must work as a team," says Ringle. "We really could not pull off the schedule we currently have if we did not have a great working environment." As is true in the various art forms we work in, building and maintaining relationships will assist in getting your goals and tasks completed. How does Ringle do that?

> *Listening and having a real discussion. It's easy to say no. It's better to say "If we say yes, then these things happen." I never want to shut down any real conversation with anyone (even if it seems out of place), but sometimes you just have to find the right way or time and place to have these discussions, and it's not always easy to do.*

RELATIONSHIPS IN ORCHESTRA OPERATIONS

When working with orchestras, the production manager's primary relationship will most likely be with the conductor of the orchestra. This person may also be referred to as maestro

Figure 13.2
Credit: Image © iStock

(Italian meaning "master" or "teacher") or maestra (a female teacher) or music director. Also, like other artistic directors, this person sets the vision for the concert season through programming (determining which music is performed on each concert), inviting guest artists and having the long-term artistic vision for the organization.

In addition to the conductor, you will have other relationships similar to those found in theatre, including the stage manager, stage crew (oftentimes an IATSE (International Alliance of Theatrical Stage Employees) union crew in major U.S. cities), facilities manager, artistic and administrative staff, and musicians (who might be members of a professional musician's union known as the American Federation of Musicians or AF of M.)

Oftentimes, the production manager will meet with the board of directors or other fundraising committees to talk about the organization from a production point of view. These meetings are important because not all of the financial decision makers have a clear understanding of what production is or what it takes to produce a concert. The more they know, the more they can be willing to provide financial support.

WHAT WE DO AS PRODUCTION MANAGERS

How exactly does a production manager fit into orchestra management? Why does a symphony organization need to employ a production manager? Similar to theatre and special events, production values are beginning to increase in the orchestra world, and technical demands are being put on the production staff more and more. With increased artistic elements comes a need for increased organization. While the tasks of the production manager may vary from organization to organization, you can assume that the production manager is involved from the beginning to the end of the creative process. Season planning may be one of the tasks that the production manager gets involved in. Planning plays an essential part of the organization: It establishes the artistic vision through programming, it is used to create the budget and it creates a platform to publicize the season to its subscribers and potential ticket holders. It also can lead to the development of new projects and the need to fund those projects through grants and donations.

Once the season is established, the production manager takes on the daunting task of building the budget. This is one of the most important tasks the production manager does each year. The number of musicians required, venue rental fees, piano rental and tuning costs, guest artist fees, and musician travel expense are just some of the figures you will need to get your season budget approved by the board of directors.

Another important role of the production manager is to determine the rehearsal and performance schedule along with other artistic staff and administrators. The American Federation of Musicians (AF of M) regulations for many of the major orchestras dictate the number of hours per day and per week the musicians can work. This is done to avoid musician fatigue and to avoid overworking their bodies. The production manager must be fully aware of the amount of "services" (a term that refers to each rehearsal or performance) that are allowed per week and be involved in creating the weekly rehearsal schedule. Oftentimes, the production manager is involved with hiring guest artists and arranging housing and transportation.

Figure 13.3

Credit: Image © iStock

Other times, the production manager is securing venues for rehearsal and performances if the concert takes place in an offsite venue.

Once the venue is determined, ordering stage equipment is next on the list of tasks. How many risers are required, and in what configuration will they be needed? Most often, it is the conductor that makes the final determination, but it is your job to get the riser plot executed. Determining the number of chairs required for each "section" of the orchestra is also the job of the conductor and the production manager. (A section is a grouping of musical instruments: first violins, second violins, violas, cellos, double basses, woodwinds, brass and percussion are typical. Section sizes vary depending on the number of musicians required for the piece of music or concert.) You can start to see why this relationship is so important.

The orchestra stage plot typically looks like this: (Note that the woodwinds and brass are made up of different instruments within that section family.)

After the sections are established and chairs and music stands are put in place, the orchestra librarian places the music on the stands. Like a theatre script with blocking notation, all the sheet music has been "bowed" and marked up for each section and for each chair. (Bowing ensures that all string instruments in that section are going in the same direction.) The amount of work preparing music for a symphony orchestra should not be underestimated. The job of librarian requires specific training, organization, attention to detail and concentration.

At this point, the production manager has determined stage shifts (if any), piano moves (if any), guest artist entrances and any other technical needs for the concert and gives that

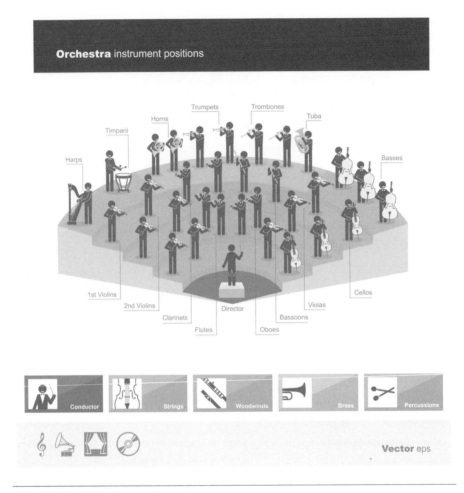

Figure 13.4

Credit: Image © iStock

information to the stage manager, who can now begin to get their book in order. Providing this information to the crew at this point is vital. Audio needs, video playback, stage moves involving chairs, risers, pianos, etc., all need to be communicated as soon as possible.

Once all of these concert factors have been determined, rehearsals can now begin. Typically, a union symphony orchestra will rehearse for 2.5 to three hours per day, four days per week. A typical concert schedule is Friday and Saturday evening and Sunday afternoon. Many of the orchestras also have a touring component, so the production manager is involved in much more than just managing a performance. In the case of the San Diego Symphony, Jennifer Ringle recalls some of the more difficult tasks of taking an eighty-five-piece orchestra to China.

Instrument transportation—because it had the most challenges and angles to deal with. The regulations on cities with ivory, rosewood and other imported woods are difficult to navigate when you are transporting instruments for eighty-five players. Since many of the players had not toured previously, documentation on instruments proving that were made many years prior to restrictions on the materials was tedious. Cargo limitations on shapes, sizes, temperature and weights traveling internationally took multiple hours creating the accurate plan and paper-trail. Also, getting cargo in and out of China and actual transportation within China was also challenging. Lastly, keeping the instruments off the "tarmac" while waiting for baggage loading and passing through customs was one of our other concerns.

Working for a symphony orchestra can be a very rewarding experience for a production manager; producing a major symphonic concert is a challenge and requires a large collaborative effort. The production manager in orchestra management is a vital part of that senior team. Paige Satter, a seasoned production manager in the orchestra world, has this final thought on how to best deal with managing an orchestra.

Blend and balance: it's all you need to know when working with a symphony orchestra. Orchestras work as one unified group. Early on, musicians are taught to listen for "blend and balance" while playing, thus ensuring that no one instrument stands out. This idea holds true when production managing orchestras as well. The orchestra is set up as one group, the musicians enter and exit the stage as one group and concerts occur one series at a time. I find this way of thinking easier to manage than a group of individuals acting independently.

The world of production management in the music business can be a fun and fulfilling job and an alternative to other production management jobs in the performing arts. Many of the same skills used in other disciplines are used in the music business. Use these skills to be the best production manager that you can, either on the road or in the venue.

CASE STUDY—SYMPHONY ORCHESTRA TOURING IN CHINA

CONTRIBUTOR: JENNIFER RINGLE—PRODUCTION MANAGER, SAN DIEGO SYMPHONY

It was two months out, and we were on our way to our first tour in China set to play at the Mong Man Wai Concert Hall in Beijing. I started to connect with each contact at the venues that we were traveling to. I sent an email requesting the piano in Beijing and went about my daily business.

As I was wrapping up my other duties to get ready for China, I had realized that I had not heard back from this particular venue. I had the original email with the requests, including a piano, but I never got a response. When I asked my contact in the administration office about the piano, I was told, "Don't worry. It has been

Figure 13.5   Jennifer Ringle

handled." I didn't worry too much, and away we went on tour. All seventy-five members of the San Diego Symphony, a sea container full of very expensive orchestral equipment and our staff all departed for our tour, beginning at Carnegie Hall in New York, then on to China. It was an exciting time.

When we arrived at the venue, the piano wasn't out onstage. I talked to a young stagehand and asked for the piano. The translators were off with another group of the staff, so I was on my own as far as requesting the piano. It wasn't great, as the stagehand went and got his crew chief, who then came back and in very broken English was able to say, "We didn't know you needed a piano."

After a slight pause, we again requested the piano, and the crew chief said, "No problem—we will go get one for you." So down the huge pit elevator we went, four stories below the orchestra level, and pulled out what seemed to be the best piano in the inventory.

The next words are what you don't really want to hear at a time like this, which were, "This piano hasn't been tuned in months." We giggled at first and then requested a tuner, much like we do when we are in the United States. The problem was, in China, you needed to reserve a tuner two weeks in advance, and we were literally three hours away from the show. I was told no tuners were available, but they would try. I asked feverishly for them to find a tuner, and we continued our ascent to the stage level with the piano.

Upon getting the piano set, my next job was to come up with an alternative solution if we couldn't find a tuner. We had to get the piano tuned. There wasn't an option for it to not happen. The building staff was still frantically looking for a tuner to come in on an emergency run. It was proving more difficult by the phone call.

My staff and I huddled and came up with the idea that perhaps Igor, our concert master, could tune the piano. He was certainly talented in violin playing and had a great ear. So we got Igor. Now we asked, does anyone have a tuning key for the piano? No one had a tuning key available at that moment. We huddled back. Our director of operations had a crescent wrench, and one of our artistic administrators had an iPhone app that had a tuner in it. It was crude, but we were ready to go.

As we were about to start the tune (this was now thirty minutes before doors), the tuner showed up in a harried state. We held doors for five minutes and got the job done. We all held our breath for a little while there. The show went on, and the San Diego Symphony sounded amazing.

In hindsight, I should have known better. Never trust someone else's answer unless it is from the source . . . and in writing. I should have had a confirmation email from the venue confirming our need for a piano. I showed them the email I sent, but they just missed the piano. A simple follow-up on my part would have alleviated some of the anxiety on show day. Lesson learned. Oh, and I also carry a tuning key in my kit now.

Presenting

"The only thing you have to sell is service."

- Carolyn Satter, Production and Facilities Manager
for the San Diego Theatres

It may be difficult to imagine that production managers may actually have to "sell" something. Mostly, we are expensing and spending money on things such as materials, supplies, venue rentals, etc., and we aren't really in the business of "selling" anything. But that is different for the production manager in a presenting theatre. Unlike the production manager in a producing theatre, where we have to answer to directors, designers and upper management, the production manager in presenting theatre has to answer to "clients" who are renting the theatre to produce their own event. Being a presenting theatre production manager has a mixed and varied set of job duties and functions; this chapter will help you determine the similarities and differences of this exciting world.

Carolyn Satter, Production and Facilities Manager for the San Diego Theatres, agrees and says that

> the theatre that creates a product and develops a set, costumes, lights, etc., is a "producing" theatre. A "presenting" theatre means we, the theatre managers and owners, present a wide span of entertainment or other types of presentational options for a paying audience. We may have a dance recital one day, a two-day university graduation the next day and then the national tour of Wicked loading in for a three-week run." She continues, "We don't limit who we rent to. We are a four wall rental house."

The presenting theatre can be known as a four wall rental because when you rent the theatre, it comes basically with "four walls" and little else. Some four wall theatres come equipped with

Figure 14.1 Carolyn Satter

some basic lighting and sound gear or they can have no equipment at all. One analogy may be to consider the producing theatre as a film studio, complete with writing staff and directors to produce and make the movie. On the flip side, the presenting theater may be seen as a movie theatre, simply a place to present the movie. Either way you look at it, production managers in presenting theatres not only have the traditional duties of the production manager, but they also have an extra level of customer service they will need to master in order to be effective in their jobs.

So just what is customer service all about, and how do you define "service"? What extra steps does the production manager have to take? Satter goes on to say that

> *customer service means that you have to hear what the client is saying, what they are trying to say and understand what they would like the event to look like in the end. We need to talk about the concept; we must offer suggestions and help them produce their event. That's our job. We have an embracing attitude in our venues. That's what customer service is all about.*

For Eric Fliss, Managing Director of the South Miami-Dade Cultural Arts Center, customer service is all about response time to the client:

Figure 14.2

Credit: Photo by Ryan Knapp

The client is expecting me to be able to turn around a cost estimate quickly. That is customer service. In order to do that, I need my team to evaluate the technical rider. By evaluating the rider carefully, it tells the client that "we care" about your event. The rider will help the production manager figure out what equipment we have and what we need to get and to submit estimated expenses to me. That also has to be done in a timely manner. And THAT is how a production manager provides customer service.

"A great skill for a presenting production manager to have is amnesia: forgetting entirely what you did last time. By having amnesia, it makes the producer be obliged to look at it with new eyes and tell you exactly what is coming in the door in the current show. If anyone ever says to me, 'it is like last year,' I immediately tell them, "I have no recollection of what you did, so let's start at the beginning."

- Bill Foster, Production Manager at the John F. Kennedy Center for the Performing Arts

Production managers in presenting theatres are in a unique situation where they must answer to clients renting or producing in their theatres. While there are riders to adhere to and contracts in place to help guide us, oftentimes the group renting the theatre may be new at producing or in the city for the first time, and the production manager is instrumental in helping to get the show up and running. The skill sets for being a production manager in a presenting theatre model are the same as in the other artistic disciplines: understanding the communication process and how to get things done efficiently. This is extremely important when it comes to dealing with clients and listening to what they need. Satter continues and says that

> Our core skill sets are the same, with an additional skill added, what I call 'insight' skill. That's the ability to stand back and watch a series of events unfold while being aware of any red flags that may be coming down the line. That takes time and experience. You can't really teach insight, but if you've had enough errors on your production management judgment, your toolbox gets filled with ways to solve problems. That's what I mean by insight.

As you begin to gain experience, you will begin to gain the insight that Satter discusses, and you, too, will be able to apply that to a situation where you can help the client save some money or time.

"The production manager is oftentimes the person that has the most contact with the client or artist. It is essential that they understand the vision and are sympathetic to that vision and to the artists. You should instill confidence that you are working toward that shared vision by demonstrating that you are balancing costs and cost controls along with maintaining a high level of service."

- Eric Fliss, Managing Director for South Miami-Dade Cultural Arts Center

ADVANCING THE SHOW

To "advance" is to "get ahead in position or time." To "advance a show" means to get out in front of the show as early as possible and start getting the production details worked out. Many production details will need to be advanced, and clear, concise information should be at the forefront of your work. Additionally, understanding the technical contract rider is of great importance for the production manager in presenting theatre. Much like the music business, the presenting theatre production manager must be adept at reading and interpreting the rider. The presenting production manager doesn't need to be an expert on the show that's coming in; rather, they need to be an expert in understanding the physical limitations of their own venue.

Figure 14.3 Eric Fliss

What are other core duties that the presenting production manager deals with? Some smaller shows that come in may not have a production manager, and the presenting production manager may have to act as the client's production manager. Here are a few things you will need to know in order to be an effective production manager in presenting theatre.

GET THE SHOW INFORMATION / READ THE RIDER

Once the booking department of the presenting theatre has signed the contracts for the show, they should send you, the production manager, the technical rider to peruse. This rider will look similar to the riders found in the music business and will contain information such as labor calls, ticketing needs (or production holds) and technical equipment requirements, such as line set schedules, light plots and audio plots. If there is no technical rider, then the fun for the production manager really begins, as you will have to do your best to track down as much information as possible from anyone who will help you. Rely on your lighting staff, audio staff and other key personnel to help you come up with a basic lighting plot and audio input list based on what you know.

> **TIP**—Try tracking down where the act or talent has played before. You may be able to contact the production manager at that venue and ask what details you may need to know.

LABOR CALLS AND MANAGEMENT

Labor calls, labor budget estimates and labor management will be one of your larger tasks that will need to be completed, and it is your job to try and have a good working relationship with the crew. Know your crew and help them understand what you are working toward. Fliss agrees and says that

> *every venue or facility has a mission, and it is essential for everyone working in that venue to know and understand that mission. It is the production manager's job to convey the mission and to establish expectations that are aligned to the mission.*

With regard to the rider, it should clearly indicate how much labor is needed for the load-in, run of show and load-out. In the case of the event that doesn't have a rider, you, as the production manager, will need to determine the labor calls based on your past experiences or previous show files. Additionally, you will be the labor liaison between the client and the crew chief to ensure that breaks are taken and that no overtime is being anticipated. No one likes surprises, especially the client and especially when it comes to money. Once you assess the event labor needs, you will need to create a budget for the client. Make sure the client knows all of the anticipated expenses ahead of time. You should prepare a written estimate and have the client sign the estimate.

> Most of the larger "road houses" will have an IATSE contract or "yellow card" in place, so you should be sure you understand all of the working conditions with regard to breaks, meals, hours worked, etc. On many IATSE calls there will be a crew chief, also known as a steward. This steward will work with you to ensure that proper breaks are taken and that crews are properly released at the end of the day.

The labor budget should be built around the worst-case scenario, taking into account the various rules that you might be under. Some production managers will do a "contingency" line item on the labor budget that covers unforeseen issues, including a longer load-in or technical challenges with equipment. This contingency can be anywhere between 5% and 10%. Some production managers prefer to not use a contingency (contingencies were covered in chapter 2 on the Money and Budget). The labor call will include the number of load-in crew needed, number of run crew needed for the performance and number of crew needed for load-out. As mentioned earlier, supervising the labor crew will be your main focus for the run of the event, as the production manager acts as the "crew chief" and must be sure that the load-in and event are happening on schedule. Keeping a careful watch on the situation and assessing the labor needs of the production happen regularly. This is where it's helpful to have that "insight" that Satter discussed earlier. Being able to quickly assess and ascertain the labor needs if things aren't going as planned is a true skill of the production manager. It is your job to keep labor on track and on budget.

> **TIP**—If you start to see that things aren't going as planned and that the load-in schedule may be affected, make sure you talk to your client as soon as possible about the possible overages with regard to the labor budget. Try to do so without an "alarmist" approach but rather with a clear and concise conversation on "where we are at" and what needs to be done to stay on target both schedule-wise and financially. This would also be a good time for you to present options for saving money or offer a different solution to a problem that could result in a cost savings.

TICKETING NEEDS OR PRODUCTION HOLDS

One of the first things you should do as the presenting production manager is to scan the rider for any production holds for ticketing or seating. A production hold means that some technical equipment may either take up the existing seat or obstruct the view of the audience member, thus making the seat unsellable. Once you review the rider, get with your box office manager to secure the production holds prior to tickets going on sale. Share this information with your client. This is a very important step and shouldn't be overlooked, as the consequences on show night are not fun for the house manager. Having to relocate patrons that can't see around a speaker stack or other obstruction is an unnecessary and avoidable step for the front-of-house staff if the production manager does their job with regard to production holds. Don't forget that part of your job as production manager is to release the production holds once the show loads in and you can check if the originally planned obstructions are still an issue. If not, you will then be able to release the tickets back to the box office for sale to the general public. As in rock and roll and other artistic disciplines, you shouldn't forget this very important part of your job and your day.

TECHNICAL EQUIPMENT NEEDS

Much like the riders in the other artistic disciplines, the rider for show in the presenting production manager's world will contain information on either the equipment that is being provided by the production or what equipment needs to be sourced locally. Make sure you read this thoroughly and do as much as possible to acquire the elements needed for the production. If the show doesn't have a rider, then it will be up to you to discuss the needs of the event with the client. This is where your customer service skills will come into play a great deal. Satter says:

> as we speak to a perspective client at our theatres, the first thing I ask is "What is it that you're doing, and how do you want to do it?", and we then offer suggestions regarding the technical and labor elements. Some clients we will become far more involved with, and some we may not get involved with at all from a technical standpoint.

DRESSING ROOMS

With regard to dressing rooms, the presenting production manager may get involved with the touring stage manager or the local producer to assign dressing rooms for the show. Careful note should be taken when reading the dressing room rider, as it may contain language that allows certain performers to be on stage level or have a restroom in their dressing room. Sometimes minor hospitality requests will need to be addressed. Proper signage should be put up indicating directions to dressing rooms as well as dressing room assignment postings on the dressing rooms doors.

MANAGING THE EVENT BUDGET/SHOW SETTLEMENT

> "Budget, budget, budget . . . because many things are contingent on an accurate estimate, such as artist fees and ticket pricing, a good advance is essential in establishing accurate costs to avoid surprises."
>
> - Eric Fliss, Managing Director for the South Miami-Dade Cultural Arts Center

Another one of the other main duties of the presenting production manager will be to monitor costs associated with getting the show presented, primarily in the area of equipment and labor. Monitoring labor calls involves keeping track of regular and overtime hours worked, meal breaks, meal penalty pay, etc. Keeping your client informed of the status of the labor budget should also be one of your top priorities throughout the day. All of these costs are then sent to the theatre manager, who will do a night-of-show "settlement" and pay the client the profits from the evening after deducting costs of venue rent, crew costs and equipment costs.

Figure 14.4

Credit: Image © iStock

> "We have to be transparent in order to be successful. You must understand that every decision you make has a financial impact on the people who rent your venue. The last thing I need to do is surprise someone at the end of the night when I present the invoice to the client who has rented the theatre."
>
> - Carolyn Satter, Production and Facilities Manager
> for the San Diego Theatres

Being a presenting production manager can have its challenges. It can also have great rewards, as you will get to work with a large group of very diverse projects and people. You get to be the one who is in on many of the decisions, both financial and operational or creative. You get to be the one that understands how the pieces fit together and how the collaborative relationships between front of house, ticketing, security, etc., all work together. You have to know what successful collaboration looks like, and that simply comes with experience and time. Satter closes with this wisdom:

> *During the event, you have to be the cheerleader of the team you're working for. You've got to be the one . . . whether it's the client, a stagehand, a security guard or a member of housekeeping, if they come to you with a situation, you've got to be the one that says let me take care of it.*

And THAT is selling service!

CASE STUDY—YO-YO MA

CONTRIBUTOR: BILL FOSTER—PRODUCTION MANAGER AT THE JOHN F. KENNEDY CENTER FOR THE PERFORMING ARTS

One of the most difficult things for the production manager in presenting theatre to deal with is the "cycle" you get into when doing repetitive shows. Because you have shows that come in with some regularity, or the presenter comes in annually, they get into the habit of thinking, "Now that we have done this show, we know what we are doing." They tend to give you less and less information with the notion that "it was just like last time," but the reality is that no two shows are ever alike.

A great example is world-renowned cellist Yo-Yo Ma. Because he had come to the Kennedy Center regularly for a few years, we all assumed it was the same show when we saw his name pop up on the calendar. It's just Yo-Yo Ma. How complicated can it be? All you need is a chair and music stand and concert lighting. That's it. Well, it can be very complicated, especially when the production manager neglects to ask "what is your show this year?" A week or so before the show, we see some marketing information that mentions Yo-Yo Ma with the Silk Road Ensemble, a twenty-five piece orchestra, which needs to be fully amplified, with a stage monitor system, as well as theatrical lighting. Luckily, we have a fabulous stage crew, and the resources to respond to changes like this gracefully.

We get into the cycle. It's especially difficult when doing a repeat show each year. Yo-Yo Ma is a radical example, but we have done repeat shows here at the Kennedy Center many times, and we tend to hear over the years "it's the same as last time," so no one writes anything down from the producer's side of the production.

Figure 14.5   Concert Hall at the John F. Kennedy Performing Arts Center

Figure 14.6

Credit: Image ©iStock

You go to your files from the past few years and see that nothing has been written down or saved. You keep your own production files, of course, but everyone's files and everyone's recollections of "last time" are different.

Remember that NO two shows are EVER the same. The exact same orchestra, a year later, on the same date, into the same concert hall can be radically different. A new conductor may want added risers or some new percussion configuration, and it will be much different than last year. Also, the theatre's schedule will have something to do with how the current year's show may go. In an organization like the Kennedy Center, we may have had a different orchestra rehearsal the previous night. I may have 120 chairs, music stands and orchestral lighting set, and we would be halfway set up for the current show to come in. In that case, I may only need an hour to set up. If I had a rock and roll gig the night before and we had to leave by midnight, we may have three hours of strike to do before loading in the simple orchestra show. All of these factors affect how we work. So, the bottom line is that even if it seems like it's the same show; no two shows are ever the same. It's also getting more and more important to ask more questions these days. For the first twenty years of my career, you could count on a string quartet being a string quartet.

Today, a string quartet may come with a video wall behind them or an aerialist swinging high above their heads. The moment you start thinking it's just a string quartet, you're done.

Another example was that we were presenting a Broadway vocalist as part of a cabaret series. I called the producer and asked if he had any information about the next presentation. His response was "it's just a guy and a piano, how hard can it be?" Well, after a couple of phone calls, I come to find out it was a guy with a piano, six other musicians, backup singers who needed an in-ear monitor system and a complicated rehearsal schedule, which made things more challenging.

"It's just a guy with a piano."

It's a temptation for everyone involved in presenting shows to get into the cycle of "it's just like last year." Treat each show as if it was new, because the reality is that it *is* new, it *is* different and, yes, you do need to get answers to all of the questions again.

Co-productions

Popularity is increasing for performing arts organizations to work together to produce a show or event. This growth in co-productions (or "co-pros" for short) can be motivated by companies hoping to decrease costs and time constraints or expose their audiences to different work from across the country or internationally. A complete explanation and exploration of co-productions could fill an entire book, but here are a few key points to consider if you find yourself producing a show with another organization.

WHAT IS THE GOAL OF THE CO-PRODUCTION?

You should understand why this project was proposed and conceived. Often, the artistic leadership of the partnering organizations initiates the process. Perhaps the organizations have similar artistic goals, and they hope an artistic partnership will allow the organizations to learn from each other. Or the opposite could be true—the partnering organizations are artistically different and want to explore those differences through the co-production process. It is also possible that the artistic leadership of the partnering organizations had a previous relationship and are excited to work together once more. Whatever the reason, understand it, for it will guide your work to come.

> "Not every partnership is a co-production. Imprecise use of language can lead to confusion from the start."
>
> - Co-Production Handbook, resource from the OPERA America Technical/Production Forum

WORKING WITH ANOTHER PRODUCTION MANAGER

As we have stated before, the role of a production manager can be a lonely one. Working on a co-production is a great way to collaborate with a knowledgeable and kindred colleague. This

Figure 15.1 *A Midsummer Night's Dream*—a co-production between the University of Maryland, College Park and the National Academy of Chinese Theatre Arts in Beijing

Credit: Photo by Stan Barouh

collaboration allows you the opportunity to learn new techniques and practices. However, this can also be challenging, as there are now two (or more) people making decisions normally made by one. For a co-production, establishing positive working relationships with everyone is important, but the working relationship you establish with your fellow production managers could be vital. Clear communications early on about how you will work together and regular check-ins will make certain communication is effective and feelings are not being hurt, nor are toes being stepped on.

> "Working on an international co-production was the largest learning curve I have ever experienced. Not only did we all need to understand the culture differences, but their way of producing theatre is completely different than ours. They did not have a production manager nor understand what that position was for. I had my work cut out for me and, in the end, won them over to the necessity of our profession!"
>
> - Cary Gillett, Production Manager at the University of Maryland, College Park

BUDGET

As mentioned before, co-productions might be a way to use funds more economically. More can be achieved with funds from two or more partnering organizations, or savings can be achieved with each organization spending less. Clearly communicating the budget and cost-sharing expectations should be done at the beginning of the co-production process so there is never any confusion. Create an itemized list of expected expenses and which organization is going to pay for what. The importance of careful budgeting and clearly identifying financial obligations is paramount. The bane of many co-pros has been ambiguous communication on financial matters. Not only should you clearly identify and communicate budget responsibilities but make certain to have a discussion about what occurs if production expenses exceed projected budgets. Are there emergency funds to cover unforeseen expenses? Make sure that budget conversations happen continually. Managing a co-production can be a complicated endeavor. Foreseeing every budget concern or possibility will better prepare you for the entire process.

SCHEDULE

Scheduling is not as simple as placing two different production schedules next to each other and calling it done. Scheduling a co-production can be incredibly challenging, as you now must consider at least double the amount of items, personnel and scenarios. Begin with deciding who will open the show first and when, then work backward from this date to schedule the rest of the originating production and work forward from the same date to schedule the subsequent productions.

Important things to consider:

- How does each organization structure their tech process? Should they match for ease of the co-pro?
- How much time will it take to strike, move and load in to another theatre?
- Will brush-up rehearsals be needed prior to the second tech?

PHYSICAL PRODUCTION

It is unlikely that the partnering organizations will have identical performance venues. Every theatre is unique. Even two proscenium theatres can be different from each other in many ways. It will be important for your designers to have venue drawings for the spaces early in the process so that they can design effectively for the uniqueness of each space. For example, if one of the spaces is smaller, it might make sense to select the dimensions of the smaller stage to use as the footprint for the set. You will then be assured that the set will fit in every space.

Another important determination to be made is whether or not all elements of the physical production will be shared by both organizations. If there is a shared cast, then costumes will likely be shared. Props (depending upon the size) can usually be shared. It might cost more to

Figure 15.2 The College-Conservatory of Music at the University of Cincinnati

Credit: Photo by Adam Zeek, www.zeekcreative.com

transport a set to the next venue than it would be to build it a second time; however, this dupli-cation of materials might not appeal to your organization's environmental consciousness. The partnering organizations will have to decide what is the most cost effective and stays within the organization's guiding principles.

STAFFING

In most situations, permanent staff of the partnering organizations will participate in the co-production (i.e., technical directors, master electricians, costumers), but what about those who need to be hired in—performers, designers, stage managers, run crew, etc.? Hiring the same performers and design team for each presentation of the project is important so as to establish continuity. There is nothing stopping you from changing the stage management team or run crew if necessary; however, if it can be avoided, it will certainly help the productions run smoother. If the partnering organizations are located in the same city, these hiring decisions will be much easier. If the performance spaces are a great distance apart, the logistics (i.e., travel, housing, per diem) for sharing stage managers and/or running crew will become more complicated, no more complicated, however, than the sharing of performers. One way to overcome this challenge is to hire people who are native to each location. For example—half the cast and crew live by location A and the other cast by location B. This way, for each sec-tion of the production, only half of the people need to be housed. This could work similarly with the design team.

AFTER CLOSING

Before the co-production process begins, you should have a discussion with the partnering organization(s) about what happens after the production has concluded. If one organization paid for the costumes, then it seems likely they would keep the costumes, but if the costs were shared, then who gets them? Perhaps they stay as a shared resource, and one organization agrees to store them. Or perhaps both organizations cover the cost of a shared rental facility.

The future of the production is always something to keep in mind. Is it possible for one of the two organizations to remount the show on their own? If so, how would that work in terms of billing, income, etc.? If another organization wants to rent part of the physical production, who would receive the rental income? These are important questions to consider before they come up.

> **TIP**—Put it all in writing! Make a contract that both organizations sign with all of the details that have been worked out. Don't risk jeopardizing your relation-ship with another organization or production manager.

CASE STUDY—CO-PRODUCTIONS IN OPERA

CONTRIBUTOR: KAREN QUISENBERRY—PRODUCTION DIRECTOR OF MINNESOTA OPERA

Co-productions and co-commissions are very common in opera. If it's a new production of an existing opera, then you would be co-producing with a group of opera companies, but if it's a new opera, you are most likely co-commissioning. It's too cost prohibitive to produce a whole season of shows on your own. If one company can pay $100,000 into a production that will eventually cost $700,000 to produce, it allows them to know they have a product for their season. To be able to produce these shows with other companies is the only way some opera companies survive. There is always (or should be) an administering co-producer who takes care of contracting all of the key personnel—composer, director, designers, etc. This is not a term I have heard outside of the opera world. I don't think they have this in regional theatre.

We often solicit other companies to co-commission with us. It helps lock it in and give it a little weight and strength to the work, knowing it will have a second life. Even though we've workshopped a new opera, it just isn't quite finished, and it needs a second or third life. We'll keep seeking co-producers throughout the process; many want to wait and see what it's going to look like or if it's getting good

Figure 15.3 Karen Quisenberry

reviews before they sign on. It's possible to have a company come on with a new opera as co-producer following the premier, but they take on a different financial responsibility in that they don't contribute toward the pay of the composer and librettist; they just come on for the physical part of the production.

We are in the process of co-commissioning a new opera called *Dinner at Eight*, which will premiere in March 2017. I am trying to infuse it with the knowledge I have gained in the last three years so we can try to avoid the pitfalls we have suffered through before. A unique situation with this production is that the composer has set deadlines for when the co-commissioners must be known. I think this was driven by his agent. This is very uncommon, but it's okay. If you are truly co-producing and only engaging with people who are a part of the creative process from the beginning, then the early dates allow for that. It also guarantees that it will be seen and not die on the vine. It's good motivation for us as the originating producer to get the right companies involved.

We've gone about selecting our co-commissioners in a very strategic way. The director of the opera is the general director of another company, so naturally they want to be involved. We've engaged a conductor that is also a general director of their own company—so we have three right there. Now we're really trying to target additional companies that are interested in new work and/or this composer. We try to keep our ear to the ground to find where this might fit. I hope I'll have six partners in the end. I'll draft a letter of intent for them to sign agreeing that they are coming on board. I have high hopes for this one, since the three partners are all deeply invested. It seems to be the better way to go about it. The more investment they have financially and creatively, the better the process will be.

We will all need to agree on the creative team. That's mostly director driven. If all of the companies trust the director, then they will trust the team the director puts together. If they don't, they will likely want to have more of a say. They want to know they are getting a good product, and having confidence in the team and the process will help that. Most companies want the premiere, but the truth is you don't; you want to let the first company work out the kinks. Really, you want to be the third presenter, because by then you are getting a mostly finished product. We've learned an important lesson that we need to premiere the piece if we are administering and initiating it. If it's in our theatre first, then we can work out the kinks and get things right before it moves on to other companies. We administered a work recently that we did not premiere, and it put a big strain on our relationship with the company that did. We just were not in a situation to be able to address things in the way we want to do them.

A production that was very successful for this company was *Silent Night*. It was a behemoth of a production, but it worked really well. Every company that has produced it after us has had to make some major accommodations to make it work in their theatres, but they are willing to do so since the production was really good. Everyone is willing to make it work if they know it's a good product. It premiered in 2011 with us and four co-producers. It was rented three times last year, and every one of us is getting a little bit back from that income. It's not a bad thing at the end of your fiscal year to get a rental check from another company.

Figure 15.4   Silent Night

Credit: Photo by Michal Daniel for Minnesota Opera

It costs about $60,000 to rent the set and costumes. The percentage of the rental income each company receives is equal to the percentage they paid into the original production. Designers also get a royalty that is based on the size of the company. Opera America ranks companies from level 1–4 (similar to a LORT theatre breakdown) depending upon their operating budget. The larger the company's budget, the higher the fee the designer would get. It's important to keep those royalties fees manageable so that it does not become cost prohibitive and that the work keeps getting produced. It's a win-win if we can keep it all in a scale that allows for everyone to participate in the right kind of way.

Whenever another company wants to rent one of our productions, I always recommend our cast and musical director. They know the show and, in the case of the performers, the costumes already fit them. Most companies want their own people, so they will rarely use the original cast. I wish our discipline paid more attention to this so we did not have to alter clothes. The administering producer is the one who creates costumes, and it's best to make sure you have a seam allowance built into all costumes for this reason.

Another project that is in the works for us is *Cold Mountain*. It premiered at Santa Fe Opera this past summer, and we will take it on in spring 2018. It's been interesting to be in the non-producing end of the production. Right now, I'm just watching all the info grow in the Dropbox. I've made some specific choices about how we will engage with the production. Sante Fe is an outdoor space, and I did not think it would be helpful to send my technical director to see it loaded in there. I'm going to wait until Philly does it, since they are another indoor venue. I think my TD will learn a lot more from that experience. And I'm glad we're not the first indoor theatre to take it on. I'm glad Philly gets to solve the problem on how to fit an outdoor show into an indoor theatre.

The time between the Santa Fe production and Philly's production is not long. Artistically, it's unlikely there will be many changes due to this. Then there is a big span of time before we get it, so we anticipate lots of changes to the music, as the composer and librettist will have had two productions under their belt and the time to reflect back and see what has worked.

Creating co-productions and co-commissions is an interesting business model, but I think in this art form it's important. For a production manager, it creates different challenges, because you have to have a broad perspective. It's important to create strong relationships with other companies and production managers.

Touring

> "As a touring production manager, I represent the production, the company, the look, the entire picture and the way everything works together. Know your show, and know what's critical and what's ideal. That way you know when to fight, when to compromise and when to really make a stand, and that's diplomacy."
>
> - Perry Silvey, former Director of Production, New York City Ballet

Broadway tours and other large tours are very different from standard regional theatre productions. Touring is about bringing a great show *to* the guests. As you learned in chapter 9, the scale of the show is usually much larger than regional theatre, and the tour will always have a technical rider. A tour, which loads in and out, has to go together, come apart, go into and out of trucks every single week and has to be built to withstand the rigors of touring. The show must also conform to fit into a truck, typically 8 feet x 9 feet x 53 feet. Because of this, truck space and efficiency are paramount on the road. Understanding how this all works with the technical rider is essential for the successful production manager.

As we have learned in previous chapters, production managers must be flexible, adaptable and diplomatic. As a touring production manager, you will have to rely on these very important traits. On tour, it's about learning other ways of adaptation and being flexible, as every show in every city may call for a different set of answers for different circumstances.

> "The theatre and touring business is flexible and always changing. Have an open mind and understand that, to do your best job, you need to be flexible, and understand that different circumstances call for different answers, and that's ok."
>
> - Kim Fisk, Production Stage Manager,
> first national tour, *The Book of Mormon*

Figure 16.1
Credit: Image © iStock

In the flexible world of touring, some touring companies are able to bring in their own full production, and some travel with partial or no production. Partial production means that you are only bringing a part of your show's requirements to the venue, and the rest of your needs will be supplied locally via the contract rider. Carrying no production at all means that 100% of the tour's needs will be supplied locally via the rider. Once the show's production company or production manager has been selected, they, along with the show's lead carpenter, will put together the show's technical contract rider. The technical rider, one of the most important documents to a production manager, will include such items as the show's lighting plots and lighting equipment needs, as well as audio plots and audio equipment needs. Power and other electrical items and needs are also discussed in details. Dressing room, quick change booth space and size of the front of house mix positions are all included in the rider that the production company and production manager create and maintain.

The production managers on tour must be ready to make changes on a moment's notice based on the limitations of other resources such as time, the venue's physical limitations and labor requirements. All will need to be taken into account when making decisions on the road. On tour, questions need to be answered quickly and efficiently so we do not waste our resources.

The best way to prepare for answering these questions quickly and efficiently is to know your show inside out and understand all of the inner workings of not only the scenic elements but the rigging plot, light plot, focus chart, audio cues, etc. Perry Silvey, former Director of Production for the New York City Ballet, says, "Not every theatre is the same. You know you're going to adapt. You have to quickly decide if that's a compromise I can live with or that's the one I can't. The earlier you make the right decisions, the more time you save and the better your show ends up looking. Knowing when to be flexible and when not to be flexible is also very important. There are times you have to demand for things and times you have to save your fight for the important moments." As you can see, knowing your show is important. So what tools can we use in order to know our show? Start out with getting it all out on paper. Get your load in and performance schedules done early so others can comment and get back to you.

TIP—Remember that shows on the road always seem to need more time, so plan accordingly when preparing your schedules.

Starting with a site visit is also always advisable when resources allow. Having a real look at the actual site can answer many of your questions ahead of time. If, for instance, the front of house mix position is too small, accommodations must be made to accompany the footprint of the front of house mix position. Seats may need to be *killed*, and that would obviously affect the box office. During your site visit, you may also look at the backstage space, looking for wing space for set carts and quick change booths. (For more on site visits, see chapter 17)

During the 1990s, many large touring theatres were reconfigured to accommodate the huge production spaces needed for Andrew Lloyd Webber's *Phantom of the Opera*. That tour really set the standard at the time for theatre renovations, as many theatres had infrastructure changes to accommodate the huge production. Today, it is not uncommon to hear that "If your theatre can fit *Phantom of the Opera*, it can fit any show!"

You should also get to know the building you are going into. Get the venue's technical specification packet, or check their website for technical specifications. By understanding the theatre's layout, you will have a much better chance of figuring out if the show will fit into the venue. Compare what is in the theatre with what is required by the rider. By knowing this information, you will have a better communicative process with the venue's production manager, and this will make your *advance* go much smoother.

Early in the process, you should establish a relationship with the venue's production manager and get the advance started. Getting this relationship solidified early will help relieve or resolve many of your potential issues. It is always nicer to get off the bus and meet someone you have already established a relationship with.

Figure 16.2
Credit: Image © iStock

You should also understand any labor regulations in that city or that particular building you are going into. Find out if the venue uses IATSE labor, and make sure you understand all of the working conditions of the contract beforehand. Is this an IATSE yellow card show? (More on yellow cards later in this chapter.) Knowing when overtime begins or what triggers a "meal penalty" becomes your responsibility. Are separate truck loaders or separate equipment pushers required on this contract? There will always be new challenges with labor when you get to the venue, so you should be prepared to discuss any such challenges. Maybe the full crew didn't report at the call time, or a rigger forgot a piece of climbing equipment. Things happen, so be flexible and ready to alter your labor plan if needed.

> Many IATSE stage calls may have "none working" department heads. Don't fear, as that doesn't mean they aren't working. It just means that they are managing people and are not required to be part of the counted crew for load-in, show and load-out.

You should try to know your local crew's names. This will go a long way with creating a good working relationship and diplomacy while you are visiting another venue. According to Silvey,

> *Diplomacy is an important element to touring. You should know the local crew's names, be a calm production manager and give the local crews a good feeling that you know what you want. Crews really appreciate it when the production manager knows the*

show needs. If you're calm and have a view and have clear knowledge of your show, your crew will respect that.

As for setting high expectations for the local crew, Silvey says,

Most people respond well to striving for high standards, as long as they are treated with respect and directness. It seems to me a way to get the best out of people. We try not to scream and yell or make derogatory jokes, but make the local crew feel like they are an important part of what we are trying to achieve, the same way our ballet masters and dancers and musicians make us feel. We are a team, and we try to give the locals a chance to join the team.

Always remember, when on tour, you are a guest in their venue, not the production manager of that venue!

The production manager on tour also has the cast and touring crew to take care of. The proper nurturing of the talent is no different on the road than it is in a home-based venue.

When going into the venue for the first time, you, along with stage management, should make sure the dressing rooms are clean and workable and appropriately marked. Clear way-

Figure 16.3   Brooklyn Academy of Music—Harvey Theatre
Credit: Photo by Ryan Knapp

finding or signage should be put up around the venue, indicating clearly where things are, such as the green room, exits to front of house or the wardrobe department. Many times when on tour, large "runways" of white gaffer's tape on the floor indicates which direction the talent should go. Either way, make sure you have a clear pathway and proper signage backstage.

> **TIP**—Before you put tape on the floors, check with the local venue manager to make sure tape is allowed on the floors' finishes!

The wardrobe department and technical staff will need their space and their work boxes in the right place. Company management needs their room, as well. As the production manager, you should try to anticipate what everyone will need in the theater. The musicians also need some care, whether in laying out the orchestra pit or making sure they have changing rooms, as well. The first day in a new theater is always a bit of a challenge, with people trying to find their way around the theatre and the neighborhood. Production managers should do their best to be ready to answer the plethora of questions that may come their way. "Where can we get coffee?" is always a favorite.

Many factors will determine if a show is going to go on the road or not. The most likely of these factors is the ability to make money for the show's producers or investors. If the show is a hit, it is most likely destined to be put on a national and sometimes global tour. In New York City, this is where a production "company" comes into the planning process. The general management of the Broadway tour will hire the production "company" to design, build and production *manage* the Broadway tour.

Aurora Productions in New York is an example of a production company that produces first-class Broadway productions and tours of shows that have already happened in New York. (Some tours can run simultaneously as the Broadway show.) Usually brought on early in the process, Aurora, which has the production manager on staff, begins to put the show together. Usually working six months to a year out, scenic plans are sent out to scenic studios for the competitive bidding process. Simultaneously, the production manager is getting bids on lighting packages, audio packages and video equipment. Labor requirements for loading in, running and loading out the show are also under the watchful eye of the production manager assigned to that show from the production company.

If a Broadway show decides to tour, the production manager is usually offered the Broadway tour if the same production company produces the tour. This is known as "right of first refusal" in some contracts. (For more on right of first refusal, see chapter 7.) If that production manager decides that they do not want to continue in the role as the production manager, another production manager will be assigned to the show. The same "right of first refusal" usually holds true for Equity production stage managers and Equity stage managers who have completed the Broadway run. (It should be noted that there are also non-union (both Actors Equity and IATSE) tours that travel around the U.S.)

"Road people oftentimes just want to be road people for a long time. You do have an opportunity, although a little harder now, to live off your per diem and put your money away in a bank account. You do that for a few years, you end up with enough to put a down payment on a house, and on tour, you can get a leg up on doing that."

- Ben Heller, President of Aurora Productions

The production company's production manager usually travels to the venue when the show goes into production at its "production city." (For the first national tour of *The Book of Mormon*, the production city was Denver.) In a process that takes about four weeks, Aurora's Production Manager Ben Heller (now President of Aurora) loaded the show in, put the show into tech and dress rehearsals and made sure the production got into previews safely. Heller than left the Denver company and went to Los Angeles to oversee the first "jump" from Denver to Los Angeles.

Once the shows get into their second city, the production manager usually heads back to their home base, and the production stage manager, along with the head carpenter and company manager, take on the role of the production manager while on tour. At this point, the production manager is back at home base, working on getting another Broadway tour together. Oftentimes "leap frogging" cities, the head carpenter will then take over and fly to each city to do an advance site visit if needed. As mentioned earlier, if the physical limitations of the theatre are in question, such as the front of house lighting and sound mix position, the carpenter will work out the spacing details while visiting the venue. Discussion on what lights to cut, what scenery may not be used or any other issues will be resolved ahead of time. This makes for an efficient use of everyone's resources, as knowing as much ahead of time as possible will obviously help you problem solve. The head carpenter on tour is a major help to the production manager and production stage manager, and attention should be paid to this very important relationship.

At some point, the touring crew is also hired by the production company. For the *Book of Mormon*, the show has what is known as a "pink contract" status with the IATSE union. That allows the production company to hire their own technical IATSE staff to travel on the road. Having your own staff, such as carpenters, electricians, audio crew, props and wardrobe crew gives the shows consistency and gives producers the best chance at success. Local crews are brought in to supplement the load-in and running of the shows in the various cities on what IATSE calls a "yellow card." The yellow card (yes it's actually still yellow!) lays out the local crew numbers in each of the cities the *Book of Mormon* travels to. Using upwards of twenty to thirty local crew, it takes a virtual village to get the show loaded in, sometimes in one day. Trained very quickly, the local crews often get less than two hours to prepare for the opening of the show!

The spirit of "WHO you know" is alive and well in the world of touring and hiring. It's still all about relationships. Heller says this about relationships:

At the end of the day, the general manager hires the production stage manager. There are only so many talented and seasoned road production stage managers, so when you have a show like The Book of Mormon, *you can go after who you want. Many times a director will have a favorite production stage manager they use. Other times, the production company may bring forth a name for a recommendation. It certainly is about relationships. We have done enough shows and have been around long enough to know most of the key people on tour in the country.*

> **TIP**—As we have mentioned repeatedly, relationship building is a key component for a successful production manager. You should start early to begin creating this network.

As for getting work in the industry, Heller says,

You need to see the whole process come together. You can only learn so much without "doing" in the theatre business. Try and be a production assistant on a show that's on tour in your city. Producers, stage managers and venues often times get the opportunity to hire a local production assistant. It lets you see the whole process come together.

He continues and suggests that you "Volunteer at the theatre where the show is happening. Get an opportunity to watch a load-in. You will be amazed at what happens in twelve hours!"

Production management for tours is very much like production managing for the other various disciplines. Attention to detail, flexibility, ability to multi-task and excellent personal relating skills are still at the top of the list of tools being used in this discipline of touring. Life on tour is all about flexibility and diplomacy. Remember that you are a guest in someone else's house. Each house may have its own set of rules that need to be followed. Do your best to follow these rules, and you will be welcomed back. At the end of the day, the venue's production manager should say, "That was a good group. We want them back again in our venue"—a good goal for any production manager to have!

CASE STUDY—NYC BALLET IN ST. PETERSBURG (PART TWO)

CONTRIBUTOR: PERRY SILVEY, FORMER DIRECTOR OF PRODUCTION

In the summer of 2003, New York City Ballet toured to the Russian city of St. Petersburg to perform at the Mariinsky Theatre. It was a historic occasion, marking the company's first visit to Russia in thirty years, and occurred during the 300th anniversary of the founding of the city. We came with a lot of trepidation, having heard stories of the difficulties others had encountered there and having gone through myriad problems in our attempt to plan the trip. We were also quite excited, looking forward to a week

Figure 16.4 Perry Silvey

in a fascinating city, performing in a beautiful theatre with the ghosts of Tchaikovsky and Petipa, and revisiting the place where Mr. Balanchine performed as a child for the Tsar.

The first obstacle began with finances, as the Mariinsky could not afford to pay our fee, and extra money was needed to support our visit. Some extremely generous members of our board took care of that problem, and plans proceeded. Anne Parsons (our general manager) and I made a trip to St. Petersburg early in the year to meet with the administrators and technical directors of the theatre to work out schedules and advise them of our needs. We were shown several hotels, at least one of them quite unacceptable, others fine. Certain terms were agreed upon, including the use of studios and dressing rooms, the building of special lighting booms for our use and other details that would allow us to give performances as close to our standards as might be possible within the limitations of the Mariinsky. There seemed to be a spirit of cooperation, a willingness to do whatever they could to help us and an air of optimism surrounding our talks.

The difficulties continued upon returning to New York. I emailed a long letter of specific needs and requests, a more exact schedule and several questions, and the response was silence. A few weeks later I emailed again, then sent the same message through two other offices, but still heard no answer. It was two months later that I heard, "Oh, yes, they got your message, and everything is fine. No problem, don't worry." Now I am not a novice (this ain't my first rodeo, as they say), and usually when someone says, "no problem, don't worry," that is the time to start worrying, because there are definitely problems ahead.

The problems for Anne, our general manager, and her staff were many, including difficulties with plane tickets, hotel reservations and other logistics. When the company finally arrived in St. Petersburg, the hotel that most of the dancers and crew were taken to was a horror (and was one that we were not shown on our previous visit). The hotel had no air conditioning to alleviate the terrible heat and humidity, the mosquitoes swarmed through the open windows, some people had no sheets on their lumpy beds and prostitutes in the lobbies were almost as numerous as the mosquitoes. We had read about some of these problems before arriving but on asking about them were assured that this was old news, that the hotel had been recently renovated and that our personnel would be housed only in the good section. This was not the first or the last time we would be misled, if not lied to outright.

Our schedule would have been brutal under the best conditions. We closed our Saratoga season with a final performance on Saturday night, July 26. Sunday, the company traveled to New York, boarded planes at JFK on Monday, arriving in Russia on Tuesday, with rehearsals and the first performance on Wednesday. Added to the jet lag and the challenge of adapting to a raked stage, the dancers had to contend with the heat (it was as hot inside the theatre as outside) and the uncomfortable living conditions. Anne immediately went to work finding alternate hotels and heroically was able to move everyone out of the Oktiabrskaia Hotel (remember that name if you ever visit St. Petersburg, and avoid it) after a couple of days.

I had left Saratoga a few days early, with Penny Jacobus, our assistant lighting director, and John Healey and Darrell Beasley, electricians. Mark Stanley, our lighting director, came a day before the company, and the five of us were there to do the initial set up in advance of the company's arrival. The rest of our production staff flew with the company, but, by the time they arrived on Tuesday, we needed to be ready for the first program. Our exact work schedule had not been confirmed before our arrival (no problem, don't worry), so we had several meetings to try to pin it down. Originally, we were to work on the stage on Monday during the day and Tuesday all day and evening. I had seen on the internet that the Royal Ballet was performing at the Mariinsky through Monday evening, so I knew that we could do very little on Monday, but expected at least the whole day Tuesday to be available to us. I was told by the Royal Ballet staff (not, please note, by the Mariinsky staff) that instead of loading out on Monday after their last performance, they would load out on Tuesday morning. When I questioned the Russians, they said, yes, this is true, but they will start early and only need three or four hours, so we could still begin our set up by noon. As it happened, the Russian crew started at 9 a.m. instead of 8 a.m., and finished around 4:30 p.m. But please, don't worry, no problem.

Sending all our equipment, sets, costumes, make-up cases and paraphernalia was another challenge. We had purposely brought the simplest ballets to Russia (simplest technically, that is—certainly not simple for the dancers or the musicians), knowing we would not have time to deal with large sets or complicated lighting cues. A month before our arrival, we loaded a forty-foot container with linoleum, drops, costumes: anything we needed in Russia but could do without in Saratoga. This container was to travel by sea and arrive in plenty of time for our load-in. The rest of our gear had to travel by air, and we had worked with our freight forwarder to make sure we could load-out in Saratoga after the last performance on Saturday night and load into the Mariinsky by Tuesday, or Wednesday morning at the latest. We had reserved space on a Lufthansa cargo plane to Frankfurt, then a separate flight on to St. Petersburg. A couple of weeks before the big move, Lufthansa cancelled the second leg of the flight, and we were left to scramble. Eventually, we chartered a flight from Frankfurt to Russia, and the airfreight did arrive on time. We had also heard that Russian customs sometimes took three or four days to clear air shipments, which would have made our stuff two or three days too late for the first performance, but then we were told that if we went through the "special" customs we could get it right away. We built an extra $5,000 into the budget for "special" customs.

Meanwhile, the trucker who was to deliver our container to the dock decided he had something better to do that day and literally missed the boat. The container was loaded onto a later sailing but missed the connection in the German port and had to be trucked across Scandinavia to Helsinki, then to St. Petersburg. It did arrive in time. The airfreight also made it. (Our forwarder had driven a dry run to make sure he could make it from Saratoga to JFK in time to load at 4 a.m. on Sunday.) We had contacted the agency in Russia that works with the Mariinsky, and they helped us clear customs, so we had everything in the theatre by Tuesday afternoon. Whew! (Don't worry, no problem.)

The load-in went reasonably well when we finally started, though the Russians didn't seem to be prepared for the size and weight of our crates and had some difficulty off-loading. I asked if they had a forklift, and they looked at me funny, then said, "no problem, we bring twenty men." For the rest of the week we joked, "What is a Russian forklift? Twenty men." We also discovered that the Russians have a slightly different view of time than we do. Though not as bad as some countries (in Brazil, a 9 a.m. call usually starts after 10), there was a cavalier attitude about starting times, though that was not true when it came to performances, and they were always ready to start the shows on time.

One oddity I had noticed during my previous trips to St. Petersburg and saw even more apparently this time was the separation between the electricians and the carpenters. There was a lot of animosity between the two crews, even more than is normally found in other theatres, to the point that several times during our stay there were shouting matches. In Russia, when the carpenters say "left" they mean stage left, but when the electricians say "left" they mean house left or stage right. The two parts of the crew are so separate, they even orient themselves differently, and it is important to know which sect someone belongs to if you plan to point them in a direction. And then get out of the way if they disagree.

After our last performance ended, we began our load-out. We took down and folded our scenery, rolled up the linoleum, trundled wardrobe and equipment crates down the long hallway behind the stage that leads to the loading door and prepared to load two containers that would be sent directly to Copenhagen, Denmark, where we were to perform for a week at the end of August and beginning of September. Once again we had asked for a forklift, and this time they told us they would provide a truck with a lift gate, which would be almost as good as a forklift. When it was time to load, however, it wasn't there, so we used the "Russian forklift" instead, a group of Russian and American men lifting crates up a wooden ramp into the container, and in one case unloading the crate, putting it on the container empty, then re-loading the crate. As we finished loading our second container, the promised truck arrived, just two hours late. For our crew, this was the end of a surreal week, and they left to go back to their hotels not long after midnight. For a couple of them it would be a short night, as the bus was scheduled for a 4:30 a.m. pick-up to take them to the airport for the flight home.

Special Events

> "You don't have to be a great technician to be a successful technical director or production manager in special events . . . you do have to be a team-builder and a problem solver."
>
> - Tom Bollard, Production Manager / Technical Director
> for Meeting Services Inc.

All special events have a great deal in common with theatre. Both have audiences, lighting, audio, décor, scenery and performers. Scripts are often used, and sometimes even costumes are a big part of the evening. There is no doubt that corporate and special events contain elements of theatre, and a good production manager is essential to the overall success of the event.

There are many types of special events, including not-for-profit fundraisers, awards ceremonies, corporate theatre (meetings and conferences) and exhibitions. In all of the various types, it is the production manager's main responsibility to take the designer's or client's concepts and bring them to a physical realization. Acquiring lighting, video and sound vendors, managing labor, working with computer assisted drafting (CAD) drawings and dealing with ongoing problem solving are all a part of the day's work for the production manager.

As in the other performing arts, the production manager's checklist is an important part of the pre-production process. Having everything accurately listed on one document will greatly aid you in the planning and laying out of the physical production. The checklist should contain every element needed in order to successfully produce a special event. Additionally, CAD drawings have become an important tool in the production manager's toolkit. Having an accurate, scaled drawing of the venue will help identify any potential challenges of fitting the physical elements of the production into the venue.

Figures 17.1/17.2 Special events can occur almost anywhere, even on an old ship or an aircraft carrier. It just takes careful planning!

Credit: Image © Jay Sheehan

One thing is a constant for the production manager, whether it be the performing arts or special events: Nurturing and maintaining relationships is crucial for success. Oftentimes, the client is the first relationship you will need to establish. The client will usually provide you with the overall concept of the event as well as the extent of the production and design elements expected. It is the production manager's responsibility to set, maintain and manage the client's expectations. Many times, certain aspects of the production may not be able to be realized due to limited resources, such as time, money or space. Learning how to have an alternative option or how to say "no" to the client properly and in a timely manner is another important tool in the production manager's toolkit.

> "Production managers should review a project's budget, timeline and expectations/job description before committing. By understanding what you are getting yourself into, you'll be better able to manage your client's expectations. Be very specific regarding how much time the client is buying when signing onto a project. Send time cards to them every week. This helps manage their expectation, as well. Be brutally honest regarding what you can and can't do. Learn how to say 'no'; the producers respect that. Experience helps here, of course, but even the young production managers need to quickly develop their sense of what can be done given the time and budget for the project."
>
> - Tom Bollard, Production Manager / Technical Director
> for Meeting Services Inc.

Once this relationship has been established and the venue has been confirmed, the next relationship that you should establish is with the venue management. At this point, you should also begin to identify who other key players are on the team and start creating those relationships as well. Lighting and audio vendors as well as video and labor providers should all be called and introduced to the production manager.

> **TIP**—In many venues, there may be an "in-house" event and production planning company. These are separate companies from the venue, but they have the "exclusive" contractual rights to provide production-related services and equipment to hotel clients requesting the service. You may also get a list of "preferred" vendors. Preferred vendors are those friendly with the local venue, but the producer does not have to use them. It is important to know and understand the differences between "exclusive" and "preferred" when it comes to working with vendors and venues.

Once you have identified the in-house production contact, connect by phone or e-mail and begin discussions on technical requirements for your event. Let them know the basics, such as what lighting, sound and/or video will be used. Providing the in-house contact with a production or load-in schedule is also an important task for the production manager. The venue and

Figure 17.3 Parking Lot Event Space—6 Post Truss Structure Up

Credit: Image © Jay Sheehan

Figure 17.4 Add backdrop, tables and chairs

Credit: Image © Jay Sheehan

Figure 17.5 Add video, linens and centerpieces

Credit: Image © Jay Sheehan

Figure 17.6 Final results from the tech table

Credit: Image © Jay Sheehan

in-house production staff are a big part of the production manager's team, and giving them as much information as possible will make your job easier on show day.

> "There are no notes too small to be taken seriously . . . attend to EVERYTHING!"
>
> - Tom Bollard, Production Manager / Technical Director
> for Meeting Services Inc.

It is important to note that in addition to providing information to the venues, the venues will need to provide information to you. These are called production guidelines. They will tell you the rules and regulations for activities in the venue, such as driving a lift on the floor surfaces, putting tape on the walls, the use of cable ramps, how you order power and other physical engineering needs you may have. You should take the time to thoroughly read these guidelines. Often, a signature will be required from either the production manager/producer or the client, confirming you will adhere to the information contained.

VENUE LOGISTICS

Every venue will have its own set of physical attributes that the production manager should be aware of. They will affect the layout and design of the event. The following is an introduction to the production elements used in special events.

One of the first pieces of information that you will need is the height from the floor to the ceiling. This is important information for the production manager to have because many vendors and designers will require it for their pre-production planning. Height of the stage, length of drapes and size of video screens allowable in the room are just a few of the production elements affected by the height of the ceiling. Once the ceiling height has been measured, the rest of the venue planning can now begin. Careful consideration and collaboration should be taken as you get into the details of laying out the venue with the various team players.

> **TIP**—Not all ceilings are the same shape or size. Many have soffits, chandeliers, or other unique characteristics. Make sure you measure all the various ceiling elements in the room that are relevant to your production. Having a good, reliable, digital tape measure as well as a 100-foot tape measure or measuring wheel are essential tools in the toolkit for the successful production manager!

STAGE HEIGHT AND STAGE PLACEMENT

The placement of the stage is one of the first steps in laying out and designing the room. Typical hotel stage platforms are usually 4 foot × 6 foot or 6 foot × 8 foot and are usually set at either 16 inches, 24 inches or 32 inches in height. In addition to the main stage, there may be other staging requirements for your event, such as risers or platforms for the tech area front of house,

IMAG (Image Magnification) cameras, follow spots or drum risers. The actual size of the stage will be determined by the production's needs, including entertainers and their equipment, presenters or speakers, and décor or other physical equipment needed on the stage for the event.

Stage steps and placement are also an important part of the production manager's checklist. Having proper entrances and exits to the stage is essential to a smooth-flowing traffic pattern on the stage. Make sure that all of these factors, as well as any other flow of people or entertainers on and off stage, are discussed with your design team and hotel or production company representative.

> **TIP**—Stages over 32 inches in height will usually require safety railing. The production manager should check with the local staging provider or venue for codes in your local area if planning anything taller.

DRAPE LINES—SOFT GOODS—MASKING

Masking and soft goods are a big part of the design in many special events. Some of the uses of drape lines include:

- Entrances and exits to the stage
- Creating backstage spaces such as a green room or performers' waiting area
- Providing masking for equipment, such as rear projectors
- Covering the back of the stage or the back of the entire upstage wall
- Storage for equipment, such as empty road cases
- Decorative covering for interior walls of venue

Figure 17.7   Business Incentive Trip W5, Creative and Meeting Services
Credit: Photo by Chris Oosterlink

- Show control drape or "front of house" mix position drape (used to cover up the unsightly look of the backs of audio and lighting boards as well as hide extension cords and other technical equipment at the tech riser, usually located at the back of the venue or ballroom)

> **TIP**—If your event involves food service, verify that you leave large enough openings in your drape line to allow food servers carrying trays to perform their duties throughout the venue. This will help you in creating a good working relationship with the catering team, as well!

BACKSTAGE SPACES

For a majority of special events, backstage space is usually at a premium. You should make sure that anyone needing backstage space discusses their needs as soon as possible. Many times, "video villages" consisting of playback monitors, switchers, rear projectors and other video equipment are created from drape or soft goods as part of the backstage set-up. Other uses for backstage space can include a performers' green room. Backstage spaces may require a lot of additional production elements, such as tables, seating, lighting, mirrors, etc., so make sure that you go over any backstage needs in detail.

> **TIP**—Use a bright colored tape and make sure you tape out areas that are off limits to guests that might be going onstage. Nothing is worse than having a shadow image cross your video screens because the backstage guest walked through the rear screen projector beam! Also, use white tape to create directional arrows for drape openings, entrances and exits.

SEATING

Seating can be in many different styles and configurations. For most of the events that happen in hotel and convention type rooms, the seating will either be "theatre" style, that in which the rows and aisles are lined up neatly, or "banquet seating" where round or square tables with chairs are arranged in the space. "Classroom seating" is another style of seating. As the name indicates, audience members are in a classroom setting with smaller, narrower tables and are usually required to take notes. "Chevron seating," or that in which some of the sections are at an angle to the stage, is also commonly used. No matter which type of seating is used, you should familiarize yourself with the drawing or discuss with the team what type of seating is being used at your event.

SIGHTLINES

The area that the audience sees from their seat to the stage is called the sightlines. Sightlines are sometimes moving objects and will vary from seat to seat. Questions should be asked early in the design process to assure that possible sightline issues have been addressed

Your checklist should look something like this:

- Where is the lectern placed on the stage?

- Does everyone in the seating area have a clear and unobstructed view of the guest speaking at the lectern?

- Does everyone in the seating area have a clear and unobstructed view of the video screens or projection surfaces that need to be visible to all guests?

- Will any sightlines be compromised by other production elements, such as ground supported trussing, audio speakers, lighting equipment, etc.?

> **TIP**—If the venue sets the tables and chairs ahead of your load-in, which is often the case due to the venue's schedule, make sure you address any potential sightline issues as soon as you arrive at the venue. Be prepared to ask the venue staff to move tables and chairs to accommodate sightlines!

RIGGING

Whenever equipment such as lighting, audio, video or scenic elements is used, the design team must first decide what is the best way to mount the equipment. Many factors, such as the event design, time, money and labor, will all affect the decision of how the equipment will be rigged, or set up. Identifying immediately if the show is "ground supported" or has a "flown rig" is the first step in figuring out what production elements will be involved. A ground supported rig is a structure usually made of trussing and is supported by the ground or floor. A ground supported rig can be lighting trusses, audio systems or video screens lifted by ground supported structures such as Genie Lifts or Sumner Lifts (www.sumner.com). A "flown" rig, as would be indicated, is flown above the stage or above the heads of the audience members. Flying a rig is always more costly, but many times it is the only solution to some of the more challenging production issues, such as weight of equipment and sightlines for the audience members.

Once the decision has been made to fly the rig, it is the responsibility of the production manager to find out how many riggers are required for the labor call. "Up riggers" (those usually suspended high above the ground) and "down riggers" (those on the ground assisting the up riggers in the air) will be needed to install. These riggers are usually on four- to five-hour minimums for both a load-in and a load-out. This is the beginning of the budgeting process for rigging.

Understanding rigging costs is important for a production manager, as the production manager is usually responsible for keeping track of the overall production budget. Costs per "rigging point" (everywhere the equipment attaches to the ceiling is called a rigging point) and hourly rates are a few of the line items found on the production manager's budget checklist. If you don't know or understand the costs, make sure you find out. Because rigging costs for a simple four-point/two truss install can run a client into thousands of dollars in costs, it is important to make sure you and your client understand that rigging costs are usually added by the venue and are usually above and beyond the normal production costs of using equipment.

Figure 17.8   Luncheon event with ground supported drape and soft goods and flown truss for lighting

Credit: Photo by Tom Bollard

LIGHTING

Almost every event you work on will have some sort of lighting. As with the other areas of technical equipment, the production manager should be familiar enough with various types of lighting equipment to be able to speak competently with the lighting designers and technicians about it. Making sure the designer (if there is one) is getting their expectations met is a key component of the production manager's job, and the production manager must assure that the event has the correct resources, such as the right amount of crew and working equipment, for example, man lifts and ladders. If there is no lighting designer, then you, as the production manager, may have to fill in. If you do, here are some other points to consider when thinking about the lighting component of the event:

- When is load-in and load-out?

- If the lighting is ground supported, are there any sightline issues preventing the audience members from seeing a clear picture of the stage?

- If the lighting system is flown, how much does the equipment weigh? This is important information for the rigging company! How many points will be used?

- How far is it from the tech table/front of house tech area to the stage? This helps determine length of control cables needed to run the show from the lighting console.

- How much power is needed for lighting, and where is it located in the venue? How far is it from the power panel to the stage? This information helps your technicians prepare properly with the correct amount of cable.

- Are there follow spots? If so, are they on any type of staging or platforms?
- Is additional lighting needed for other areas, such as silent auction tables, food stations, cocktail bars or dessert stations?
- Will you need cable ramps to cross door openings for food servers or guests?
- How will you focus the lighting rig? Is a lift needed? Is a ladder needed? If so, what is the trim height of the lighting rig?
- Do you have cue sheets or a script for show calling purposes?

Having all of the information found on the checklist will also aid you greatly in the creation of the CAD drawing, which is highly recommended for event planning. All of this information above will need to be reviewed prior to every event, so use your checklist wisely.)

Figure 17.9 The College-Conservatory of Music at the University of Cincinnati
Credit: Photo by Adam Zeek, www.zeekcreative.com

AUDIO

In addition to lighting, almost every special event has an audio component. The bigger the event, the bigger the audio package. Variables such as who is speaking at the lectern, what is the entertainment on the stage and how much stage space is available for equipment all need to be discussed. Every scenario will be different, and careful audio planning is another step in the creation of a successful event. Remember that it is the production manager's responsibility to have all of these questions answered and have the information disseminated as soon as you can, and as is the case with the other design elements, you should work closely with the audio designer or technicians to meet the expectations of the client.

> **TIP**—Many of the answers to your audio preproduction questions may come via the technical rider that is usually supplied by the entertainment. The rider will contain such information as a stage plot, input list and "hook-up" chart for audio. Having this information handy will aid you greatly in your advance work or pre-production. (More detailed information on the rider and the contract can be found in the Rock and Roll chapter.)

As with lighting, it is imperative to make sure the audio technicians are getting their expectations met. Make sure that the audio team has the correct resources, such as the correct amount of crew and working equipment such as man lifts and access to power. It is also important to note that the production manager should make sure that any sound checks or other "ring outs" (a term used to equalize the sound systems) are clearly indicated on the schedule, or timeline. Having adequate time in the schedule to address such issues as wireless microphone radio frequency interference (it happens), correct patching of the system and other various tasks is essential.

Like with all of the other equipment being used, the production manager should have a working knowledge and speak the language of the sound designer and technicians. "Front Fills," "Side Fills," "IN ears" and "Monitor wedges" are just a few of the terms that will become part of the everyday language used when discussing audio requirements.

The audio checklist should include the following bullet points, and the production manager is responsible for collecting and disseminating this information:

- Is the audio system flown or ground supported?
- Are we using wireless microphones or wired microphones?
- If ground supported, what are the speaker cabinet sizes, weights and locations? Are they on the CAD?
- If the audio system is flown, what are the speaker cabinet sizes and weights?
- Will the entertainment be using monitor wedges or "in ear" monitors?
- Are there multiple speakers at the lectern at once? Will each need their own microphone, or will they share?
- Will the speakers at the lectern use a lapel microphone or an over the ear microphone?
- How far is it from the tech table/front of house mixing console to the stage?

  (This is important to know so you can order the correct length of audio snake, the cable connecting the stage equipment to the front of house sound board.)

- What is the path that the audio "snake" will take? Is it flown? If it is ground supported, will you need cable ramps to cross door openings for food servers or guests?

- Where is power coming from? How far is it to the power panel? How much power is needed for audio?

- Who is supplying source material, such as walk in music, recorded audio cues, etc.?

- What playback capabilities for source material are needed for audio?

- Are we using an iPod, laptop, cellular device, compact disc? (Yes, they still exist.) Is there a signal or feed from video to audio that needs an input on the audio board? Are there cue sheets or a script prepared for the audio portion of the event?

THE SOUND CHECK

The sound check is a very important part of the day's schedule. Sound check details and lengths can vary based on how complicated the event is. If the event has one presenter at the lectern and one microphone, chances are the sound check will take less time. If you have entertainment, such as a musical group, you will need to plan for a longer sound check. The bottom line is that you should always do a sound check and test your microphones and equipment prior to the doors being opened to let guests into the venue.

VIDEO AND IMAGE MAGNIFICATION (IMAG)

Many special events will have some sort of video component such as PowerPoint slides, video clips and live action camera shooting (IMAG) that will need to be projected onto large screens. The production manager should be familiar with these components as well as common screen sizes and shapes, projector brightness, throw distances and rigging options. The discussion of rear vs. front projection should also be clear and thought out properly. Both front and rear projections have special needs with regard to throw distance, and placing the projectors on your CAD will help immensely in the process of deciding front vs. rear projections. At this point, you should also determine if the video screens will be ground supported or rigged, as discussed earlier in this chapter. The most common screen size for larger events are usually 9' × 12' and 10½' × 14', with the height being the first dimension and the width being the second dimension. This is with the common aspect ratio of 4:3. A 9' × 16' is also commonly used when the aspect ratio is 16:9. More and more events are beginning to use LED video walls, consisting of several small panels put together to create one large video wall. The sizes of LED video walls can be from as small as one panel to many hundreds of panels, creating a wall close to 60 feet wide and 20 feet in height. The limitation for the size of the video wall will depend on many factors, such as rigging capabilities, desired size of the screens, locations for the screens and budgets. LED video walls are significantly more expensive than standard projectors. One of the major benefits of using an LED wall for projections is that, unlike projectors, they work well outdoors and in full daylight.

> **TIP**—Understanding the limitations of video equipment and the surrounding environment is another tool in the production manager's toolkit. Such questions as—are you indoors or outdoors, what time is sunset, if outdoors, and how bright are your projectors?— are all great questions to ask when advancing your event. Having a "Sunrise/Sunset" app on your personal phone or device is a great idea. Oftentimes, this question will come up at a walkthrough, and having this information is a valuable asset to your planning.

Here are some other thoughts about video and its components

- What type of playback does the video vendor need to provide? Laptop? DVD Player?
- What inputs are needed for the video components? HDMI? VGA?
- Do you have cue sheets or a script for video operators?
- Is there enough electricity at the video front of house position or backstage position?
- Are remote control slide advancers needed for the presenter onstage?
- Is a "confidence monitor" needed at the edge of the stage? (This is so the presenter onstage can see what is being shown on the screens.)

Like the audio and lighting components of the event, you should make sure that you have ample time in the schedule to go over the video content and cues.

> **TIP**—Make sure that any video playback that has audio on it (such as film clips) is all tested prior to opening the doors of the venue to the public. You should personally hear the video playback and NOT rely on someone else to tell you "it worked."

For larger scale events, the use of a camera or a multi-camera shoot for image magnification (IMAG) on the large screens within the room is also commonly used. Carefully placing cameras and platforms on the CAD becomes the production manager's responsibility, as well. Deciding what camera shot to bring up at what point during the event is also under the careful eye of the production manager.

Many of the events using a video component will need a playback device, and the laptop computer is still the most preferred way. This playback device will almost always need a line input to the audio board in order to hear the dialogue on the video. It is important to find out from your client what format the projected media will be coming to you on. This will help in properly planning what equipment will be needed for the event.

> **TIP**—If possible, have the show files loaded in and played on the actual laptop that will be at the event. Oftentimes, media can be created on earlier versions

Figure 17.10

Credit: Photo by Ryan Knapp

of software, and fonts and formats may not match. Having the video played on the actual show laptop will help prevent any last-minute crisis of the media not being played properly.

Video and digital imaging of events is quickly becoming more and more of an integrated design concept, and as with lighting and audio, make sure you know the basic language of the video team. Having this knowledge will make you a valuable asset to the client and the production team.

ORDERING POWER: HARD POWER VS. GENERATOR

Ordering electrical services can be a big responsibility for the production manager to wrangle. The first order of business is to find out what electrical services are available in that particular venue. This can often be found on the venue's website, but a call to the in-house production company or engineering department will provide the most current information and inform you of any other details you need to know with regard to ordering power.

In addition to finding out how much electrical service is available in the venue, you will also want to know what type of connectors the electrical service ends in. Camlock connections are the industry standard for most hotels and major convention centers around the country. You may also find 30 and 50 amp twist lock connections. Make note of what type of connections the hotel has. You will also want to pay attention to the type of power that is needed for the event. It can be called "three phase" or "single phase."

Three phase power is electricity capable of delivering 220 volts, as opposed to single phase, which can only deliver 110 volts. The power the venue provides must match the needs of the equipment. The production manager must ask the various vendors (lights, audio, video, etc.) what their requirements are and carefully order and oversee the distribution of the electrical loads to the various areas by way of breaker panels and large power cables. During this part of the process, the production manager should make sure that there is a separate power service for lighting and a separate power service for audio and video (who usually share power).

> **TIP**—By separating the equipment and power, you greatly reduce the chances of having a "buzz" in the audio system, which usually happens when you share power with lighting and audio. Make sure you fully understand the power requirements and create a final power distribution plan to double check your power loads. You should also keep an eye out so that the audio snake and main power cables are not run next to each other!

For non-traditional venues and events that are held outdoors, large portable generators (usually towed by a truck) are used to get the amount of electricity needed for the event. In this case, the production manager would calculate all of the power needed for the event and contact their local generator provider to discuss sizes of generators and amount of cable needed to get the power from the generator to the stage or other area needing power. The generator company can also provide you with cable ramps for safety, which are used in entrances and exits to prevent people from tripping on the large power cables.

> **TIP**—Once you have established how much power is available in the event space, make sure you know the distance from the power panel to the stage or area containing lighting dimmers or audio amp racks. This information should easily be found on the CAD drawing. This is helpful for the lighting and audio vendors providing the power cables that extend from the power panel to the stage or other distribution points.

WORKING WITH LABOR

Much of the work of the production manager on show day is about managing the various crews and maintaining the fast pace of the production schedule. You will need to find out if the labor on your event is International Alliance of Theatrical Stage Employees labor (IATSE) or non-union labor. The working conditions and hourly rates will vary based on what city you are in and what labor contract you might be under. You should make sure you understand these hourly rates and working conditions (i.e., overtime hours, meal penalties, etc.) for whatever situation you find yourself working with.

> **TIP**—Not fully understanding your local contract or labor agreement could result in a costly mistake to those paying the bills at the end of the night.

On most events, crews are divided by departments, and the production manager must make sure that each department is adequately staffed with labor. Lighting, audio, video, staging, décor and rigging crews are all managed by the production manager, and a careful watch should be kept by the production manager to make sure that no area falls behind in the production schedule. At times, you may find yourself having to move labor from one department to another if one falls behind. This is at times challenging if all departments are behind and you have no extra staff.

Keeping a labor checklist will help you as well. Some of the items on this checklist might be:

- Crew call time for load-in—load-out
- Amount of crew needed for truck unloading and loading
- Amount of crew needed for "pushing" the equipment from the dock into the room. (Some IATSE venues will contractually require separate "pushers" from the rest of the crew. Check your local contract!)
- Amount of crew needed for lighting
- Amount of crew needed for audio
- Amount of crew needed for video
- Amount of crew needed for scenery/drapery installation
- If it is non-IATSE crew, is there a crew chief on the call that you are working with?
- Is crew parking paid for or validated at the hotel or other venue?

> **TIP**—Make sure that you give the crews their proper break periods throughout the day. Some may be contractual, so make sure you know the local rules. Your crew will appreciate this!

As you can see, managing labor is all about time management and people skills. Making everyone feel like they are part of the team and that they contributed to the event's success is all a part of the production manager's job.

> "Always listen first . . . it's amazing how often your crew will have a better idea than yours."
>
> - Tom Bollard, Production Manager/Technical Director
> for Meeting Services Inc.

Figure 17.11   Tom Bollard

THE INITIAL SITE VISIT OR VENUE WALK-THROUGH

Once your team has been identified, use your contact sheet to schedule a venue walk-through. Though the participant list may vary from event to event, generally they will include: the client, venue staff (such as catering managers) and in-house production company representatives, as well as event designers and vendors (décor, lighting, sound, and video). This will often be the first time that everyone is in the room together, so this will provide an opportunity for relationship building and practicing good communication techniques.

Start with introductions and have your contact sheet ready for distribution. You should have a written agenda and try to stick to it. If too many side discussions are occurring and it overwhelms the meeting, it becomes your job to get the others on task and focused. You should note that not all questions will be answered at the first walk-through. Oftentimes, the walk-through creates more questions than it answers, so be prepared for it to go either way. Make sure you capture the information and notate it either with a pad and paper or tablet-type device.

ENTRANCE

The walk-through should begin at the entrance of the event. At this point, the production manager should be on the lookout for any design elements discussed. This could include lighting, audio and/or video elements.

TIP—You should look at the way your patrons or guests are entering the venue. Is it well-lit and safe, and are there enough ways out in case of emergency?

LOBBY/FOYER

The lobby, foyer or entrance to the main ballrooms in the hotel is usually the next stop on the site visit. Oftentimes with corporate theatre meetings and conventions, the lobbies and foyers are filled with registration tables, silent auction tables, alcohol bars or other items that may come as a surprise later. Again, look for electricity needs, lighting needs and possibly another sound system for production elements such as background music, a live band or auctioneer.

Larger scale and higher budget events often use the foyer as an additional performance space. Bringing in production elements is not an uncommon experience in these spaces.

THE MAIN BALLROOM OR CONVENTION CENTER ROOM

As the site survey moves into the main ballroom, the realization of the physical production should start to take place, and walk-through will cover a myriad of topics.

Placing the stage at the correct location in the venue is usually the first decision to be made. This can be decided by physical limitations or by the client's specific requests. Once the stage is placed, the rest of the design team can now concentrate on locating other production elements. For the production manager, the questions will start to accumulate. What is the size of the stage? What are the audio, video, lighting components needed for the event? Where will they go? Where is the tech table set up? Many other discussions will be happening once you get in the ballroom. Seating styles (theatre, banquet, classroom), table sizes and placement, decorations (décor), thematic interpretations of the event—all will start being discussed as it pertains to the main ballroom. Be prepared to listen in to discussions about seating, sightlines, schedules, meal menus, décor and color themes. Table centerpieces, video elements and talent needs will all be discussed as well. Much like a theatre production meeting, all of the various topics need a place on the agenda.

Once you conclude the meeting, you should find time to walk the venue again either by yourself or with an assistant. Having these details ahead of time will help you be more effective on show day. First, find the loading dock and check how many trucks can unload at once. Check the height of the dock to determine if an additional ramp or forklift is needed. Now check the loading dock door size to make sure your production elements will fit. Also, check the route that the equipment is going to have to follow to get loaded into the room. Are you loading equipment through the hotel kitchen, with many obstacles? Is there a freight elevator near the loading dock if the event is on a different level in the hotel? How tall are the ceilings in freight elevators? Do you have to share elevators with room service staff at hotel venues?

You would be surprised how many hotels are not set up for a smooth load-in for the audio-visual crews. By walking the route ahead of time, you will have a head start on show day. With that knowledge, you can inform the stagehands about the various challenges ahead of time, thus saving time and saving money.

OTHER ITEMS ON THE PRODUCTION MANAGER'S CHECKLIST

The production manager's checklist is filled with details that need to be constantly addressed. Here are a few other details that the production manager may or will need to handle:

Truck and vehicle parking: The production manager is oftentimes the person responsible for securing parking arrangements for any trucks that need to remain on the property. Equipment vendors are not always just delivering equipment and leaving. At times, the production manager may need to find available parking for trucks that stay on site. At other times, the truck may be left at the loading dock. Find out from the vendor if their trucks are staying onsite and need parking. Start with the security office if you need onsite parking for trucks. Keep the parking costs for your budgets, as well. Again, find out how many trucks can unload at one time at the loading dock and how much freight the elevators can handle. This will help you in making the proper crew calls for both the unloading and loading of trucks.

> **TIP**—Find out where the local crew needs to park for your event. Having this information communicated to the crew assists with having everyone on time and ready to work at the call time.

STORAGE

As mentioned above, the use of backstage space for the storage of road cases and extra equipment is usually recommended. Having the storage cases ready for load-out in an organized and efficient manner can help keep labor costs down. But what if there isn't any backstage space for storage? What if all of the space is being used up by technical elements or the design of the show doesn't allow for any backstage space? If you are in a hotel or convention center-type ballroom, ask the hotel contact for an additional room for storage, if at all possible. Most of the times, hotels are used to production being brought in, and most have a plan for storage. Make sure you talk it through and understand where the storage room is in relation to the room your equipment is in. In some cases, the only place to put empty road cases is back on the truck. Knowing this information in advance will help you, as a production manager, schedule proper amounts of labor and time to get empty road cases back off the truck and into the room for load-out.

The production manager in special events, like the production manager in the other performing arts disciplines, is by no means a small job. As technology advances and the productions become more and more complicated, a properly trained production manager may be the difference between a successful event and one that may not go so well. The plethora of details cannot and should not be overlooked, as no detail is too small for the production manager. By using your relationships created along the way as well as your checklist, you, too, can become a successful and competent production manager in the exciting world of special events.

CASE STUDY—HOOVER DAM CELEBRATION

CONTRIBUTOR: KEN FREEMAN—MEETING SERVICES INC.

We were brought into this project by a local producer in Las Vegas to help the Bureau of Land Management turn the Hoover Dam into a theatre and event space suitable for 3,000 guests. The program was to include a celebration of the 100-year history of the Bureau, complete with a custom video, several live performances and commemorative presentations by local officials from both Nevada and Arizona. In addition, we were told to expect several key members of the White House cabinet and possibly the vice president. The media would be here, and we were expected to record and document the entire proceedings.

From a production standpoint, two things stood out:

- No one had ever attempted to produce this type of event before at the Hoover Dam.
- All of the various vendors, from lasers and fireworks to audio-visual production and food services, would share the same resources and access via a single narrow tunnel.

The sense of scale and scope of this venue and project were not apparent from first look. The river valley is almost 1,200 feet deep. The face of the dam runs 726 feet, and the Hoover Dam's power plant generates about 4 billion KWh per year. To say it is awe-inspiring would be an understatement.

We were contracted to look after the project in August of 2001. Our first site survey was to be on September 13, 2001. Our country had been attacked two days earlier, and all forces that were currently in motion were now at an immediate halt. The Hoover Dam was now on the list of possible terrorist targets and went into immediate lock down. We were asked to reschedule and possibly cancel the event all together. It would take eight weeks to make the decision, but it was determined that we should move forward with the event, and we proceeded to do two site surveys in November and January of 2002.

Technically, the venue was going to be a difficult one to create from scratch. The audience seating area was along the service roads for both Arizona and Nevada Wing power transformers.

Figure 17.12   Ken Freeman

The stage placement would be equally challenging. There was enough space on the stage for nine chairs and a five-foot walking aisle. With this set up, it meant we would have guests seated as close to 100 feet from the stage and as far as 700 feet from the stage.

Other technical questions would have to be answered as well. From an audio stand point, the question was how to make a cohesive event system that covered an area 600 feet long and 20 feet wide? For video, we had similar challenges, along with the question of how to make the screen big enough for optimum viewing? Since our event was at night and there are essentially no real lighting instruments on that part of the dam, we would have to come up with an efficient house light system that was capable of turning on and off from one main house light switch (again, covering an area 600 feet by 20 feet).

As for power, we would need our own generators, as well. Dinner would also be served to 3,000 guests, and the logistics of that was also placed on our production team. With no real cooking facilities on site, hot water sinks and additional restrooms had to be brought into the venue. With no crew facilities, we had no production office. We went camping, complete with pop up tents and all the food and water we needed for the day.

As for temperatures, we saw them in excess of 130 degrees on the dam's concrete surface. It was grueling, and on the second day, we adjusted our production schedule to work from 4 a.m. to 2 p.m. By 11 a.m., we had to move to indoor projects to avoid the heat and finish our work day.

Access to the venue was also a new challenge, as the Hoover Dam, post 9/11, was to be a "secure site." All production staff were given complete background checks, and intense screenings happened anytime a staff member came on or off the dam's property. As for vehicular access, the biggest truck we could get through the access point was a 24-foot stake bed truck. All equipment would have to be cross-loaded from one truck to the other.

We were also informed at this point that because the Hoover Dam is a part-time power station and a key national asset, it may be pressed into action at any time. With that in mind, each area of production needed a 10-minute "stop and drop" plan. The challenges just kept coming.

With a one week load-in period, we pushed on in the heat and completed the tasks at hand.

While the challenges were many, a few key ones come to mind.

- In 2001, long before the widespread use of flat-screen monitors, we had cathode ray tube monitors, which spill off a tremendous amount of magnetic energy. It turns out these same monitors were also very sensitive to the same magnetic energy that the Hoover Dam generators emit. Our first tests indicated that we could only use conventional CRT sets if the dam's generators were off.
- 1,500 feet of fiber optic cable runs were needed to get from the event area to the press riser high above the dam's surface.
- Communications between the stage manager, Jay Sheehan, and all of the technicians was also hampered by the large generators' magnetic fields inducing a hum on the normal intercom channels.
- Video would be challenged with a 600-foot camera shot in a venue that vibrates at 60Hz when the generators are on. Sony came to the rescue with a new image stabilization technology.
- Audio had the biggest challenge: how to get even audio signals down two 600-foot venues that were 20 feet wide. We also needed to do this without any delay in the signal. We did this with a system not normally seen on an event site: spaced 70 volt with no delays. Low volume, but lots of speakers!

The solution for these challenges was the result of many people collaborating on the idea of how to solve the problem. We ended up using 10-foot-tall vertical truss that was spaced about every 30 feet. On the truss was a speaker and lighting instruments and also the first deployment of what was then a state-of-the-art 42-inch plasma display screen.

Patience and flexibility were two keys assets for our team that year, as it turned out to be a spectacular event with everyone in attendance in awe at the firework and laser show at the end of the program.

Oh yeah . . . and then there was load-out . . .

Concluding With Balance

> "In our industry, balance in life seems to be a lesson learned only through the bruising effects of the lack of balance in our lives."
>
> - Tom Bollard, Production Manager / Technical Director
> for Meeting Services Inc.

The preceding chapters have all been about the job of the production manager. What does it take to network, to make the client or director happy, and to have a successful production? The bottom line is that it takes hard work, long hours and extreme dedication to the art form in which you are working. The job of the production manager is not for the faint of heart or those not seeking out some excitement in their everyday job. Careful thought should be given before taking on the job. One must think of balance, define it for oneself, and decide on how to achieve that in each circumstance.

BALANCE? WHAT IS THAT?

Balance, equivalence, equity, proportion, harmony and evenness are words that the production manager may hear in a design meeting. While these words do help us to describe design thoughts and ideas, it is also important to think of these words as the way we should strive to run our busy production manager lives. Every one of these harmonious sounding words has a counterpart, though, and the wise production manager should also be on the lookout for such things as unbalanced, inequity, disproportionate, discord, unevenness and instability.

What does balance in life actually mean, or what is it that we are trying to achieve? Originally a Latin word for "having two," it is also a condition in which different elements are equal or in the correct proportions. So balance in life would be equal proportions of work and life. But balance is not always equal. Balance is often times asymmetrical. An artist may add

Figure 18.1

Credit: Image © iStock

something to an asymmetrical piece to make it symmetrical and bring something back into balance. We, as production managers, must do the same so we do not stay out of balance too long. We must make corrections to swing the pendulum back in order to bring us back into equal balance.

> "Balance to me means giving 100% to what you are doing and/or what you have in that moment, but not 100% of the time. This way you are not compromising your personal life or your work, but simply doing your best to be present in both arenas."
>
> - Kim Fisk, Production Stage Manager,
> first national tour, *The Book of Mormon*

PAIN IS INEVITABLE, SUFFERING IS OPTIONAL

So what exactly happens when we get out of balance? What can suffer? The answers will vary person to person, but, for the majority of us, being out of balance can have some serious consequences. Let's look at a simple example of what happens when we get stressed and out of balance:

- We lose focus on the projects.
- We lose interest in the work.

- We make simple mistakes.
- The work doesn't get done.
- We get depressed.
- We become introverted.
- We distance ourselves in our relationships.

None of these things are conducive for a production manager in show mode. We must be able to think clearly and effectively, and in order to do that we must be able to handle stress well. The fact is that it's not about the stressful job but how you handle the stress. That's what is meant by suffering is optional. We have the ability to help control this by looking at ways to reduce our stress and limit our "suffering."

According to researchers at San Diego State University, an eight-level approach to wellness is best. Here are some ways in which you can reduce your stress and have a healthier, happier life:

- *Physically:* Caring for your body in order to stay healthy now and in the future; eating well and being active
- *Socially:* Maintaining healthy relationships; enjoying being with others; developing strong friendships and intimate relationships; caring about others and letting others care about you
- *Emotionally:* Managing your emotions in a constructive way; understanding and respecting your own feelings, values and attitudes; appreciating the feelings of others
- *Occupationally;* Developing a sense of your strengths, skills, values and interests in your career; maintaining a balanced life between work, family, play and taking care of yourself
- *Multicultural:* Being aware of your own cultural background and becoming knowledgeable about, respectful of and sensitive to the culture of others
- *Environmentally:* Awareness of how your behavior impacts the earth, as well as how the physical world impacts you; demonstrating a commitment to a healthy planet
- *Spiritually:* Finding purpose, value and meaning in your life with or without organized religion
- *Intellectually:* Growing intellectually, maintaining curiosity about all there is to learn; valuing life-long learning and responding positively to intellectual challenges

There are many other ways in which you could approach your own stress management. The bottom line is to be aware of how you feel and make adjustments as necessary.

FREELANCING AND STRESS

The freelance production manager gets an added layer of stress that they must contend with, and that is always keeping an eye out for work. Looking for your next gig can be a full-time job, and careful attention must be made when considering how to balance looking for work and doing the work parts. While it is often advised for young production managers to take on every opportunity presented before them, the fact is that one way to reduce stress is to understand your limits and learn how to say no when necessary. Taking on too many projects becomes stressful as well. Most of your work becomes mediocre instead of *all* of your work being excellent. At some point, if you get too busy, all of the clients start to suffer as you become less and less available due to the many projects you have taken on. Your work suffers, and you suffer. All of that equates to unhappiness. It is a fine line to draw between saying "no" or taking on too many jobs. There are no clearly defined criteria for determining how many projects are too many. One must assess their own situation and make the choices best for them.

> "Balance to me means everything. Being able to do what you love while raising a family, having great friends, enjoying good food and living life with fun and laughter is the balance I strive to achieve."
>
> - Christy Ney, Stage Manager for *Wicked* on Broadway

KNOW YOUR SHOW TO REDUCE STRESS

What are some other ways that we can control stress? The fact is that production management is all about how we handle the unknown factors that pop up in our daily production lives. By limiting the amount of unknown factors, we immediately start to eliminate some of our day of show or daily stresses. Bottom line is to know your show or your event and really know it inside out. By knowing your show, you are investing your time into balance without even knowing it. By knowing your show, you are properly planning for limiting your exposure to stress. Remember what Perry Silvey said in the touring chapter: "By knowing your show, you can save time by making correct decisions." Making correct decisions reduces stress.

HAVE A FULL LIFE

> "A person with a full life has a broader perspective when making decisions and more experiences from which to draw when the going gets tough."
>
> - Neil Kutner, Director of Production for the Brooklyn Academy of Music

What does it mean to have a full life? It means balance your work life with your personal life. Take time to be with your family and friends. Go experience museums, movies, music or art or take your dog for a walk. And when we say "be with your family and friends," it means be WITH them. Be present and be focused on what is happening at that moment where you are.

Figure 18.2

Credit: Image © iStock

Use your production management skills that you use with your clients at home as well. Make your family member the most important person you are talking to at that moment. Turn off the phone and put down the email device. Be present.

> "As I've matured, I realize that, although my professional life has provided many gifts, it is a relatively small part of who I am. Work is a 'means to an end' but the end is so much more. I'm a production manager and technical director and love that . . . but being a father, husband, artist, philanthropist, gardener, volunteer and mentor is what colors my life and provides the balance I need. My approach to balance is to integrate all of these things into my work life because it makes me real. I wish I had learned this lesson as a younger man."
>
> - Tom Bollard, Production Manager / Technical Director for Meeting Services Inc.

As you get started in the business, you will learn that production management is all about schedules. One way to stick to your balancing act would be to actually schedule your life as you would schedule the rest of your production meetings. If you had a meeting with an important client or director, you wouldn't take a phone call in the middle of it or just not take the appointment because something else came up. The same must be true for your family and friends. For some people, actually scheduling time with family and friends is necessary and welcomed. While not for everyone, it can be an effective tool in your toolkit.

Now, go out and live life! Use the tools you have learned in this book to fill your toolkit and production manage to the best of your ability. Work hard, build confidence, balance, and enjoy the ride. Production management is like nothing else you will ever experience.

> "I did then what I knew how to do. Now that I know better, I do better."
>
> - Maya Angelou

Index